DIRTY VALENTINE

A J.J. Graves Mystery

LILIANA HART

ALSO BY LILIANA HART

JJ Graves Mystery Series

Dirty Little Secrets

A Dirty Shame

Dirty Rotten Scoundrel

Down and Dirty

Dirty Deeds

Dirty Laundry

Dirty Money

A Dirty Job

Dirty Devil

Playing Dirty

Dirty Martini

Dirty Dozen

Dirty Minds

Dirty Weekend

Dirty Looks

Dirty Liars

Dirty Valentine

Addison Holmes Mystery Series

Whiskey Rebellion

Whiskey Sour

Whiskey For Breakfast

Whiskey, You're The Devil

Whiskey on the Rocks

Whiskey Tango Foxtrot

Whiskey and Gunpowder

Whiskey Lullaby

The Scarlet Chronicles

Bouncing Betty

Hand Grenade Helen

Front Line Francis

The Harley and Davidson Mystery Series

The Farmer's Slaughter

A Tisket a Casket

I Saw Mommy Killing Santa Claus

Get Your Murder Running

Deceased and Desist

Malice in Wonderland

Tequila Mockingbird

Gone With the Sin

Grime and Punishment

Blazing Rattles

A Salt and Battery

Curl Up and Dye

First Comes Death Then Comes Marriage

Box Set 1

Box Set 2

Box Set 3

The Gravediggers

The Darkest Corner

Gone to Dust

Say No More

Laurel Valley

Tribulation Pass

Redemption Road

Midnight Clear

Forgiveness River

Atonement Trail

Men feared witches and burnt women.

It is the function of speech to free men from the bondage of irrational fears.

~Louis D. Brandeis
US Supreme Court Justice

For a charm of powerful trouble,
Like a hell-broth boil and bubble.

~William Shakespeare
Macbeth

PROLOGUE

KING GEORGE COUNTY, VIRGINIA

May 1725

The morning mist clung to the river like the breath of ghosts, and perhaps it was. Bridget Ashworth had learned to see omens in everything now—in the way the crows gathered in threes along her fence posts, in how her milk had curdled three days running, in the silence that fell over the tavern when she passed. Fear had a smell to it, sharp and metallic, like blood on a blade, and it had been growing stronger with each passing day.

She stood at her cottage window, watching the sun struggle through the Virginia darkness, and knew with the certainty that had always lived in her bones that this would be her last sunrise.

The gift—or curse, depending on who was asked

—had come to her as it had come to her grand-mother and her grandmother's grandmother, flowing through the women of her bloodline like water through a creek bed. She could ease a difficult birth, brew tonics that would break a fever, and yes, some-times she simply *knew* things. When the Henderson baby would come early. When the drought would finally break. When Patrick McKellar's gambling debts would catch up with him.

She'd never claimed to be a witch. Had never consorted with the devil, despite what the whispers said. She was simply a woman who listened—to the earth, to the wind, to the subtle rhythms that most people had forgotten how to hear. In England, such women had been valued. Here, in this God-fearing colony where Puritan sensibilities still ran as deep as the Rappahannock, they were feared.

And fear, Bridget had learned, was a poison that turned good people into something else entirely.

The sound of hoofbeats on the dirt road made her turn from the window. She'd been expecting them, had known they would come with the dawn. Six men on horseback, their faces set with the right-eous determination of those who believed they served a higher purpose. At their head rode Magis-trate Jonathan Blackwood, a man whose soul was as pinched as his thin lips, who saw the devil's work in everything from a woman's laughter to the way cats gathered in her garden.

Bridget smoothed her simple brown dress and checked that her dark hair was properly covered by her white cap. She would meet her accusers with dignity, even if they would show her none in return.

The pounding on her door came like thunder.

"Bridget Ashworth!" Blackwood's voice carried the authority of a man who'd never questioned his own righteousness. "By order of the King George County Court, you are charged with the practice of witchcraft. Open this door!"

She could have run. The woods behind her cottage were thick, and she knew them better than any of these men. She could have slipped away like smoke, disappeared into the Virginia wilderness, perhaps made her way to one of the other colonies where a woman's knowledge of herbs and healing wasn't seen as evidence of communion with Satan.

But running would be an admission of guilt in their eyes, and more than that, it would mean abandoning the people who still came to her door in desperation—the young mothers whose babies burned with fever, the old men whose bones ached with the changing weather, the women who whispered their secrets and sorrows into her capable hands.

She opened the door.

"Magistrate Blackwood." Her voice was steady, though her heart hammered against her ribs like a caged bird. "I have been expecting you."

His pale eyes narrowed at that, and she saw him make a quick sign of the cross. "Have you indeed? And by what unholy means did you come by such knowledge?"

"The same means by which I know that your wife's consumption will worsen before the winter's end," she said quietly. "And that your son will return safely from his voyage to the Indies, though not with the cargo you hope for."

The color drained from Blackwood's face, and the men behind him shifted uneasily in their saddles. Truth, Bridget had found, was often more frightening than lies.

"Seize her," Blackwood commanded, his voice tight with something that might have been fear.

The trial, if it could be called that, was held in the courthouse that still smelled of fresh-cut timber and the sweat of nervous men. Bridget sat in the dock while witness after witness testified to her crimes— how she'd cursed the Miller boy's leg to heal crooked after he'd trampled her herb garden, how she'd bewitched the weather to bring rain on the day of Sarah Whitman's wedding, how she'd been seen talking to her black cat as if it were human.

The accusations grew more fantastic with each

telling. She had flown through the air on moonless nights. She had turned milk to blood with a glance. She had caused livestock to sicken and crops to fail. She had, according to Widow Morrison, been seen dancing with the devil himself at the crossroads at midnight.

Bridget listened to it all with the patience of stone, speaking only when directly addressed, answering each question with simple truth that seemed to infuriate her accusers more than any denial might have. Yes, she had knowledge of herbs. Yes, she sometimes knew things before they happened. No, she had never made covenant with any dark power. No, she had never sought to harm another soul.

When they asked her to recite the Lord's Prayer, she did so without stumbling. When they searched her for the devil's mark, they found only the scars and calluses of a woman who worked with her hands. When they threw her into the river to see if she would float, she sank like any mortal woman, choking and gasping as they pulled her from the water.

But none of it mattered. The verdict had been decided before the trial began, written in the fearful eyes of neighbors who had once sought her help but now crossed themselves when she passed.

"Bridget Ashworth," Magistrate Blackwood

pronounced, his voice carrying across the packed courthouse like the toll of a funeral bell. "You have been found guilty of the practice of witchcraft. You are hereby sentenced to death by pressing, that the weight of stones might crush the devil from your body and send your soul to whatever judgment awaits."

The method of execution was deliberate, chosen not just to kill but to terrorize. Pressing was reserved for those who refused to confess, who would not bend their will to the court's demands. It was slow, inexorable, designed to break the spirit as thoroughly as it broke the body.

They brought her to the cemetery, to the section where they buried the unwanted—criminals and madmen and those who had died by their own hand. It was fitting, they said, that a witch should find her final rest among the damned.

The morning was gray and still, the air heavy with the promise of rain. They had dug a grave for her—so she would simply be pressed into the earth where she lay, the weight of stone and sin crushing her down among the roots and bones of those who had gone before.

Bridget looked up at the gray sky and felt, for just a moment, the presence of every woman who had died for the crime of being different, of being inconvenient, of knowing too much or too little or simply existing in a world that feared what it could not control. Their voices whispered to her on the wind, a chorus of the forgotten and the wronged.

"Have you any last words?" Blackwood asked, though she could see in his eyes that he hoped she would maintain her silence. A confession would have been satisfying, but her continued defiance was somehow more frightening.

Bridget looked around at the assembled crowd—neighbors who had once brought their children to her for healing, men who had secretly sought her counsel, women who had whispered their fears and hopes into her compassionate ear. Fear had transformed them all into strangers, their faces hard with borrowed righteousness.

"I forgive you," she said simply, and saw more than one person flinch as if struck. "All of you. You act from fear, and fear makes cowards of us all. But know this—the truth has a way of rising to the surface, no matter how deep you try to bury it. What you do here today will not be forgotten. This ground will remember."

They stripped her of her clothes—her dignity—tossed her in the hole and then laid the wooden planks across her chest, heavy boards that pressed the breath from her lungs. Then came the stones, one by one, each rock carefully chosen and placed with ceremonial precision. The weight built slowly, inexorably, each new stone adding to the crushing pressure that squeezed the life from her body.

But Bridget Ashworth did not scream. Did not beg. Did not confess to crimes she had never committed. She looked up at the gray sky and thought of all the women who would come after, all the daughters and granddaughters who would inherit both her gifts and the burden of living in a world that feared them.

As the last stone was placed and the darkness closed over her vision, she felt the earth beneath her back accepting her sacrifice. The ground drank her blood and her breath and her bones, weaving her essence into the very soil of King George County.

Death, when it finally came, was almost a relief.

But death, Bridget discovered, was not the end.

The magistrate and his men departed, satisfied that justice had been served and the devil's influence purged from their community. The crowd dispersed, returning to their homes and their daily concerns, eager to put the unpleasantness behind them.

They left her there, beneath the weight of stones, in ground that was already heavy with the accumulated sorrows of the unwanted dead. But something of her remained—not a ghost, exactly, but an essence woven into the very fabric of the place. Her blood had fed the roots of the ancient oaks. Her bones had enriched the dark soil. Her final breath had joined the wind that whispered through the cemetery grounds.

The truth would rise, as she had promised. Justice would come, though it might take centuries to arrive.

And in some distant spring morning, when another soul lay broken on her grave, Bridget Ashworth would be there to witness it—to see if this time, finally, the weight of lies would be lifted and the stones of truth would crush those who deserved crushing.

The cemetery remembered everything.

And sometimes, on nights when the mist rose thick from the river and the moon hid behind storm clouds, visitors would swear they could hear her voice on the wind—not crying out in pain or calling for vengeance, but simply whispering the same words she had spoken on that gray morning so long ago.

The truth has a way of rising to the surface, no matter how deep you try to bury it.

This ground will remember.

CHAPTER ONE

Death had a sense of humor.

My name is J.J. Graves, and I've spent enough time with the Grim Reaper to appreciate his twisted sense of timing. As King George County's coroner and a fourth-generation mortician, I've built my life around the inevitable—that final exhale that comes for everyone, whether they're ready or not. Most people find my dual professions unsettling. Jack, my husband and the county sheriff, considers it practical. Between us, we handle both sides of mortality—the peaceful passings that keep Graves Funeral Home in business, and the violent endings that require yellow tape and evidence bags.

After years in this business, you'd think nothing would surprise me anymore. But the Grim Reaper had a gift for creativity that would put any artist to shame. Today's masterpiece came courtesy of twenty-three seventh graders, one overwhelmed teacher, and what appeared to be a murder victim arranged on top of a three-hundred-year-old grave like some kind of macabre historical reenactment.

"Well," Jack said, surveying the chaos of tweens scattered around the historic section of what locals called Olde Towne Cemetery. "This is a new one, even for us."

I followed his gaze as I pulled on my latex gloves. Some kids were crying, others were taking selfies with the crime scene in the background, and at least three had thrown up and contaminated the crime scene. One enterprising young man was livestreaming on his phone while providing commentary.

"I'm pretty sure that kid just violated about six different laws with that livestream," I said, stepping carefully around a fresh puddle of vomit. "You think a thirteen-year-old kid has a following?"

"Stranger things have happened," Jack said. "My mother was telling me about a rabbit that rides around on the back of a pit bull in a saddle and they have over two million followers. Let's just hope none of the kid's followers comes to check things out for themselves."

A harried-looking teacher with gray hair

escaping from what had probably started the day as a pristine bun was frantically trying to corral her students. Her sensible cardigan was buttoned wrong, and she looked like she was about three seconds away from a complete breakdown.

"You couldn't pay me enough to be a teacher," I said, watching as she blocked a redheaded boy from slipping under the police tape.

Cole and Martinez had arrived just minutes after us, responding to Jack's call for backup. They were both senior enough in rank that they usually acted as the lead on their own cases, so it was unusual to see them both here. But it wasn't often we saw something like this, so I couldn't blame their professional interest.

Detective Cole was a man's man—a modern-day cowboy with eyes that had seen too much in his years on the force. He wore his usual uniform of Wranglers, a white dress shirt, a gray sport coat, and his ever-present Stetson, though today the hat sat slightly askew as if he'd been running his hands through his hair. He was currently trying to convince a group of seventh graders to stop taking pictures of the crime scene, his usual stoic expression strained with the effort.

Detective Martinez, on the other hand, approached us with his notebook already out. Even at a crime scene in a cemetery at ten thirty in the morning, he was impeccably dressed in pressed slacks and a button-down shirt, his dark hair perfectly styled. I'd come to find out recently that Martinez came from money—not just a little money, but the stupid kind of money that his children's children would inherit.

Except I'd also found out he'd had a vasectomy because the money had messed up his family and he didn't want to pass the crazy along. But as far as I knew, I was the only person to know that little secret. Other than his expensive lifestyle, Martinez was just a regular guy. His need for justice was what drove him to work alongside the rest of us.

"Please tell me this isn't going to be another case where we have to interview every person in a five-mile radius," Martinez said, eyeing the chaos of the kids behind him. "Because I already have a headache. Seeing all these kids is the best birth control there is."

"Amen to that," Cole said, having escaped from wrangling children. "Remind me to ask Lily if she's up to date on her prescription."

My lips twitched, but I kept my head down. Jack and I hadn't announced that I was pregnant yet, and I had the worst poker face on the planet.

"I thought you wanted kids," Jack said, arching a brow.

"I just need some time to recover from this many

in one place," Cole said. "Maybe we'll just have one kid. One kid can't possibly get into that much trouble."

I snorted and pointed to Jack. "You're looking at the king of being an only child. Why don't you tell him how much trouble one kid can get in?"

"To be fair," Jack said, grinning, "I was usually the one trying to keep everyone out of trouble."

"Because you have that fast brain and cute dimple," I said. "Not because you weren't guilty."

Jack shrugged sheepishly and said to Cole, "You'll be fine. When the time comes."

"Maybe I'll wait another twenty years and then I'll be dead by the time he's a teenager," Cole said.

"Good advice," Martinez said. "You should write a parenting book." He rolled his eyes. "Y'all are ruining my breakfast with all this talk of having kids. Can we get back to murder please?"

"Yes, murder," Cole agreed, the relief obvious in his voice.

The corner of Jack's mouth twitched, but he complied. "Riley was first on scene and he got a quick statement from the teacher," Jack said. "Lois Warren is her name. She brings her seventh-grade history class to Olde Towne Cemetery at the end of every school year to see the graves of local prominent historical figures—founding fathers, war heroes— that kind of thing. But a few of the kids wandered off to this side of the cemetery. According to Riley, the kids said it looked, and I quote, 'spooky.'"

"I guess they were right," I said. "Naked dead guys that have been crushed by rocks are pretty spooky."

Cole snorted. "And it's not even Halloween. It's always comforting to know psychopaths are crazy year-round."

I looked around and felt a chill that had nothing to do with the morning air. We were standing in what was clearly the forgotten section of King George Cemetery—the part where respectable families didn't want to be buried. Ancient headstones tilted at drunken angles, their inscriptions worn smooth by centuries of Virginia weather. Gnarled oak trees stretched arthritic branches overhead, creating a canopy so thick that even the bright May sunshine could barely penetrate the gloom. Shadows pooled in the hollows between graves like spilled ink, and the air itself seemed heavier here, weighted with the accumulated sorrow of three hundred years.

This was where they'd buried the unwanted— the criminals, the insane, the accused witches. The section was separated from the respectable part of the cemetery by a low stone wall that had crumbled in places, as if even death couldn't maintain the social barriers that had existed in life. Moss covered everything with a green velvet shroud, and the only sound was the whisper of wind through dead leaves that rustled despite the fact that it was spring.

The victim lay directly on top of a grave marker so old and weathered that the inscription was barely visible.

"Bridget Ashworth," I said. "1689–1725. I remember learning about her in school."

"Executed for witchcraft," Jack said. "It was a gruesome tale. I was fascinated when I was a kid."

"We all were," I said. "Think how many times we crept out here in the middle of the night when we were kids because Jimmy Slokum said her ghost haunted the graves of the men who killed her."

"The same Jimmy Slokum that got arrested for distributing methamphetamine last month?" Martinez asked.

"The very same," Jack said. "He was always a good salesman."

"Hell, the high school kids still try to come out here to get drunk or make out," Cole said. "Nothing like ambiance, adrenaline, and hormonal teenagers."

Martinez snorted. "Yeah, those were the good old days. Whoever killed our victim certainly knew how to set a scene."

The victim's head, arms, and legs were clearly visible, his naked body pale against the dark earth. But his torso was completely hidden beneath wooden boards and a carefully arranged pile of stones. His graying hair was matted with moisture from the morning dew, and his arms were positioned at his sides, hands turned palm up as if in supplication. His legs were straight, feet together, the whole arrangement giving the impression of someone laid out for burial.

"Pressed to death with stones," Jack said grimly, studying the deliberate positioning. "If I remember right that's how Bridget Ashworth was killed."

"It's certainly not something you see every day," Martinez observed, circling the scene with professional interest.

"Yeah, I've been getting pretty tired of stabbings and gunshot wounds," Cole said. "I was hoping for something different to liven things up."

"Who found him?" I asked.

"Madison Fletcher and Ashley Yang," Jack said, pointing to two girls who were sitting on a nearby bench, wrapped in emergency blankets despite the warm morning.

"Has anyone touched the body?" I asked, even though I was pretty sure I knew the answer.

"Mrs. Warren thought it was a dummy at first," Jack said. "When she realized it wasn't she checked for a pulse. But she was smart enough not to disturb anything else once she realized what she was dealing with. Though I'm not sure the same can be said for the kids."

As if on cue, a shriek erupted from somewhere behind us. The redheaded boy was pointing excitedly at something near the cemetery's wrought-iron fence.

"There's another dead person over there!" he yelled. "This place is like a zombie apocalypse!"

"That's a statue, Kevin," Mrs. Warren called wearily. "It's been there since 1847."

"Are you sure?" Kevin asked, clearly disappointed. "It looks pretty real."

"Maybe we should get these kids back to school before they contaminate any more of my crime scene," I suggested. "This is going to take a while, and I don't need an audience critiquing my technique."

"Riley's working on transportation," Martinez said. "We'll need formal statements from the kids who found the body, but that'll have to wait until their parents come to get them."

"We'll need to find an expert who can tell us exactly what we're looking at here," Jack said. "We can assume the way the body was discovered is some kind of symbolism or historical reenactment. I'll make a few calls when I get back to my office. I'm sure the historical society has a recommendation of someone we can consult with."

I grunted and said, "Let's see what we're dealing with," and then I pulled out my measuring tape. "I need to document everything before we start moving stones."

The victim was a white male, probably in his fifties based on his graying hair and the lines visible on his face and hands. His clothes were folded neatly and placed on a nearby headstone. They looked expensive—slacks, a button-down shirt, and nice leather shoes that had a label even I recognized.

"Any ID?" I asked, though I doubted our killer would have been thoughtful enough to leave the victim's wallet intact.

"Nothing obvious in the clothes," Jack said. "But maybe once we clear these stones and boards we'll find something more."

The process of removing the stones was painstaking. Each one had to be photographed in place, measured, and carefully catalogued before being moved. Some were the size of softballs, others were larger than my head. All of them had been selected for their flat surfaces and arranged to distribute weight evenly across the wooden boards.

"So here's the million-dollar question," Cole said. "Where did these stones come from? Did the killer come prepared? Seems like a lot of work to load up your trunk with stones ahead of time. These things aren't light."

"Definitely not a crime of passion," Jack said, bending down to heft up another stone. "This was calculated and well planned. Our killer needed time. The gates to the cemetery are supposed to be locked after nine o'clock, and a deputy does a drive-by on regular patrol to make sure kids aren't doing stupid things. But somehow our killer unlocked the gate, drove in their vehicle and kept to the perimeter road, got the victim to this location..."

"Not only that, but the killer got him to be compliant," I said. "Most victims fight back while they're waiting for their murderer to get the job done."

Jack nodded and said, "And as we can see, moving these stones takes a little time."

"Which suggests the victim was already dead," Cole said. "Or drugged."

"He wasn't killed here," I muttered as I worked. I lifted his thigh since it was easily accessible. "Look at the lividity." I pointed to the bluish-purple skin where blood had pooled to the lowest part of his extremities after death. "He's got striations. This body has been moved. Looks like he was lying on his side when he died. He's got faint coloration along his entire left side. And then when he was placed here on his back the blood pooled again." I pointed to the second line of discoloration.

"We need to talk to the grounds crew," Jack said. "Whoever was on duty to lock up last night. Maybe he just got lazy and didn't lock the gate."

"Already got the name," Martinez said, handing Jack a piece of paper. "Al Contreras. Works for the city. Said to give him a call if you need to talk to him."

"Helpful," Jack said, taking the piece of paper.

Once we'd cleared the stones, the wooden boards were revealed—two thick planks that had been placed across the victim's chest and upper abdomen. As we carefully lifted them away, the victim's torso was finally visible. There were clear impressions from the boards across his skin, but something still felt off.

"Jack," I said, leaning closer to examine the victim's face and exposed torso. "Look at this."

The victim's eyes were closed, his face relaxed. While there were marks from the pressure of the boards across his chest, there were no signs of the prolonged agony that should have accompanied death by crushing. No protruding tongue, no bulging eyes, no indication that he'd struggled against the weight for an extended period. I pulled back the victim's eyelids to check for burst capillaries, but there was nothing but the milky film that covered his blue irises.

"This isn't right," I said, sitting back on my heels. "The staging is elaborate, but he didn't die from being crushed."

Jack's eyebrows rose. "You're sure?"

"I won't know for certain until I get him back to

the lab," I said, pulling out my thermometer and a scalpel to take a liver temperature reading. "But while there's evidence of compression from the boards on his chest, this doesn't look like death by crushing. He wasn't even restrained. No ligature marks on the wrists or ankles. If someone was piling stones on my chest and I had mobility I'd be doing everything I could to get them off."

I made a small incision and inserted the thermometer, checking my watch to note the time. "Core temperature is seventy-nine degrees. Given the ambient temperature and exposure, I'd estimate time of death between 3 and 4 a.m."

"The witching hour," Martinez observed, looking up from his notes. "How perfectly appropriate for our location."

"So our killer had plenty of time to stage this scene," Jack said. "Martinez, I need you to expand the perimeter to include the entire section of the cemetery. Look for any evidence of how the killer got here—tire tracks, footprints, anything disturbed."

"Already started a preliminary sweep," Martinez replied. "Found some tire impressions. Looks like someone drove a vehicle right up to the edge of this section."

I continued my preliminary examination, checking for obvious wounds while documenting the position of the body. "No visible trauma to the head, neck, or extremities. I'll need to examine the torso more thoroughly once we get him back to the lab."

"Martinez, you and Riley start a grid search of the access roads leading to this section. See if there are security cameras. If I remember right, the county council voted against them because of the expense, but maybe one of the nearby houses has cameras."

I snorted and said, "Hey, at least the council president got them to confirm a brand-new Cadillac as his city vehicle. You'd think he was part of the presidential motorcade."

"Well, priorities," Cole said dryly.

Martinez's mouth quirked in a smile and he said, "I'll grab Riley and get started." And then he headed off, making a detour around where the group of kids was huddled waiting to get on the school bus.

"I need to find the real cause of death," I said. "This is smoke and mirrors."

"Could be a copycat like that Jack the Ripper case we had," Jack said. "Could be someone trying to send a message. Or..."

"Or?" I asked.

"Or could be our killer is just plain crazy."

"My favorite kind," Cole said.

As if on cue, a cool breeze rustled through the ancient oaks overhead, sending shadows dancing across Bridget Ashworth's weathered headstone. The whisper of wind through the leaves sounded almost like voices—the accumulated whispers of three centuries of the forgotten dead.

I shivered despite the warm temperatures, suddenly aware that we were standing in a place where justice had been perverted once before. Where an innocent woman had been crushed to death by the weight of lies and fear and small-town politics.

"We need to find out who he is," I said, taking one last photograph of the victim's peaceful face. "He wasn't picked at random."

"CSI team just pulled up," Martinez said, his voice coming through the radio attached to Jack's belt. "And I can see the news van right behind them."

"Perfect," Jack muttered. "Nothing like having the media turn murder into a circus."

I looked down at our victim one more time—at his peaceful face that belied the violence of his final hours, at the careful arrangement of his body on top of Bridget Ashworth's crumbling grave. The killer had chosen this spot for a reason. Had positioned him here like an offering to the dead witch beneath the stone.

"You know what bothers me most about this?" I said, my voice barely above a whisper.

"What's that?" Jack asked.

"Whoever did this knows our history. Knows about Bridget Ashworth, knows about the pressing, knows exactly which buttons to push to get our attention." I stood slowly, my knees protesting after crouching for so long. "This feels personal."

The wind picked up again, rustling the leaves overhead and carrying with it the faint scent of decay that seemed to seep from the very ground beneath our feet. In the distance, I could hear the news crew setting up their equipment, ready to turn our investigation into entertainment for the masses.

But here in this forgotten corner of the cemetery, surrounded by the graves of the unwanted and the damned, something darker was stirring. Something that had been waiting three hundred years for the right moment to claw its way back to the surface.

And whatever it was, it had found its voice in death.

CHAPTER TWO

THE DRIVE BACK TO BLOODY MARY SHOULD HAVE BEEN peaceful. Spring had settled over King George County like a benediction, painting the rolling hills in every shade of green imaginable. Dogwood trees lined the winding roads, their white blossoms scattered like confetti against the deeper emerald of old oaks and maples. It was the kind of day that made you believe in new beginnings and second chances.

Too bad we were hauling a corpse.

The irony wasn't lost on me as Jack's Tahoe led the way through countryside that had witnessed three centuries of Virginia history. I followed behind him in the Suburban, past weathered tobacco barns that had sheltered Confederate deserters and around curves where Colonial militias had once marched toward uncertain battles. The past seemed to breathe in every shadow, whisper in every stand of trees.

Maybe that's why someone had chosen Bridget Ashworth's grave for their display. In King George County, the past wasn't just history—it was family.

I turned onto Catherine of Aragon Street, and the familiar sight of Graves Funeral Home came into view. The red-brick Colonial sat on its corner lot like a dowager empress holding court, its white columns welcoming the living while sheltering the dead. Two ancient oaks stood sentinel in the front yard, their massive canopies filtering the afternoon sunlight into dancing patterns across the grass.

The funeral home was comfort for me—though it hadn't always been. It was the place where I'd learned that death was just another part of life's rhythm, where I'd discovered my calling among the silent and the lost.

The Suburban's engine settled into silence under the portico, metal contracting with soft pings in the afternoon heat. Jack moved around to help me maneuver our victim onto the hydraulic lift, and I found myself watching the fluid grace of his movements—economical and sure, born from years of experience with the darker corners of human nature.

I'd known this man my entire life, had loved him in one form or another for just as long. First when we were children, then as teenagers navigating the treacherous waters of friendship, hormones, and questionable decisions. Through college we'd gone our separate ways, each seeking paths that would lead us far from Bloody Mary and the futures that somehow kept calling us back home. But loving Jack now as a man—my husband, my partner, my anchor in a world that often felt unmoored—was something else entirely.

Time had been kind to him, refining the sharp edges of youth into something deeper, more compelling. The boy's handsomeness had matured into the kind of masculine beauty that turned heads on the street and made other women look at me with barely concealed envy. The occasional strand of silver glinted through his dark hair, though he kept it cut close to his scalp, and lines fanned out from his eyes—evidence of laughter shared, sorrows weathered, a life lived fully.

But it was more than his looks that still made my pulse quicken after all these years. It was the way he moved with unconscious confidence, the quiet authority that made people instinctively turn to him in crisis. The gentle strength in his hands as he helped me guide the gurney, mindful of both the weight we carried and the dignity we owed the dead.

Sometimes I still couldn't quite believe he was mine. That this man who could have had anyone had chosen me, again and again, through all the years and changes between us.

"You okay?" he asked. "You're not going to throw up again are you?"

My lips twitched. Morning sickness had become part of our routine. One I wasn't afraid to admit I was ready to move past. I've been told the second trimester is better. I'm skeptical.

"No," I said, arching a brow. "I was just admiring the view."

He grinned and the blue of his eyes deepened to the color of a summer lake. "That kind of talk will get you in trouble."

"I sure hope so," I said. "It's not like you can get me pregnant again."

He laughed and we rolled the gurney into the oversized mudroom and toward the pressure-sealed door that led to my lab.

"You know what's bothering me?" Jack said.

"The fact that our killer knew enough local history to stage an execution from 1725?" I suggested, punching in the security code for the lab door. We maneuvered the gurney into the elevator.

"Anyone who's spent much time in King George would know the history. It's part of the reason people come to this area." Jack's eyes were thoughtful as he hit the button to take us down a level. "But it's more than that. If it was about the killing, the victim would have died by the method in which he was found. But the more I think about it, this murder was about sending a message."

"The question is whether the message was meant for us or for someone else entirely," I said.

Lights came on automatically as we descended, blindingly white and showcasing the sterile white walls and floor. My parents had built this lab as part of their smuggling ring. The main area held an embalming table—stainless and sterile with drains to keep the area clean—since preparing bodies for burial was the main function of a funeral home.

But there had been another area built with state-of-the-art autopsy table and lab equipment where they'd Frankensteined bodies to transport weapons, drugs, cash...whatever had fetched the highest price. The crazy part was it had all been funded by the government. Everything they'd done had been part of covert government operations. Of course, it hadn't always been the United States government.

Jack helped me transfer the body to the examination table. "Could be a warning," he mused, stepping back to let me work. "Someone holding a grudge or letting the community know they haven't forgotten old grievances."

"Maybe it's revenge," I said. "Three hundred years in the making."

"I've always admired people who future plan that well."

I snorted out a laugh.

But the thought sent a chill down my spine that had nothing to do with the lab's temperature. In King George County, some families had been nursing grudges since before the Revolution. If someone had decided to settle an old score, we might be looking at the kind of case that tore small communities apart.

"That's it for me," Jack said, already backing toward the elevator. The formaldehyde and antiseptic smell was getting to him—it always did. "You need anything else before I head back to the station? I need to make some calls."

"I'll come upstairs with you. I could use some coffee. I've been too sick in the mornings to drink anything but water."

"Coffee sounds good," he said, pressing the elevator button with obvious relief. "As long as I make it."

I followed him back upstairs to the kitchen and went to wash my hands while he made the coffee. He leaned against the counter while we waited. The afternoon light streamed through the windows and caught the strong line of his jaw, and I felt that familiar flutter in my stomach that had nothing to do with morning sickness.

"Have I told you lately how sexy you are?" I asked.

He got a look in his eyes I recognized, and I felt emboldened to step forward, so I was close enough to catch the scent of his aftershave.

"You might have mentioned it once or twice," he said, tucking the swing of my hair behind my ear. "But I wouldn't mind hearing it again."

I placed my hands on his chest, feeling the steady beat of his heart under my palms. "All I have to do is look at you, and I want you. Do you know what happens to a woman's hormones during pregnancy?"

Jack's eyes darkened, and I saw his jaw tighten slightly. "Jaye…"

"They go completely haywire," I continued, sliding my hands up to loop around his neck. "All kinds of…cravings. Intense needs that demand immediate attention."

"Is that so?" His voice had dropped to that husky tone that made my knees weak, and his hands found my waist, pulling me closer.

"Absolutely," I said, pressing against him until there was no space between us. "And right now, I'm having a very specific craving that only you can satisfy."

"Here?" he asked, nibbling at the corner of my mouth seductively. "Someone could come in at any moment."

"Then they'll get an education," I said, standing on my toes to brush my lips against his ear. "Besides, when has the possibility of getting caught ever stopped us before?"

His hands tightened on my waist, and I felt the exact moment his resolve crumbled. "You're going to be the death of me, woman."

"I certainly hope not," I murmured against his neck. "I have plans for you that require you to be very much alive."

Before he could respond, his mouth found mine in a kiss that tasted of pure masculine hunger. My hands fisted in his shirt, pulling him closer as heat exploded between us with the sudden intensity of a struck match.

"Twenty minutes," I whispered against his lips. "That's all I need."

"I can do a lot with twenty minutes," he said, his smile wicked and full of promise. "Want me to prove it?"

Before I could answer, the distant sound of voices echoed from the front of the funeral home, followed by the familiar sound of Emmy Lu's laughter.

"Hell," Jack muttered, stepping back just as we heard footsteps approaching the kitchen.

"—told you we should have insisted on the over-sized coffin," Emmy Lu was saying as she entered the kitchen with Sheldon trailing behind her. "Some people just don't fit standard sizes."

Emmy Lu Stout was what my grandmother would have called pleasingly plump, with silver-streaked light brown hair that she perpetually kept in a messy bun on top of her head, kind eyes, and dimples. She was as cute as a button.

When I'd hired her a couple of years ago, neither of us had known how desperately we'd needed each other—me after learning of my parents' betrayal, and her after her husband of twenty-five years had walked out on her after their youngest son had graduated from high school. She was a hometown girl, so it helped that she usually knew someone in our deceased clients' family trees.

"We should've recommended cremation," Sheldon said, and then he noticed Jack and me standing suspiciously close to each other, both of us slightly flushed and breathing harder than the situation warranted.

Sheldon was my assistant funeral home director, and the more often I was called out on cases, the more often he was needed to keep the funeral home running and in the black. He was in his mid-twenties, a few inches over five feet, and doughy in appearance. He had a comb-over, Coke-bottle-thick glasses, and he always looked like he was playing dress-up in his father's clothes whenever he was meeting clients.

He was an acquired taste, but he was sweet and his penchant for blurting out random facts was mostly endearing.

"Oh," he said, eyeing us closely. "Are you both feeling okay? You're showing signs of an elevated heart rate, and your skin looks feverish."

Emmy Lu snorted. "They're not sick."

"Did you know that people who have high fevers are worse at lying?" Sheldon asked. "It impairs the prefrontal cortex that controls executive function and impulse control. So feverish people are more likely to blurt out the truth."

"Jack and I were just discussing the case," I lied.

"If you're feverish that's probably the truth," he said, staring intently at me and blinking owlishly.

I remembered I'd come up for coffee and handed my mug to Jack to fill. I preferred to drink it black, but I took the cream from the fridge to cut the caffeine and give my system time to settle.

"Well," Emmy Lu said, settling onto one of the stools that surrounded the large square island. "We've had an adventurous morning."

"What happened?" I asked.

A flush worked its way up Sheldon's neck and cheeks. "I spent the night at Leena's house and then she got a flat tire on her way to drop me off at work.

My mom said it's because I had a sleepover with a girl and it was punishment for living in sin. Leena said it's because my mom put a curse on her."

Sheldon lives with his mother and doesn't get out much, though he weirdly doesn't seem to hurt for female attention. He's been seeing a girl that works at Lady Jane's Donuts. To say she was interesting was an understatement. I'd become pretty protective of Sheldon—he was like a puppy and someone had to watch out for him. But it seemed to me that Leena was only interested in him because he worked at the funeral home.

She was one of those girls who wore black lipstick, thick eyeliner, and painted her nails black. And she liked it when Sheldon wore his embalming coveralls. Leena was a strange one, and if anyone was putting curses out there my money was on her instead of Sheldon's mom.

"You need to start thinking with the brain in your head instead of the other one," Emmy Lu said, clucking her tongue. "Besides, that's not what I was talking about when I said we'd had an adventurous morning. You need to get a grip."

"What other brain?" Sheldon asked, confused. "I only have one."

Emmy Lu sighed and shook her head. "Tell them what happened with Mrs. Patterson."

"Right," he said, pushing up his glasses. "So

Mrs. Patterson calls this morning about arrangements for her mother. Mrs. Abernathy died yesterday at the age of ninety-three. So her daughter comes in this morning to go over preliminaries, but she has this...thing with her." Sheldon shuddered visibly.

"What kind of thing?" I asked, knowing I was going to regret it.

"Well," Sheldon said. "She said it was a cat."

Emmy Lu snorted with laughter. "You should have seen Sheldon's face when she pulled that moth-eaten furball out of a Louis Vuitton tote like it was a priceless heirloom."

"It was a taxidermied Maine coon," Sheldon said. "I might have screamed a little."

"More than a little," Emmy Lu said, patting his shoulder. "But it was understandable. I've never seen anything more terrifying. She must've had that thing taxidermied at the Dollar Store. There was an eye missing, and only a few patches of hair remained."

"And Mrs. Patterson wants it displayed with her mother at the viewing," Sheldon said.

"What did you tell her?" I asked, trying to keep my expression neutral.

"I told her we'd do our best to honor her mother's wishes while maintaining the dignified atmosphere our other families expect," Sheldon said carefully. "But between you and me, I wouldn't be opposed to it finding its way to the crematorium. No one should have to look at that."

"Agreed," Emmy Lu said. "She left it in my office. Now I have to go back in there and throw salt around or something to clear out the evil spirits."

"I'm proud of you, Sheldon," I said. "That was a very professional response."

"Except for the screaming," Jack said under his breath, making me smile.

"On that note," I said, glancing toward the basement, "I should probably get started on our John Doe."

"And I'm going to deal with the media circus and see if any missing persons reports have come in."

"You're a day late and a dollar short on that front," Emmy Lu told him. "I caught the story on the news already. Imagine finding a body on Bridget Ashworth's grave." She shivered. "It's just creepy. I used to drink Boone's Farm and make out with Roger Shofer around there when I was fifteen. Those memories will never be the same."

"Cemeteries are real aphrodisiacs," Sheldon said wisely.

Emmy Lu nodded as if this were common knowledge instead of completely weird. "If you go to the cemetery at night you can hear her talking when the wind blows through the headstones."

"You think she was a real witch?" I asked.

"I'm just saying, there's been too many strange things that have happened around her grave over the last three centuries. Everyone knows that."

"Hmm," I said, deciding I'd need to do a Google search on Bridget Ashworth once I got finished with my autopsy.

Jack kissed me and headed toward the mudroom door, but he paused and looked back at me with an expression that promised our interrupted moment would be continued later.

"We'll finish our earlier discussion tonight," he said.

"I'm counting on it." Heat rushed to my cheeks, and I didn't bother trying to hide it. "I'll let you know as soon as I'm finished with him."

Jack was almost to the mudroom door when his phone buzzed against his hip. The sound cut through the kitchen's warmth like a blade. He glanced at the screen and I watched his expression shift from heated promise to razor-sharp alert in the space of a heartbeat.

"What is it?" I asked, recognizing the look that meant our afternoon was about to take a very different turn.

"Text from Martinez," Jack said, all traces of our earlier flirtation evaporating like morning mist. "They found something at the cemetery."

The kitchen went tomb quiet. Emmy Lu's coffee

mug froze halfway to her lips, and Sheldon's nervous fidgeting stilled completely. Even the old house seemed to hold its breath.

"What kind of something?" I asked, though my stomach was already dropping with the certainty that I didn't want to know.

Jack's jaw tightened as he scrolled through the message, his face growing grimmer with each word. "After the CSI team finished processing the scene, they expanded their search. Found a fresh carving on another headstone about twenty yards away. Jonathan Blackwood, died 1725."

"Same year as Bridget Ashworth," I said. "That can't be a coincidence."

"Someone carved a message into his headstone." Jack's eyes found mine across the kitchen, and the blue depths held shadows I didn't like. "It said, *The first stone has been cast.*"

A shiver worked its way down my spine. "The first stone?"

"Could mean anything," Jack said. "I need to get back out there and see it for myself. Martinez is securing the area. Call me the second you find anything unusual with our victim. If someone's defacing graves and staging murders, every detail matters."

"Jack," I called after him, my voice smaller than I intended. "Be careful."

"Always am," he said, and then he was gone, leaving nothing but the echo of his footsteps.

I stood there in the kitchen, surrounded by the familiar comfort of afternoon sunlight and the gentle hum of the refrigerator, but something had shifted. The very air felt charged with possibility—and not the good kind. Whatever had started with our John Doe on Bridget Ashworth's grave was connected to something much older and infinitely more dangerous than a simple murder.

Behind me, Sheldon cleared his throat with the nervous precision of a man about to deliver bad news. "Did you know that the practice of public stoning was designed to distribute guilt among the community? No single person was responsible for the death because everyone participated."

I turned to face him, watching his face grow pale behind his thick glasses. "What are you saying, Sheldon?"

"I'm saying," he stammered, adjusting his glasses with fingers that trembled like autumn leaves, "that historically speaking, when someone carves *casting the first stone* at a murder scene, they're probably planning to cast more."

CHAPTER THREE

THE LAB WELCOMED ME LIKE AN OLD FRIEND, ALL gleaming steel and antiseptic comfort. Down here in my domain, surrounded by the tools of my trade and the familiar hum of refrigeration units, the world made sense in ways it rarely did above ground. Death might be a mystery to most people, but to me it was simply another puzzle to solve, another story to piece together from the evidence left behind.

I pulled my hair back into a tight ponytail and scrubbed my hands at the deep sink, letting the hot water and surgical soap wash away the lingering tension from the cemetery.

My John Doe lay waiting on the examination table, covered by a crisp white sheet. The preliminary photographs were already uploaded to my computer, but I took a moment to review them on the large monitor mounted on the wall. The staging at the cemetery had been elaborate, theatrical even. But down here, stripped of context and drama, he was simply a man who'd died too soon.

I moved to my desk and pulled out a fresh autopsy form, then picked up my digital recorder. The familiar weight of it in my hand was comforting —a talisman that helped me focus on the scientific rather than the emotional aspects of what lay ahead.

Music was essential for this kind of work. Something to fill the silence without demanding attention, sophisticated enough to match the gravity of what I was doing without becoming a distraction. I scrolled through my playlist and selected Norah Jones—her voice was like velvet, smooth and unobtrusive, perfect for the painstaking work ahead.

"Come Away With Me" began to play softly through the lab's speakers as I switched on the recorder.

"Autopsy case number twenty-four dash fifteen. May fifteenth. Time is 2:37 p.m." My voice sounded steady and professional in the quiet lab. "Victim is an unidentified white male, approximate age fifty to fifty-five years, discovered this morning in the historic section of Olde Towne Cemetery. Body was found in an elaborate staging designed to mimic historical execution by pressing."

I moved closer to the table and pulled back the

sheet, revealing the man who'd lain so peacefully atop Bridget Ashworth's grave. In the harsh fluorescent lighting of the lab, details that had been obscured by morning shadows and crime-scene chaos became starkly visible.

"Subject appears well nourished and shows evidence of good personal care. Height approximately five feet ten inches. Weight approximately one hundred eighty pounds. Hair is brown with significant graying, cut in a conservative style. Facial hair has been recently trimmed."

I continued my external examination, noting everything from the condition of his fingernails—neatly manicured—to the small scar on his left thumb that spoke of some long-ago accident. These details painted a picture of a man who took care of himself, who had people in his life who mattered to him.

But it was his hands that told the most interesting story.

"Subject's hands show calluses consistent with regular manual labor," I said into the recorder. "Palms and fingertips show evidence of work with tools or rough materials. However, the overall condition suggests this was skilled labor rather than purely physical work. Maybe an artist?"

I photographed each finding meticulously, building the visual record that would become part of the permanent file. Every scar, every mark, every detail that might help identify him or explain what had happened.

He wore no jewelry, not even a wedding ring, though there was a pale band of skin around his ring finger that showed he recently had.

"No wallet or identification left at the scene," I said into the recorder. "Missing wedding ring indicates the ring could have been taken along with the wallet. Or victim could have been recently separated."

Was someone wondering where he was right now, when he'd be coming home? I pushed the thought away and continued my examination. Emotion had no place during an autopsy. Pregnancy hormones had made autopsies challenging recently, and I'd found myself more than once crying over things I'd never shed a tear over before.

"No obvious external trauma visible," I continued, moving the recorder closer as I worked. "No defensive wounds on hands or arms. No ligature marks on wrists or ankles. Subject appears to have been positioned postmortem rather than restrained prior to death."

The lack of obvious injury was both a relief and a concern. Relief because it meant his death hadn't involved prolonged suffering. Concern because it made determining cause of death infinitely more complicated.

I moved to the computer and pulled up the preliminary toxicology request form, checking off the standard panels. He had no traces of alcohol or any substances in his system. Not even over-the-counter medicine. If someone had poisoned him it wouldn't show up here. The problem with poison was you had to know what the exact poison was before you tested for it, so you could order the right test. I hated deaths where poison was involved. It made my job much harder.

I took x-rays, but there was nothing out of the ordinary—a childhood break in his left ulna based on the remodeling, and a more recent break in his distal radius on the same side.

The Y-incision came next—the moment when external examination gave way to the deeper secrets held within. I picked up my scalpel, the familiar weight of it steady in my hand, and made the first cut from shoulder to sternum.

Norah Jones crooned softly about dreams and longing as I worked, her voice a gentle counterpoint to the clinical reality of blade meeting flesh. The music helped maintain the rhythm of the work, the meditative quality that allowed me to focus completely on what the body was telling me.

The heart told the story I'd been dreading.

"Significant cardiac abnormalities present," I said into the recorder, leaning closer to examine the organ that had failed this man. "Heart shows evidence of acute cardiac arrest. Muscle tissue appears damaged in a pattern consistent with sudden, catastrophic failure."

I photographed the heart from multiple angles, documenting the damage that had ended our victim's life.

"No evidence of coronary artery disease," I continued. "No blockages present. Subject's cardio-vascular system appears healthy for his age."

That was the problem that would complicate everything. Healthy fifty-something-year-old men didn't typically drop dead of heart attacks for no reason.

I continued the internal examination, checking liver, lungs, kidneys, brain—all the organs that might hold clues to what had killed him. Everything appeared normal, healthy, and consistent with a man who'd taken good care of himself. By all appearances he was fit, didn't have wear on his liver from excessive drinking, and didn't smoke. He'd obviously spent time outdoors and had the musculature of someone who spent time in the gym. By all appearances, he should have had years of life ahead of him.

A wave of nausea hit me suddenly, and I had to pause, gripping the edge of the examination table as my stomach churned. The antiseptic smell that usually didn't bother me seemed overwhelming, mixing with the metallic scent of blood in a way that made my head spin.

I breathed through my mouth, waiting for the moment to pass. This was becoming a regular occurrence lately—my body's reminder that I was no longer working for just myself. The life growing inside me was making its presence known in the most inconvenient moments.

After a few deep breaths, the nausea subsided enough for me to continue. I made a mental note to keep some crackers in the lab for moments like this.

The computer chimed softly as I was closing the incision, and I glanced over to see that the fingerprint analysis had completed. Results were already populating on the screen, pulling up records that would finally give our victim a name and a history.

"That was fast," I said. "Victim's prints readily available in AFIS. Thomas Andrew Whitman, age fifty-two. Resident of King George County. Married to Patricia Howe Whitman. No children. No criminal record, not even a parking ticket."

The address made me pause. Whitman Lane, just outside Bloody Mary Proper. Whitman was an old King George family name—the kind that had roads and buildings named after them, whose ancestors were buried in the oldest sections of local cemeteries. Everyone in the county would recognize the name.

I printed out the identification results, my mind already turning over the implications. Thomas Whitman wasn't just some random victim. He was local, with deep roots in the community. The question was whether that connection was coincidental or the very reason he'd been chosen.

I signed the autopsy report, listing the official cause of death as cardiac arrest under suspicious circumstances, and then I rolled Thomas into the refrigeration unit.

When I finally looked down at my phone, I saw that Jack had texted to let me know he was still at the cemetery. Perfect. I needed to see him in person, needed to share what I'd found and hear what else the team had discovered.

I secured the lab and grabbed my keys, the weight of unanswered questions heavy on my shoulders.

I was halfway to the mudroom when voices drifted from the front office—Lily's laugh mixing with Sheldon's earnest tenor in a way that suggested trouble was brewing.

"—telling you, she's bad news," Lily was saying as

I rounded the corner. "Any woman who gets turned on by dead bodies has issues."

It was rare to hear aggravation in Lily's voice. She was one of the kindest and most even-tempered people I'd ever known.

"It's not the dead bodies," Sheldon protested, his voice taking on that defensive tone he used whenever someone questioned his judgment. "Leena appreciates the artistry of what we do here. She finds death fascinating."

"Sheldon, honey, there's a difference between appreciating your work and wanting to role-play funeral director and corpse."

My nose squenched as that unholy image flashed into my brain.

I paused in the doorway, taking in the scene. Lily sat cross-legged on the floor next to Emmy Lu's desk, her long dark hair pulled back in a messy bun secured with what looked like a pencil. She was beautiful in that effortless way that made other women hate her on sight—olive skin that never needed makeup, dark eyes that missed nothing, and a body that belonged on magazine covers despite her diet of gas station coffee and carbs.

Today she wore scrubs the color of sea glass and looked like she hadn't slept in a week, which was probably accurate given that finals were approaching. Medical textbooks were scattered around her like fallen soldiers, and she had that slightly manic look that came from too much caffeine and not enough sleep. Which explained the aggravation.

And then there was Sheldon.

I had to blink twice to make sure I wasn't hallucinating. Gone was his funereal uniform of slacks and a conservative button-down shirt. Instead, he stood near the window in baggy black jeans that hung low on his hips, a black T-shirt for some band called Eternal Suffering, and what could only be described as an attempt at emo hair—his usual neat comb-over had been artfully tousled and hung across his forehead in greasy strands.

But it was the eyeliner that really completed the transformation. Thick, uneven lines rimmed his eyes, making him look like he'd either been punched or had applied makeup in a moving vehicle.

"Oh," I said, unable to stop myself. "What happened to you?"

Sheldon's cheeks turned bright red beneath the black-rimmed eyes. "Leena said I should try expressing my darker side."

"Your darker side apparently shops at Hot Topic," Lily said.

"It's called embracing the aesthetic," Sheldon said, tugging at the hem of his shirt. "Leena says conventional fashion is just society's way of keeping us trapped in conformity."

"And eyeliner is your path to freedom?" I asked.

"Don't forget the hair," Lily added. "I got here just in time to stop him from dyeing it black in the bathroom sink."

Sheldon unconsciously touched the greasy strands hanging in his eyes. "The box said it was temporary."

"It's never temporary," Lily said.

"You can hardly tell my hair is thinning when it's combed down like this," he said. "The TikTok I watched said it's emo. I might get my tongue pierced."

"Well," I said, trying to find something diplomatic to say, "it's definitely a new look for you. Maybe wait on the tongue piercing. You want to wait to put holes in your body until you know the relationship is going to last."

"Good point," Sheldon said. "And Leena's not that bad. She just dabbles in the dark stuff. No one knows what they want to be when they're twenty."

Lily's lips thinned into a straight line, and I knew she was biting her tongue.

"What were you doing at twenty?" I asked Sheldon.

"I was in mortuary school," he said automatically. "But I'm an exception to the rule. Did you know the average age of when a person finds a stable job they stick with for more than ten years is thirty-nine? So by those statistics all of us could be on a different career path soon. I mean, did you ever think you'd go from being an ER doctor to doing what you're doing now?"

He had a point, and I looked at Lily with raised brows.

"All I'm saying is just be careful," I said.

"Careful is my middle name," he said, adjusting his glasses again. "Not really. It's Ray. My mom watched *Goodfellas* a lot when she was pregnant with me, and she thought about leaving my dad for Ray Liotta."

"I guess she decided to stick it out with your dad," Lily said.

He shrugged. "Until he left with his girlfriend." He checked his hair in the small wall mirror behind a big vase of fresh flowers. "I should've used the hair dye. Leena would've liked it. She's picking me up any minute."

"In what?" Lily asked, her eyes on the pathology textbook spread across her lap. "Her hearse?"

"It's not a hearse," Sheldon said calmly. "It's a black Lincoln Town Car. Completely different."

"Right. Because the color scheme is what makes it creepy, not the fact that she bought it from a funeral home in Richmond."

I cleared my throat. "Sheldon, you know we care about you, right?"

He blinked again, his eyes magnified behind his thick lenses. "Sure," he said.

"Then I'm going to give you my opinion," I said. "This girl qualifies as creepy. You should be careful. You're too smart to ignore red flags when they're right in front of you."

Lily looked up. "Finally, someone with sense. Leena wants Sheldon to take her on a romantic midnight picnic." She closed her textbook with a thud. "In the cemetery."

"To be fair," I said carefully. "People do a lot weirder stuff than that."

"In Olde Town Cemetery," Sheldon added. "She says the energy there is perfect for communing with spirits, especially now that someone has been murdered."

"Ah," I said, narrowing my eyes at Sheldon. "And you said what, exactly?"

He shuffled his feet nervously. "I said I'd think about it."

"Sheldon," Lily said with the patience of a saint. "Normal women don't ask their boyfriends to have picnics in cemeteries. They ask for dinner and a movie. Maybe flowers. Not séances and sandwiches with a side of supernatural."

"But she's not normal," Sheldon said, as if this were a selling point. "She's unique. Interesting. She reads tarot cards and knows all about crystals and energy fields."

"She also works at a donut shop and thinks black lipstick is appropriate workplace attire," I pointed out.

"There's nothing wrong with self-expression," Sheldon said defensively, which was rich coming from someone who looked like he'd been attacked by a makeup counter.

"There's self-expression, and then there's dating Wednesday Addams," Lily said. "What's next? Is she going to ask you to help her perform ritual sacrifices?"

Sheldon's silence was telling.

"Oh my God," Lily said, sitting up straighter. "She already has, hasn't she?"

"It's not what you think," Sheldon said quickly. "She just mentioned that some herbs work better when they're blessed under certain moon phases, and that sometimes you need to offer something to the earth spirits to show respect."

"What kind of something?" I asked, though I wasn't sure I wanted to know.

"Just small things. A lock of hair. Maybe a few drops of blood. Nothing major."

Lily buried her face in her hands. "We're going to find you dismembered in a pentagram, aren't we?"

"That's not how pentagram magic works,"

Sheldon said with the confidence of someone who'd clearly done research.

"The fact that you know that is exactly my point," I said.

A car horn honked outside, and Sheldon immediately perked up like a dog hearing a dinner bell.

"That's her," he said, checking his reflection in the window and immediately regretting it when he saw the eyeliner smudged under his left eye.

"How do I look?" he asked, trying to fix the makeup disaster with his finger.

"Like you're about to become a cautionary tale," Lily said.

"You look..." I searched for something constructive to say. "Very committed to the aesthetic. And take an umbrella. It looks like it's going to rain. That won't be good for your makeup."

"Just remember," Lily added, "if she suggests anything involving blood, candles, or ancient burial grounds, the answer is no."

"What if it's just candles?" Sheldon asked hopefully.

"No," Lily and I said in unison.

Sheldon grabbed a black jacket I'd never seen before and headed for the door, the baggy jeans making swooshing sounds as he walked.

"You two worry too much. Leena's just...spiritually aware."

"That's what they said about Charles Manson," Lily called after him.

The front door closed with a decisive click, leaving Lily and me alone with the lingering scent of whatever hair product Sheldon had used and the certain knowledge that we'd probably be visiting him in jail before the week was out.

"Think he'll listen?" I asked.

"Not a chance," Lily said, gathering up her textbooks. "But at least when they find his body, we'll be able to tell the police we tried to warn him."

"I should call his mother," I said. "Except he's twenty-five years old."

"Well someone needs to knock some sense into him," Lily said angrily and then she fell back onto the carpet and put her arms over her face. "Sorry, I'm being awful. Finals are making me crazy. I haven't slept more than three hours a night in two weeks."

"I figured as much," I said. "I've been there. And to be fair, Sheldon does need a keeper."

"I know, I know. I really am worried about him." Lily dropped her arms down to her side and sat up slowly. "I should get going. These organic chemistry formulas won't memorize themselves."

"Good luck with exams."

"Thanks. And Jaye? Try to get some rest. You look exhausted."

After she left, I stood there for a moment,

thinking about friendship and family and the people we choose to protect. Sheldon might be making terrible decisions, but he was our terrible decision-maker, and we'd watch out for him whether he wanted us to or not.

It was just one more thing to worry about in what was shaping up to be a very complicated week.

CHAPTER FOUR

THE CEMETERY LOOKED DIFFERENT IN THE LATE afternoon light than it had that morning. What had been merely eerie in the soft dawn mist now felt actively malevolent as shadows lengthened between the weathered headstones and the sky above churned with slate-gray clouds that promised another round of Virginia's unpredictable spring weather.

I parked behind Jack's Tahoe and made my way through the expanded perimeter, noting how much larger the cordoned area had become since I'd left for the lab. Yellow tape now encircled nearly a quarter of the historic section, fluttering in the wind like warnings no one wanted to heed. I could see Martinez crouched beside a headstone about thirty yards from where we'd found Thomas Whitman's body, his expensive suit somehow still immaculate despite hours of investigation work.

The scene felt heavier somehow, weighted with more than just the approaching weather. There was an anticipation in the air that made the hair on my arms stand up, as if the very ground beneath my feet was holding its breath, waiting for something terrible to be revealed.

"Found something interesting?" I called out as I approached the group.

Jack looked up, his expression grim in the fading light. "More than we bargained for," he said. "Get an ID on the victim?"

"Thomas Andrew Whitman, age fifty-two, local resident."

"That's an old family name in this area," Jack said. "There are Whitmans buried all over this county going back to the early 1700s."

I was just noticing Martinez and Cole and several other members of the forensics team stationed at different headstones throughout the section, combing through grass and searching empty stone urns for clues. No one left flowers anymore for those buried so long ago—these graves had been forgotten by everyone except whoever had chosen to desecrate them.

"Well, this looks like a nightmare," I told Jack,

taking in the scope of the expanded investigation. "What is all this?"

"Take a look," he said, pointing to the grave he'd been studying. He handed me a pair of latex gloves and I slipped them on with the automatic efficiency that came from years in the medical field.

The carving on Jonathan Blackwood's headstone was precise and intentional. Someone had used what appeared to be a laser to gouge the words *THE FIRST STONE HAS BEEN CAST* into the weathered granite below the original inscription. The cuts were fresh, white stone showing through the gray patina that had accumulated over centuries like open wounds in the ancient rock.

"Very neat, very clean," I said, running my finger along one of the carved letters. Tiny flakes of stone dust still clung to the grooves. "Very fresh."

"Agreed," Cole said, stepping carefully around the evidence markers that had sprouted like metallic flowers throughout the section. "But it gets better. Or worse, depending on how you look at it."

He gestured toward the other graves they'd been examining with the weary expression of a man who'd seen too many cases turn complicated. "We found markings on four other headstones, all from the same general time period. Come see."

We made our way through the maze of burial sites,

careful not to disturb the various pieces of evidence that were still being catalogued. The grass was damp beneath our feet, and the darkening sky had turned the air thick and electric. Every shadow seemed to shift and move, as if the dead themselves were restless.

The first marked grave belonged to someone named Ezekiel Morton, died 1726. Carved into the base of his headstone was a symbol that looked like scales—crude but unmistakably recognizable as the scales of justice, the kind a child might draw but executed with the calculated intent of an adult message.

"Morton," Cole said, consulting his notebook. "I've heard that name before."

"It's an old King George family," I said, searching my memory for the connections that small-town life created over generations. "There's a Morton Road just outside town, and there used to be Morton's Pharmacy back when I was a kid, but the big chain stores put them out of business."

The irony wasn't lost on me—another old family reduced to a street name and fading memories, while their ancestor's grave was being used to send messages about justice.

"Then there's this one," Cole said, pointing to another grave about twenty feet away where Martinez stood like a well-dressed sentinel.

"Rebecca Hughes, 1698–1726," Martinez said,

looking up from his documentation. "Someone's carved Roman numerals into the side of her headstone—VI, XII, III. Fresh cuts, just like the others."

"Could be dates," Cole said. "Or some kind of sequence. Maybe a code."

Jack grunted in agreement and we moved to the next marked burial site, our small procession winding through historic section like mourners at a funeral no one wanted to attend.

The third grave showed the most elaborate marking. William Lawson, 1665–1729, had what looked like a broken sword carved deep into the stone beneath his name. The blade was fractured in two places, the hilt separated from the tip, with jagged lines suggesting a violent break rather than a clean cut. The carving was meticulous, almost artistic in its precision despite depicting destruction.

"Lawson," I said, looking at Jack with raised eyebrows. "Well, that hits close to home."

"My dad will have all the information on him," Jack said, his voice carrying the mix of pride and exasperation that came from having family roots that ran deep into Virginia soil. "But I know he's an ancestor. Lawsons date back to the 1600s in Virginia. I have no idea why his grave would have been marked, though."

"You can never say people in the south don't have long memories," Cole said.

"I've never understood why Virginia is considered the south," a woman said from behind us.

I jumped slightly at the sound of her voice, my nerves already on edge from the cemetery's oppressive atmosphere. I hadn't seen her kneeling down and searching near Jack's ancestor's grave for anything the killer might have left behind. She was a small woman with dark brown hair pulled back in a practical ponytail at the nape of her neck. Her face was narrow and sharp featured, and she was devoid of makeup in the way of someone who had more important things to worry about than appearance. She was one of those people who just blended into the scenery—even after looking at her closely I wasn't sure I'd be able to recall her features if I had to describe her to someone. I'd seen her on investigations before, but we'd never had reason to interact.

"That's because you're a Yankee, Potts," Cole said, grinning in the way that suggested this was an ongoing debate between them. "We're below the Mason-Dixon line. This is the south. And we like it that way."

Potts rolled her eyes with the familiarity of someone who'd had this conversation before. "Yes, it makes total sense to still use the Mason-Dixon line as a marker in the twenty-first century. Nothing like living in the past."

"If you understood the south, then you'd understand that's a prerequisite," Cole said. "I thought you knew that before you moved here."

She snorted out a laugh and brushed dirt from her hands as she stood. "I was just looking for a cheap place to live. Boston forensics techs make less than public sanitation workers. I figured being able to pay rent was more important than staying a Yankee."

"Once a Yankee, always a Yankee," Cole said with mock solemnity. "But we're glad you're here anyway."

"Uh-huh," she said, her tone suggesting she'd heard variations of this welcome before. "I could tell that right off when someone left a small Confederate flag and a bunch of tea bags in my locker. I figured whoever left it wasn't going to be winning any History categories on Jeopardy anytime soon."

"Jenkins," Cole and Martinez said in unison, their voices carrying the weary recognition of cops who knew exactly which of their colleagues was responsible for every stupid prank.

"Guy isn't the sharpest knife in the drawer," Cole said.

"If it gets out of hand, come see me, Potts," Jack said, and his tone carried the authority of someone who took workplace harassment seriously.

"I can handle myself, Sheriff," she said, giving me a glance for the first time—taking my measure the way cops did with civilians on active cases. "Besides, I ain't no snitch." She looked at Cole and Martinez with exaggerated innocence. "Did I use that properly in a sentence?"

"You'll do just fine, Potts," Cole said and slapped her on the shoulder with good-natured approval before leading us to the next area of the cemetery.

"Why do I smell rosemary?" I asked. "Are people planting herbs on grave sites instead of flowers?"

"It's me," Potts said. "I put rosemary oil under my nose. I've never been able to stand the smells at crime scenes, so I've been using this for years. I figure it's better than throwing up."

"You're not wrong," I said. "Every once in a while I'll get one where I still have to use Vicks to cover the smell. Remember the lady that got eaten by her cats?" I asked, turning to Jack.

"Not one I'm likely to forget anytime soon," he said.

"It wasn't pretty," I told Potts. "Maybe next time I'll try the rosemary oil."

"I'm not afraid to admit I'm glad I missed that one," Potts said with a shudder and then walked away.

"Any others?" I asked Martinez.

"Oh, yeah. Over here we've got the grave that really caught our attention," Martinez said.

The headstone read *Sarah Whitman, 1702–1731,* and below the original inscription that said *LOVING*

WIFE AND MOTHER, someone had carved a simple but chilling message. *JUSTICE SERVED*.

"Whitman," I said. "Same as our victim."

"Can't be a coincidence," Jack said, his expression darkening as the implications settled over him like storm clouds. "Now we just need to figure out why it's not a coincidence."

The weight of history pressed down on us as we stood over Sarah Whitman's grave. Centuries ago, she'd been buried here as a loving wife and mother. Today, her descendant had been murdered and staged on another grave just yards away. Whatever had started with her was finally coming full circle.

"There's one more," Cole said, moving only one family plot away, his voice carrying the careful neutrality cops used when they knew they were about to show you something that would give you nightmares.

The fifth marked grave was the most disturbing of all. Not because of what was carved into it, but because of what had been done around it. Someone had arranged small stones in a careful pattern around the headstone of Rachel Mills, 1690–1725. The stones formed what looked like a circle, with larger rocks placed at specific points that corresponded to compass directions. It was the kind of arrangement that belonged in horror movies or occult rituals, not in a Virginia cemetery on a Tuesday afternoon.

"So…is it just me or is this new?" I asked, feeling a cold chill creep up my spine that had nothing to do with the dropping temperature. As if we were getting confirmation from heaven, electricity split the sky in a jagged streak, making the hair on my arms stand up and dance. "Someone tell me this wasn't here this morning when we found the body."

"It wasn't here this morning," Jack confirmed with a tired sigh that suggested he was already calculating the additional manpower this would require. "Someone must have done it once we'd cleared out. The main area was cordoned off and I had a deputy posted to keep watch, but someone got through. But it's a big cemetery, and the historical section is a good distance from where our victim was found on unconsecrated ground.

"The only reason we found these was because we discovered the stones the killer used to place on the victim came from the fence that divides the two areas."

"Beats bringing them with you I guess," I said sarcastically. "But even with the distance this is still bold." I studied the meticulous arrangement of stones with growing unease. "Or desperate. Someone risked being seen to come back and add this."

Cole scanned the tree line that bordered this section of the cemetery with the ease of someone who'd learned that threats could come from anywhere. "Could have hidden in those woods and waited for us to focus our attention elsewhere."

The idea that someone had been out there watching us, waiting for the right moment to continue their twisted game, made my skin crawl. I found myself glancing toward the woods, half expecting to see eyes watching us from the shadows.

"So what do all the graves have in common?" I asked, trying to focus on the investigation rather than the growing sense that we were being observed.

"That's the million-dollar question," Jack said, pulling out his phone to check for messages.

The wind picked up, rustling through the oak trees overhead and sending dead leaves skittering across the graves like tiny ghosts fleeing some unseen horror. The temperature had dropped significantly since I'd arrived, and I could smell rain in the air—that distinctive metallic scent that preceded Virginia downpours.

"Well, since this case isn't interesting enough," I said, pulling out my preliminary autopsy report, "I should probably tell you my findings."

"Let me guess," Cole said with the gallows humor that sustained cops through the worst cases. "Snake bites? Exotic poisons? Death by a thousand tarot card cuts?"

"Close," I said. "Cardiac arrest."

"Heart attack?" Martinez asked, looking up from sealing another evidence bag.

"Heart attacks are different than cardiac arrest," I explained, falling back on the clinical language that helped me process the horror of what people did to each other. "A heart attack can cause cardiac arrest, but it doesn't always. Heart attacks occur because there's damage to the heart—blocked arteries, muscle death. Our victim had a perfectly healthy heart."

"So what killed him?" Jack asked, and I could see him running through possibilities in his mind, cataloguing threats and methods the way sheriffs learned to do.

"I guess today is the day for million-dollar questions," I said. "Could be a lot of things. Could have been poison, but you'll need to narrow it down before we can test for sure. We can ask for medical records to see if he had any history of arrhythmia or cardiomyopathy. Cardiac arrest can also be caused by severe physical stress."

"Like he could have been scared to death?" Cole asked.

"Pretty much," I said. "There are documented cases of people dying from extreme fear or shock. The surge of adrenaline can disrupt the heart's electrical system."

"Anything come back in the toxicology?" Martinez asked.

"No alcohol, no drugs—not even anything over the counter like aspirin or allergy medication. There wasn't much left in his stomach, but he'd had a meal of chicken at some point several hours before death. Protein tends to hang around longer than everything else."

The first rumble rolled across the sky, closer this time, followed by another brilliant flash that turned the cemetery into stark black and white for one frozen moment. The weather was moving in faster than anticipated, and the shadows between the graves had deepened to an almost impenetrable darkness despite the fact that it was barely past five o'clock.

Lieutenant Daniels was directing her team as they packed up their equipment in a hurry, the incoming tempest adding urgency to their methodical work. I watched Potts carefully secure evidence bags in waterproof containers, her movements efficient despite the pressure.

"We're heading out, Sheriff," Daniels called out, jogging toward her vehicle as the first fat raindrops began to fall. She and Potts hopped into a white van that immediately kicked up gravel as they drove toward the cemetery exit.

"Hell of a place for a murder," Cole said, settling

his Stetson more firmly on his head as the wind tried to snatch it away.

"Make sure we've got two deputies assigned here overnight," Jack said, his voice carrying the authority of someone who'd learned that active investigations attracted all kinds of unwanted attention. "I don't want anyone else adding anything to our scene. The last thing we need is someone deciding they want to do a séance or something on our investigation site."

The mention of séances made me think immediately of Sheldon and my earlier conversation about Leena wanting to have midnight cemetery picnics. The thought of his girlfriend dragging him to places like this for "spiritual communion" suddenly seemed a lot less harmless and a lot more dangerous.

A brilliant flash illuminated the entire cemetery, followed immediately by a crack that made us all flinch. The tempest was no longer approaching—it was here.

We made a dash for our vehicles, but not before I took one last look at the scene we were leaving behind. Even through the rain that had begun in earnest, fat drops that quickly turned into a steady downpour, I could see the yellow tape fluttering in the wind like prayer flags marking some unholy shrine.

"We've still got another hour or so of daylight," Jack said once we were safely inside the Tahoe, cranking up the heat against the sudden chill. "Now that you've got an ID on our victim, we can notify next of kin."

I was cold despite the heater, and I pulled my jacket tighter around me. "That would be the wife. Their place isn't far from here."

As we drove through the downpour toward the Whitman house to deliver the worst news any family could receive, I couldn't shake the feeling that we were racing against more than just time.

The windshield wipers fought a losing battle against the deluge, and through the rain-streaked glass, the countryside looked wild and untamed despite generations of civilization. It was easy to imagine how this same landscape had looked to Colonial settlers, how it had witnessed the fear and superstition that led to Bridget Ashworth's death, and how it was now witnessing the consequences of secrets that had been buried for centuries.

CHAPTER FIVE

RAIN HAMMERED THE TAHOE'S WINDSHIELD AS WE turned onto Whitman Lane, where crushed oyster shell popped and hissed beneath the tires like bones breaking. The headlights caught ancient oaks that leaned over the drive, their branches twisted into shapes that belonged in nightmares, Spanish moss hanging like shrouds.

The air tasted metallic, electric—that particular flavor of Virginia storm that made your teeth ache and your skin prickle. Lightning split the sky, illuminating a house that rose from the darkness like something that had been waiting three centuries for us to arrive.

"Jesus," Jack breathed.

The Whitman house was Georgian perfection, all hand-laid brick and towering columns that had weathered revolution, civil war, and countless storms. But perfection had an edge to it—like a beautiful woman with secrets, it drew you in while warning you to keep your distance.

Jack parked behind a mud-splattered Jeep that looked like it had been driven through hell and hadn't bothered to stop for a car wash. Field equipment crowded the back—shovels, brushes, collection bags. Tools for digging up the past.

We ran for the porch, rain slicing through the humid air like cold knives. My boots splashed through puddles that reflected lightning, and the smell of wet earth and old wood filled my lungs. The front door was massive oak with iron hinges that belonged in a museum, and when Jack's knock echoed through the house, it sounded like we were summoning ghosts.

The woman who opened the door looked like she'd been wrestling with the dead for days and hadn't quite won. Patricia Whitman stood tall in the doorway—late forties, athletic build going soft at the edges, auburn hair shot with gray and yanked back in a ponytail that had given up hours ago. Red clay caked her boots, dirt crescented her fingernails, and her field clothes carried the earthy smell of excavation sites.

But it was her eyes that made my pulse kick. Green as bottle glass and sharp enough to cut, they locked on to Jack's badge with the intensity of a predator recognizing another predator.

"Sheriff Lawson," Jack said. "This is Dr. Graves. I'm afraid—"

"He's dead." Her voice was flat as old champagne. Not a question. A statement of fact, delivered with all the emotion of a weather report.

"Yes, ma'am. We found your husband's body this morning. We're treating it as a homicide."

I waited for the collapse. The tears. The denial. Hell, even anger would have been normal.

Patricia Whitman did none of those things.

Instead, she stepped back with the controlled precision of a woman who'd been expecting us, her jaw tight enough to crack teeth. "Come in."

The foyer smelled of beeswax and old paper, leather and whiskey—the particular cocktail of scents that came with old money and older secrets. She led us to a living room where Colonial furniture mixed with modern chaos. Research materials covered every surface like she and Thomas had been trying to solve a puzzle with pieces scattered across three centuries.

Patricia went straight to a crystal decanter and poured three fingers of bourbon, neat. The amber liquid didn't tremble in the glass. Her hand was steady as a surgeon's.

"Where?" One word, sharp as a scalpel.

"Olde Towne Cemetery."

She laughed—a sound like glass breaking. "Of course. They couldn't resist the symbolism, could they?" She took a long pull of bourbon, and I watched her throat work as she swallowed. "The threats started three weeks ago."

I caught Jack's eye. In all my years working with the dead and their grieving families, I'd seen every possible reaction to death notifications. Collapse. Hysteria. Denial. Rage. But this cold, controlled fury? This was something else entirely. Jack's subtle nod told me his cop instincts were screaming the same warnings as mine.

"What kind of threats?" Jack pulled out his notebook, but his eyes never left Patricia's face.

"Anonymous at first. Notes on Thomas's car. Emails from dummy accounts saying he should stop digging." Another swallow of bourbon. "Then two weeks ago, he presented our findings to the historical society board. That's when things got specific."

"What findings?"

Patricia moved to a table buried under maps and photographs, her movements fluid despite the bourbon. "We've been documenting unmarked graves throughout the county. Bodies that shouldn't exist. People who were erased from history after being murdered for their land."

She spread out photographs. Excavation sites.

Skeletal remains. Personal effects that whispered of wealth and position—gold buttons, silver buckles, jewelry that had outlasted the flesh that wore it.

"Three centuries of murder and theft, Sheriff. And certain families have been protecting those secrets ever since." Her finger traced property lines on an old map. "Including what really happened to Bridget Ashworth's land."

"Tell me about the board meeting," Jack said.

"Richard Blackwood went volcanic. Screamed about libel, about destroying family reputations." Patricia's knuckles went white around her glass. "But Margaret Randolph was the one who scared Thomas."

"How so?"

"He said she went pale as death when he showed the evidence. After the meeting, she cornered him in the parking lot." Patricia's voice dropped, cold as winter stone. "Told him that some sleeping dogs should stay sleeping. That terrible accidents happened to people who went digging in the wrong places."

The rain lashed the windows, and thunder rolled through the house like a warning.

"When Thomas tried to argue, she said his expertise in finding bodies might serve him well when he became one."

"Did he report it?"

"He wanted evidence first. Real evidence." Patricia moved to a secretary desk, pulled out a folder. "Yesterday, he was supposed to meet with the state archaeological commission. He'd found original surveyor's notes from 1725 in the courthouse basement. Documents that proved everything—that Bridget Ashworth's thousand acres of riverfront property was stolen using forged documents."

She handed Jack the folder, and I saw his jaw tighten as he scanned the photocopies.

"Mrs. Whitman," Jack said carefully, "we'll need Thomas's phone records, appointment calendar, any notes from recent meetings."

"I'll pull it all together." She set down her empty glass with a soft click. "Sheriff, my husband knew the risks. He went anyway because he believed the truth mattered more than his safety." For the first time, something flickered in her eyes—not grief, but rage. "Don't let them bury this along with him."

"We won't. Is there someone you can call?"

"My sister in Richmond." Patricia's spine straightened like she was preparing for battle. "I'll be fine. I always am."

The words hung in the air like a confession.

Outside, we ran through the rain to the Tahoe, water streaming off our jackets, the smell of ozone sharp in the air.

"That was interesting," Jack said once we were inside, his tone deceptively mild.

"No tears. No shock. No questions about how he died." I watched Patricia's silhouette appear in the window, backlit and motionless. "Just straight to who and why."

"Could be shock."

"Could be." I turned to face him. "Or could be she's been expecting this. Could be she already knew."

Jack's fingers drummed against the steering wheel—his tell when his mind was racing. "Phone records. Alibi. Financial records. The works."

"She didn't kill him," I said, surprising myself with my certainty. "But she knows more than she's saying."

"Agreed." Jack started the engine. "The question is whether what she's hiding is relevant to his murder or just to their marriage."

Lightning illuminated the world in stark relief— the house, the trees, the rain—before plunging us back into darkness. In that brief moment of clarity, I saw Patricia still standing at the window, watching us leave.

A woman carved from stone, waiting for her moment to strike back.

CHAPTER SIX

THE RAIN HAMMERED AGAINST THE TAHOE'S windshield as we pulled out of Patricia Whitman's driveway. I couldn't shake the image of her standing at that window—no tears, no collapse, just cold fury waiting for its moment. The oyster shells crunched beneath our tires, and through the passenger mirror I watched the Colonial house disappear into darkness.

"That woman knows more than she's telling us," I said, settling back against the heated seat.

Jack's hands tightened on the steering wheel as he navigated the winding country road. "She's also just found out her husband was killed for trying to expose three-hundred-year-old murders. That's enough to process without us pushing harder. We'll circle back."

Something in his voice made me look at him more closely. "Jack? What's bothering you?"

He was quiet for a long moment, the only sound the rhythmic sweep of windshield wipers fighting the rain. "My family's been in King George County since the early 1700s," he said finally. "Lawsons were among the original landowners, built their wealth on tobacco farming and land speculation. I've always been proud of that legacy—the idea that we were founding families, that we helped build this community."

"And now you're wondering if that wealth was built on something uglier," I said softly.

"William Lawson's grave was marked just like the others. What if..." He trailed off, but I could hear the weight of the unfinished thought.

"What if your ancestor was involved in murdering Bridget Ashworth? What if he was part of the conspiracy to steal her land?"

Jack's knuckles went white against the steering wheel. "My mother used to tell me stories about William Lawson when I was a kid. How he was a respected member of the community, how he helped establish the county boundaries, how he testified in important legal cases. I named my horse after him when I was twelve."

The pain in his voice made my chest ache. Jack's family history wasn't just academic to him—it was part of his identity, part of what had shaped him into the man who believed so deeply in justice and protecting people who couldn't protect themselves.

"Jack," I said carefully, "we don't know anything for certain yet. William Lawson's grave being marked could mean a dozen different things."

"Could it?" His laugh was bitter. "Five graves marked around a murder scene, all from the same time period as Bridget Ashworth's execution. That's not a coincidence, Jaye. Someone's sending a message about those families."

I reached over and placed my hand on his arm, feeling the muscle tension beneath his jacket. "Then we'll find out the truth. Whatever it is."

"What if the truth is that my family built their fortune on blood money? What if every acre of land we own, every dollar in our accounts, came from murdering an innocent woman three hundred years ago?"

The anguish in his voice broke my heart. This was more than professional concern—this was personal in the deepest possible way.

"Whatever the truth is," I said quietly, "we'll face it together. And if your family was involved, that doesn't define who you are now. You've spent your entire career fighting for justice."

Jack nodded, but I could see the worry still etched in the lines around his eyes. He was quiet for another moment before seeming to shake himself back to the present.

"Where are we going?" I asked.

"My parents' place. If my family's name is on that grave, they could be in danger. And maybe they know something about William Lawson that could help us understand why his grave was marked."

The Lawson estate sprawled across prime Virginia countryside like something from a coffee table book about Southern living. Even through the driving rain, you could sense the permanence of it—hundreds of acres that had been in Jack's family since the mid 1600s, though the house he'd grown up in had been built at the turn of the twentieth century. The circular drive wound through towering oaks older than the country itself, their branches whipping in the storm, creating shadows that danced in our headlights.

The house was understated elegance—red brick with white columns, not ostentatious but solid, permanent, like the family itself. The windows glowed warmly against the storm, and I'd spent countless hours here growing up, more than at my own home. Seeing it always made something in my chest ease, even on a night like this.

Before Jack could even kill the engine, the front door flew open and his mother appeared on the covered porch, backlit by the warm light from inside.

Jeri Lawson stood maybe an inch over five feet, but she commanded attention like someone three times her size. Her dark hair, the same shade as Jack's, was pulled back in a casual ponytail, and she wore jeans and a University of Virginia sweatshirt that had seen better days. But her pale blue eyes were sharp as ever, and I guarantee she had already cataloged everything from Jack's tense shoulders to my exhaustion.

"Get in here before you drown!" she called out over the rain. "And don't tell me this is a social call. You've got that official look about you. And I'm not going to take offense that it's been a week since I last saw you and you're not just here because you missed my cooking."

I chuckled and we dashed through the rain to the porch, and Jeri immediately pulled Jack into a fierce hug despite being soaked.

"You look terrible," she said bluntly, then turned to me with arms already opening. "Come here, my girl. You look hungry. Why aren't you feeding her, Jack? She's always been skin and bones."

"I've been trying," Jack said, water dripping from his jacket onto the porch floor. "She's stubborn."

"She's always been hardheaded too," Jeri said, pulling me into a hug that smelled like vanilla and the coffee she'd probably been drinking. She pulled back, studying my face with those keen eyes. "You need some real food. Rich! The kids are here! Come on, y'all come inside and get dry. This weather is driving me batty. I just washed my car yesterday." She took a quick breath and then said, "I made a pot roast for dinner. There's plenty left over."

I was used to Jeri's rapid-fire speak. She had the gift of being able to talk about everything and nothing all at the same time.

Jack's father emerged from somewhere deeper in the house, reading glasses perched on his nose and what looked like financial papers in his hand. Richard Lawson had passed his blue eyes and strong jaw down to his son, though his hair had gone silver years ago. He moved with the easy confidence of someone who'd never met a situation he couldn't handle.

"Jack, you look like someone just told you the Redskins moved to Dallas," Rich said, setting down his papers to pull his son into a back-slapping hug. "What's wrong?"

"That's what we need to talk about," Jack said.

"Well come on into the kitchen," he said. "I'm sure your mother is dying to feed you. Jaye, you look beautiful. Give me a hug."

And I melted into his embrace and held on a little longer. Jack was the best man I'd ever known. And he'd learned everything about what it meant to be a man from his father. It's why I wasn't worried about the parenting part of having a baby. Even if I didn't know what I was doing, Jack had the experience of being raised by two people who'd done things right.

The kitchen was exactly as I remembered—warm yellow walls that seemed to glow in the lamplight, copper pots hanging from a wrought-iron rack, and a massive farmhouse table that could seat twelve but usually just held Jeri's latest projects. Tonight it was covered with what looked like tax documents and estate planning papers—the kind of paperwork that came with managing centuries of accumulated wealth—and at the far end was her sewing machine and a stack of fabric squares.

"Ignore the mess," Jeri said. "Your dad is running numbers to do upgrades to some rental properties, and I'm making a quilt."

"That looks like a baby quilt," I said, looking at the cute fabrics she'd chosen.

"It's always nice to have one as backup when a baby shower pops up," she said. "Or when someone has unexpected news." She fluttered her lashes at me and it was everything I could do to keep my face blank of expression.

"Pot roast smells good," Jack said, diverting her attention.

"I haven't even put anything away yet," she said, hurrying over to the stove to scoop up mashed potatoes and cover it with her pot roast and gravy. "It's still nice and warm. Y'all sit at the table. Rich, clear some space."

"Already done," he said. "And maybe while you're getting things ready Jack can explain what's going on. Do we have any pie?"

"Of course we have pie," Jeri said. "I made a cherry pie this morning. You already knew that."

Rich winked at me and said, "Yes, but I wanted to make sure you didn't forget you made a cherry pie. Go ahead, son. You look like you're about to burst at the seams."

"I don't know if you've seen the news about the most recent murder," Jack said without preamble. "Thomas Whitman was found on Bridget Ashworth's grave."

Rich nodded, pushing his reading glasses up to rest on his head. "It's all that's been on the television. Is it the same Thomas Whitman who wanted permission to dig up some of our property? Archae-ologist, right? He could never prove there was anything to dig up, so he wasn't able to get the permits he wanted since it's our private land."

"He's the one," Jack said, nodding. "But the case has taken an interesting turn—there were other graves marked—old graves—and it's related to the murder. William Lawson's grave was one of those marked."

The knife in Jeri's hand stilled. Thunder rumbled overhead, making the lights flicker for just a moment. "Good grief. Why in the world would William Lawson's grave be tied to a murder?"

"That's what we're trying to find out," Jack said, looking at his father. "What do you actually know about William Lawson? Other than the family stories that have been passed down."

Rich leaned back against the counter, crossing his arms. The rain drummed against the windows, creating a steady rhythm that somehow made the kitchen feel more insulated, safer. "More than you might think. We've got quite a bit of our history locked away upstairs. Your grandmother was quite fascinated with our genealogy. It was her hobby. Other old ladies put together puzzles and played dominoes, but Edith Lawson researched dead people."

"I remember her," Jack said. "She was always telling me some tale or another any time I'd go to stay with her and Grandpop."

"She was so into it you'd have thought the Lawsons were her direct bloodline," Rich said.

"And before she passed," Jeri said, "she gave everything to me. Hoped that I would continue the work she'd started. I supposed I should now that technology has made things easier." Jeri grabbed my hand and looked dead into my eyes. "There's nothing

I hate more than sitting in a dusty old library staring at pages that make no sense. But give me a good movie and a box of art supplies and I'm your girl. When you and Jack have kids I'm going to be the fun grandparent."

I chuckled, knowing without a doubt that she would.

"Edith had boxes and boxes of documents," Jeri continued. "Journals, letters, legal documents going back three centuries."

"And?" Jack leaned forward.

"William Lawson was a revered man," Rich said, settling into a chair that creaked in protest. Lightning flashed outside, illuminating the room in stark white for a moment. "Have you seen the letters from the governor? The man was the county's chief constable, responsible for keeping law and order. He was called to Williamsburg to help investigate a smuggling ring that was threatening Colonial trade routes—the governor specifically requested him because of his reputation for being incorruptible."

"That's why he wasn't here during Bridget Ashworth's trial," Jeri added, her small hands folding together on the table. "He was in Williamsburg on the governor's orders, tracking down smugglers and pirates. There are travel documents, official correspondence, even a letter from him to his wife expressing frustration that he couldn't get home for the trial because he knew it was a farce."

I felt Jack's shoulders relax slightly. "He knew?"

"Oh, he knew." Rich's expression darkened. "The family stories all say the same thing—when William got back from Williamsburg and found out what had happened to Bridget Ashworth, he was furious. Supposedly he tried everything to get the verdict overturned. Wrote letters, filed complaints, even tried to get the governor involved. But by then it was too late. She was dead, and the other families had already divided up her land. They had too much power, too much influence."

"But here's the interesting part," Jeri said, leaning forward despite another rumble of thunder that shook the windows. "They offered William part of the Ashworth land, hoping that would keep him quiet. But he refused them. The Lawsons never took any of the Ashworth land. Not one acre. In fact—" she looked at Rich, who nodded, "—William secretly sent money to Bridget's husband and daughter after they fled north. Helped them start over."

"How do you know that?" Jack asked.

"Family records," Rich said simply. "We have William's original ledgers—his widow preserved everything after he died. Which was only a few years after Bridget. He wasn't an old man, by any means, but times were harder and wilder back then. Apparently he was trying to break up a drunken brawl between Nathanial Blackwood and Joseph Hughes and he got a knife in his gut for his troubles. Lived long enough to tell his wife and children goodbye."

"He was killed by Blackwood and Hughes?" Jack asked, brow arched. "They're two of the families whose graves were marked."

"They're also two of the families who got part of the Ashworth land," Rich said. "But that was three hundred years ago." Jeri put a piece of pie down in front of him and a fresh cup of coffee. "I guess it makes sense why his widow would keep all the documentation about the trial and the money transfers to Jedediah Ashworth.

"Maybe she felt like she'd need them later down the road. Since both Virginia and Massachusetts were British colonies at that time, William hired a private courier to deliver British pounds to the Green Dragon Tavern so Jedediah could pick it up. The name listed on the correspondence was Jed Ashford, and from what I understand, once he received the money he and his daughter changed their names and disappeared."

The lights flickered again as the storm intensified, and Jeri got up to light some candles, just in case. The warm glow added to the kitchen's coziness, making the violence of the storm outside seem distant.

"So why would someone mark his grave?" I asked. "If he was trying to help?"

"Maybe because he failed," Jack said slowly. "He had the power and position to potentially stop it, but he wasn't here. If he'd been at that trial…"

"Or maybe," Rich said quietly, "Someone blames him for dying before he could get justice. He was the only one with enough authority and respect to challenge what happened, and when he was killed, any hope of overturning the verdict died with him."

"He died trying to keep the peace between the very families who'd stolen from Bridget," I said, the irony not lost on me. "And they killed him for it."

Jack set down his fork, pushing his empty plate aside, and I saw him take a breath. "Mom, Dad—whoever killed Thomas Whitman is targeting all six families from the trial. Someone carved symbols on the headstones. Messages."

"What kind of messages?" Rich asked, his voice quiet.

"Scales of justice. Roman numerals. Things about bearing witness." Jack picked at the edge of his napkin. "Like someone's been planning this for a long time."

"And they marked William's grave," Jeri said, not a question.

"Yes," Jack confirmed. "Someone wants us to know we're all connected to this."

The rain hammered harder against the windows, and for a moment nobody said anything.

"Well, that's just peachy," Jeri said, setting down her coffee with a sharp click. "Three hundred years later and someone's still holding a grudge? People need hobbies."

"Mom, please," Jack said softly, and I saw Jeri's expression soften. "I can't do my job if I'm worried about you."

She studied her son's face for a long moment. "No."

"Mom—"

"I said no. This is our home. We're not running because some lunatic has a grudge about something that happened three centuries ago."

"Jeri, be reasonable," Rich said.

"I am being reasonable. We have the security system, we have the dogs, we have neighbors who'd notice if something was wrong." She crossed her arms. "We're not leaving."

Jack stood up, frustration clear in every line of his body. "Someone is killing descendants of these families. Dad's ancestor is on that list."

"Your ancestor too," Jeri pointed out.

"Which is why I need you safe!"

They stared at each other across the kitchen, and the resemblance had never been stronger—same stubborn jaw, same refusal to back down.

"What about Martha's Vineyard?" Rich said suddenly.

Both Jack and Jeri turned to look at him.

"The Stewarts have been begging us to visit their place. It's an island—one way on, one way off. Easy to monitor." He looked at his wife. "You've been wanting to go. And I could check on that marina investment while we're there."

Jeri's eyes narrowed. "You're trying to trick me into a vacation."

"I'm trying to keep you alive while also looking at a business opportunity," Rich said calmly. "Two birds, one stone."

"I don't like it."

"You don't have to like it. But Jack's right. Until this is resolved, we're targets."

She was quiet for a long moment, then threw her dish towel on the counter. "Fine. But I'm not happy about it."

"Noted," Rich said, already pulling out his phone. "I'll call the Stewarts."

"And I'll pack," Jeri said, then pointed at Jack. "But you call us every day. None of this protecting-us-from-worry nonsense. We get updates."

"Deal."

"And make sure your wife eats actual food. Not just coffee and donuts from that Lady Jane's place."

"Hey, their donuts are really good," I protested.

"They're sugar and grease," Jeri said flatly. "Jack, promise me you'll get some vegetables in her."

"I promise," Jack said, clearly trying not to laugh.

She headed for the stairs, then paused. "Rich, tell the Stewarts we'll be there tomorrow afternoon. I need time to pack properly and arrange for someone to watch the dogs."

"Tomorrow?" Jack started to protest.

"Tonight we're locked up tight with the alarm on," Jeri said firmly. "I'm not driving to Richmond to catch a ferry in this weather. We leave first thing in the morning."

Jack looked like he wanted to argue, but Rich held up a hand. "Your mother's right. We'll be fine tonight. I'll make sure the security system is armed, doors and windows locked. We've weathered worse storms than this."

An hour later, after Jack had done his own check of the house's security and made them promise to call if anything seemed off, we finally left. Rich handed Jack a weathered wooden box as we stood at the door.

"Your grandmother's collection on William Lawson," he said. "Maybe it'll help.

Jack took the box carefully.

Jeri pulled him into a fierce hug, having to stand on her toes to do it properly. "You find whoever's doing this. You stop them."

"I will."

She turned to me next, and her hug was softer but no less intense. "Take care of each other," she whispered against my ear. Then, louder: "And you know, we're not getting any younger. Be nice to have some grandkids before we're too old to enjoy them."

"Seriously?" Jack asked. "That wasn't subtle at all."

"I wasn't trying to be," she said, grinning. "Your second cousin Keith had a baby. Named him Keith Junior." She shuddered. "Keith Junior. Can you imagine? Sounds like he should be selling used cars in Petersburg."

"We get it," Jack said, but he was fighting a smile.

"I'm just saying. Good genetic material shouldn't go to waste." She winked at me, and I had to bite my lip to keep from laughing.

Rich pulled Jack into a quick, hard hug. "Watch yourself."

"Always do."

"And Jack?" Rich paused at the door. "William died trying to do the right thing. Murdered by the very people he was trying to stop. Don't let that happen again."

The rain had eased to a steady drizzle as we walked to the Tahoe. The box sat between us like a passenger, full of secrets that had waited three hundred years to be told.

"Feel better?" I asked as we pulled onto the main road.

"Yeah," Jack admitted. "They'll be safe on the island tomorrow. And now I can focus on finding a killer without worrying about them."

We drove in comfortable silence for a few minutes, the rhythmic sweep of the wipers the only sound.

"Your mom wasn't exactly subtle with all those grandchildren hints," I said finally.

Jack laughed. "She never is. The baby quilt was a nice touch though. Very smooth."

"She knows, doesn't she? About the baby."

"She always knows. It's deeply unsettling." He glanced at me. "She's right about one thing though. You do need to eat a vegetable occasionally."

"Hey, french fries are vegetables."

"They're really not."

"They're made from potatoes. Potatoes grow in the ground. That's basically a salad."

Jack laughed, and some of the tension that had been riding his shoulders finally eased. "Your logic is terrifying."

"You married me."

"Best decision I ever made," he said, reaching over to squeeze my hand. "Even if you think french fries are health food."

CHAPTER SEVEN

JACK SEEMED MORE SETTLED AS WE PULLED BACK ONTO the main road, the rain still coming down but not quite as violently as before.

"We should head home," I said, stifling a yawn. "It's been a long day."

"Actually," Jack said, glancing at the dashboard clock, "Martinez gave me Al Contreras's number earlier—the maintenance guy who was supposed to lock the cemetery gates Monday night. He works nights at city facilities, so this is actually the perfect time to catch him."

"Of course he works nights," I muttered. "Because why would anyone in this case have normal hours?"

Jack was already pulling out his phone. "If

someone got into that cemetery through an unlocked gate, I need to know. This can't wait until morning."

I listened to Jack's side of the conversation as he explained who he was and asked if Al could meet them somewhere to talk. After a few minutes, Jack hung up.

"He suggested Martha's Diner," Jack said. "He's about to start his rounds but can meet us for a quick coffee."

"Well, at least there'll be coffee," I said, though what I really wanted was my bed. "And maybe pie."

Martha's Diner was one of those roadside establishments that had been serving truck drivers and insomniacs since the Eisenhower administration. The neon sign buzzed and flickered in the rain, casting pink and blue shadows across the puddle-strewn parking lot. Half the letters in *Martha's* had given up the ghost years ago, so it now read *Ma ha's*, which Emmy Lu always said made it sound like a laugh track for people with bad timing.

Inside, the familiar scent of coffee mingled with the smell of bacon grease and industrial-strength disinfectant. The black-and-white checkered floor was worn smooth by decades of work boots, and the red vinyl booths had been patched with duct tape in so many places they looked like they'd survived a knife fight.

Al Contreras sat alone in a corner booth,

hunched over a cup of coffee that steamed in the fluorescent lighting. He was a small, wiry man in his sixties with weathered hands and the kind of deep tan that came from working outdoors year-round. When he saw Jack approaching, he half stood and extended a calloused hand.

"Sheriff Lawson," he said, his voice carrying a slight Hispanic accent. "Thanks for meeting me here. I figured it was better than trying to talk over the rain."

"No problem, Al. This is Dr. Graves, our coroner." Jack slid into the booth across from Al, and I settled in beside him.

"Doctor." Al nodded respectfully. "Heard about what happened at Olde Towne Cemetery. Terrible thing. Makes a man feel responsible, you know?"

The waitress—a woman named Dorris who'd been working at Martha's since before I was born—appeared with coffee cups and a pot that looked like it had survived both World Wars. She poured without being asked, which was Martha's Diner policy. If you didn't want coffee, you went somewhere else.

"Tell me about Monday night," Jack said, adding cream to his cup. "Walk me through your routine."

Al's hands fidgeted around his coffee mug. "I start my rounds at nine thirty, usually finish up around midnight. Got the cemetery, the municipal building, the parks, couple other places. Cemetery's always last on my list 'cause it's the easiest—just check that the main gate's latched proper and the grounds are clear of any troublemakers."

"What time did you get there Monday night?" I asked.

"Around eleven fifteen, maybe eleven twenty. I was running behind because Mrs. Jorgenson had locked herself out of the library again." He took a sip of coffee and made a face that suggested it tasted exactly as it looked. "Third time this month. Woman's the head librarian but can't remember to take her keys when she goes to empty the trash."

"So you were late getting to the cemetery," Jack prompted.

"Yeah, and it was a clear night, nice and warm. I pulled up to the main iron gate—the public entrance —and it looked closed. I always give it a shake to make sure it's latched proper, but..." Al's voice trailed off, and he stared into his coffee cup like it might contain absolution.

"But?" I encouraged.

"But I was already running so late, and I could see the gate was pulled to. I figured it was locked and just drove on." He looked up at Jack with guilty eyes. "I know I should've gotten out and checked it proper. The back entrance where we keep the maintenance equipment is always locked—only grounds crew and funeral directors use that one. But the main gate, that's the one the public uses, and that's the one that should've been secured."

"Al." Jack's voice was gentle but firm. "Someone was determined to get into that cemetery Monday night. If the main gate had been locked, they could have tried the back entrance or found another way. A locked gate doesn't stop someone with bolt cutters or determination."

Al nodded, but I could see the guilt was going to eat at him for a long time.

"Did you see anything unusual while you were there?" I asked. "Any cars, people, anything that seemed out of place?"

"Well," Al said slowly, "there was a dark car parked over by the gas station across the street. Didn't think much of it at the time—people pull in there all hours to use the restroom or grab snacks from the vending machines. But it was just sitting there with the engine running."

"What kind of car?" Jack asked, his attention sharpening.

"Couldn't tell you the make or model. Too dark to make out details, even under those streetlights. But it was a sedan, dark color. Blue or black, maybe dark green. Hard to say."

"Did you see the driver?"

"Nah. Windows were tinted, or maybe it was just

too dark. But whoever it was, they were just sitting there. Waiting for something."

Or someone, I thought.

Jack nodded, committing the details to memory. "You've been helpful, Al. If you think of anything else, give me a call."

"I will, Sheriff. And I'm real sorry about not checking that gate proper."

"I bet you'll never do it again," Jack said, making Al smile.

"You got that right."

Jack caught Dorris's eye. "Could we get some pie to go?"

"You got it, honey," Dorris called back. "Give me ten minutes."

Jack left a generous tip on the table and we waited only five minutes for our order.

Outside, the rain had intensified, if such a thing were possible. We ran to the Tahoe, but by the time we got inside, we were both soaked.

"Well," I said, wringing water from my hair, "that gives us something to follow up on. A dark sedan near the cemetery around the time of the murder."

"Could be nothing," Jack said, starting the engine and cranking up the heat. "Someone stopping for gas or using the restroom. But it's worth noting. We'll see if Cole and Martinez can track down any security cameras in the area."

As we drove through the darkness toward home, I found myself thinking about the partial information we'd gathered. Al's oversight with the gate, a dark car that might or might not be significant, and a killer who'd managed to get into the cemetery undetected. We had pieces, but not enough to form a clear picture yet.

"Jack," I said as we turned onto the winding road that led to our house, "what if this isn't just about covering up historical land theft? What if someone's been planning this for a long time—waiting for the right moment, the right research, the right threat to their secret?"

"You mean Thomas Whitman might not have been the first person to stumble onto this conspiracy?"

"I mean maybe he wasn't the first person to die because of it."

The thought hung between us as we pulled into our driveway, the motion-sensor lights illuminating the three-story structure that rose majestically from the cliff like something carved from the landscape itself. It was a modern-day log cabin of polished golden logs and glass that had become our sanctuary, perched on the edge of the Potomac with towering pines surrounding us like natural guardians. But tonight, even home didn't feel completely safe. Somewhere out there, a killer was still free, and we were just beginning to understand how deep this conspiracy ran.

"Come on," Jack said, taking my hand as we made another dash through the rain. "Let's get inside and see what we can dig up about our five families. Something tells me the real story is going to be even uglier than what we've seen so far."

As we reached the porch, I realized I was looking forward to diving into the research. Because somewhere in the historical records and family trees, a killer had left tracks. And by morning, we were going to start following them.

CHAPTER EIGHT

JACK'S OFFICE WELCOMED US LIKE AN OLD FRIEND, ALL warm lamplight and the lingering scent of the cedar logs that made up the cabin's walls. I kicked off my wet shoes and padded across the Persian rug in my bare feet, already mentally organizing the research we needed to tackle.

The office was one of my favorite rooms in the house—as spacious as our living room but infinitely more functional. The stone fireplace dominated one wall, flanked by built-in bookshelves that held everything from Virginia legal codes to Jack's collection of Civil War histories. Floor-to-ceiling windows lined the west wall, though tonight they were covered by the automated blackout shades for privacy.

The business end of the room featured Jack's L-shaped desk and the conference table constructed from a restored barn door, but the real star was the electronic whiteboard system that covered two corner walls. The touchscreen interface could display multiple databases simultaneously while allowing us to annotate and cross-reference information in real time.

"Coffee or tea?" Jack asked, already moving toward the small wet bar tucked into one corner of the room.

"Coffee," I said automatically, then reconsidered. "Actually, make it tea. I've had enough coffee today."

Jack's movements stilled for just a moment, and I saw him glance at my still-flat stomach with that mixture of wonder and protectiveness that had been appearing more frequently since we'd learned about the baby.

"Tea it is," he said softly. "You want to get started on the murder board while I put the kettle on?"

"Already on it." I was already touching the screen to activate it, the familiar blue glow illuminating the room as the system came online.

I started with Thomas Whitman's DMV photo in the center of the board, then added the crime-scene photos Cole had uploaded to the database. Even seeing them again, the elaborate staging struck me as both theatrical and deeply personal. This wasn't random violence—it was a message.

"What are you thinking?" Jack asked, setting a steaming mug of Earl Grey at my elbow.

"I'm thinking our killer has a serious flair for the dramatic. Look at this staging—the careful positioning on Bridget Ashworth's grave, the historical re-creation, even the timing. This person wants us to understand the connection to the past."

"The question is whether they're using history to confuse the scene and make us chase after things that have nothing to do with anything," Jack said. "Even the witchcraft angle for that matter. At first I thought maybe it was some creepy satanic ritual, but after looking at the scene I'm not so sure. I worked a case in DC when I was on SWAT that dealt with black magic and the occult. It's not something I'll ever forget. This is nothing like that."

"Creepy," I said, shuddering.

"You have no idea."

"It's certainly not a coincidence that Thomas Whitman is a descendant to one of those newly marked graves. Someone connected dots somewhere. We just don't know our history."

"Yeah, I don't remember Mrs. Vogle teaching any of this stuff in seventh-grade history."

I grinned, thinking of the sturdy and hard-of-hearing Mrs. Vogle. "'Cause she was superstitious. When we got to the witch trials section of Virginia history she kept crossing herself and kept assuring us there was no such thing as real witches."

"That's because my class scarred her for life," Jack said. "Dickie and Vaughn put some black horsehair from one of the mares on the farm on her desk and sprinkled a ring of salt around her desk. Then Eddie swore up and down he saw the ghost of Bridget Ashworth and that it had to be her hair, and Mrs. Vogle believed him because it was Eddie."

My eyes were wide with disbelief. I knew of the prank of course. Everyone in school had heard what had happened. But this was the first time I'd heard who'd been behind it. I should have guessed.

"And Eddie never got in trouble," I said, understanding how things how gotten so out of hand. Eddie had always been a straight arrow. Teachers loved him, and if Eddie said something it was as good as true.

"Of course, Eddie felt so guilty after he did it he had to go to the bathroom and throw up. Ended up missing two days of school because he made himself sick."

"Punishment enough, I guess," I said, laughing.

I pulled up the database search function and began entering the names from the marked graves. "Let's find out who these people really were."

The search results began populating the screen,

and I felt my eyebrows climbing toward my hairline as the family information filled the display.

"Well, well," I said, pointing at the Blackwood family tree. "Here's our friend Richard Blackwood in all his glory. No wonder he got so bent out of shape at that historical society meeting.

Jack leaned over my shoulder, and I caught a whiff of his aftershave mixed with the lingering scent of rain from our clothes. "Richard Blackwood has always been a hothead. He sits on the historical society board and several other committees around town, likes to throw his weight around and remind everyone who his family is. Patricia Whitman said he went volcanic when Thomas presented his findings —screaming about libel and destroying family reputations."

"I've met him a time or two," I said. "I've heard he has a son that's a chip off the old block. Emmy Lu said he's the same age as her oldest son and has gotten busted for DUI a couple of times."

"Emmy Lu is better than the news," Jack said, grinning. "Yeah, the kid got pulled over both times in Richmond, so out of our jurisdiction thank God. I heard Blackwood donated money to the mayor's opponent for not dismissing the chief and got a new guy elected who promptly fired the chief of police and had the arresting officer demoted."

"Sounds like a peach of a guy," I said. "Can't wait to interview him about murder."

"I sense sarcasm," Jack said, kissing the top of my head. "The Blackwoods have owned that property on River Road since the early 1700s. The original manor house is still there—it's on the historic registry now—but they built that big Colonial behind it back in the eighties. My mother always said there was something not right about that place."

"Your mother's not wrong," I said, scrolling through property records that showed an impressive accumulation of land over the centuries. "I always got the creeps driving past there as a kid. Remember how Richard's mother used to stare at us from that upstairs window?"

"God, yes," Jack said, settling into the chair beside me with his tea. "Mrs. Blackwood was terrifying. And the way she died was even worse—drowned in the pond behind their house."

I scrolled through the Blackwood history and said, "It looks like tragic deaths aren't an uncommon event in their family."

"Richard's grandmother fell down the stairs and broke her neck," Jack confirmed grimly. "And before that, his great-grandmother got kicked in the head by a horse. The Blackwood women have a real problem with living past fifty."

"And then there's Richard's first wife, Caroline," I said, "I don't really remember her, but I know she was an acquaintance of my mother. And everyone remembers how she died."

"That was the summer before my senior year," Jack said.

"Fourth of July Celebration at the Towne Square," I said, remembering. "Crazy how big the county has gotten in fifteen years. It was much smaller then, and everyone was there. I don't think I'll ever forget the sound her body made as it hit the pavement after that car launched her into the air."

"It was definitely weird circumstances," Jack said. "It was crowded, but the main road was still open to let cars through. Witnesses all said she just walked into traffic. There was nothing the driver could do to avoid her."

A chill ran down my spine. "That's an awful lot of accidents for one family."

"Or an awful lot of convenient deaths," Jack said grimly. "Richard collected a hefty life insurance payout after Caroline died. Enough to renovate that Colonial house and buy another hundred acres of riverfront property."

I moved on to the Morton family records, and found what looked like a more straightforward family history.

"Well, here's Judge Harold Morton," I said, pulling up the current family information. "At least he's not accumulating mysterious deaths."

"Harold's always been straight with me," Jack said, reading over my shoulder. "Fair judge, doesn't play politics. Though that doesn't mean his ancestor wasn't dirty as hell back in the 1720s."

"True," I said, scrolling through the property records. "The Mortons still own about two hundred acres of the original land grants. Could be they inherited stolen property and just never knew it."

"Or they knew and kept their mouths shut for three centuries," Jack said.

Next up was the Hughes family, and I immediately recognized several names from high school.

"Oh my God," I said, pointing at the screen. "Rachel Hughes—remember her from high school? She was the one who got caught skinny-dipping in the river with half the basketball team."

Jack nearly choked on his tea. "That was Rachel Hughes? I thought that was just an urban legend."

"Nope, totally true. She was in my class. I saw the pictures. And then Rachel's parents came in and withdrew her from school, and I never saw her again. I wonder what she's doing now?"

"Last I heard, she was on her third divorce and working as a bartender at that dive bar outside town," Jack said. "But her family's got some interesting connections. Her father's a lawyer, handles a lot of real estate transactions for the older families."

"Real estate transactions," I repeated. "Like property transfers and land deals?"

"Exactly the kind of work that would give him access to historical records and current land values," Jack said. "If the Hughes family has been the legal muscle behind covering up the original land thefts..."

"Then they'd know exactly who to threaten and how much money is at stake," I finished.

I moved on to the Mills family records. "Dr. Victoria Mills," I said, pulling up her information. "She's got a family practice out near the river. The Mills have been the primary physicians for this area for generations."

"Good reputation," Jack said. "My mother always spoke highly of Dr. Mills's grandfather. Said he delivered half the babies in King George County back in the day."

"Five generations of doctors," I said, scrolling through the family history. "That's impressive. And look—they still own significant portions of the original Mills land grant. Another family that might be unknowingly living on stolen property."

"Starting to see a pattern here," Jack said. "All these families still own the land their ancestors acquired right after Bridget Ashworth's execution.

The question is whether the current generations know how their ancestors really got it."

Finally, I pulled up the Lawson family records, and Jack leaned forward with interest.

"William Lawson, 1665–1729," I read. "Let's see if the official records match what your parents told us." I scrolled through the Colonial documents. "Here it is. Confirmation that he was definitely in Williamsburg during Bridget Ashworth's trial. His name appears on a legislative document dated the same week as her execution, just like your dad said."

"So the family stories were true," Jack said, relief evident in his voice. "He wasn't here to stop it."

"And look," I said, pulling up another document. "The records confirm what your parents said about him refusing the Ashworth land when it was offered. The other families divided it up, but the Lawsons didn't take a single acre.

"But someone still marked his grave with a broken sword," I said slowly. "Why mark the grave of someone who tried to help?"

"Maybe because he failed," Jack said. "He had the authority to potentially stop it, but he wasn't here. And then he was murdered before he could get justice."

I studied the screen, something nagging at me. "But wait—our killer went to all this trouble to stage an elaborate historical murder, researched these families, knew about Bridget Ashworth's execution method. But then marked the grave of someone who wasn't even there? That doesn't track."

Jack leaned forward. "You're right. Either our killer doesn't know the real history as well as they think they do..."

"Or they're deliberately including the Lawsons for another reason," I finished.

Jack leaned back in his chair, the weight of the evening's discoveries settling over both of us. "We've got a three-hundred-year-old land theft conspiracy, families who may or may not know their wealth is built on stolen property, and a killer who's either making mistakes or deliberately trying to confuse us."

"And somewhere in all of this, Thomas Whitman died because he got too close to the truth," I said. "The question is, what truth? The historical conspiracy, or something happening right now?"

"Maybe both," Jack said grimly. "Tomorrow we start talking to these people. Starting with Richard Blackwood and Margaret Randolph—the ones who threatened Thomas at that Historical Society meeting."

As we finally headed upstairs to bed, I couldn't shake the feeling that we were only seeing the tip of the iceberg. The historical conspiracy was real—Thomas Whitman had died for uncovering it. But someone was also using that history for their own purposes, weaving past and present together in a web of secrets that stretched back three centuries.

Tomorrow we'd have to start untangling the truth from the lies. And pray we could do it before anyone else died.

CHAPTER NINE

THE ALARM'S SHRILL CRY PIERCED THROUGH MY dreams like a blade, dragging me from the blessed darkness of sleep into the harsh reality of another day. Before I'd even opened my eyes, my stomach was already staging its morning rebellion, rolling and pitching like a ship caught in a hurricane.

I barely made it to the bathroom before the nausea hit with the brutal efficiency of a sledge-hammer to the gut. The cool porcelain against my knees was a small mercy as my body purged itself of whatever imaginary toxins pregnancy hormones had convinced it were poisoning my system.

Jack appeared behind me like he had every morning for the past two weeks, his warm hands gathering my hair away from my face while his other hand rubbed steady circles between my shoulder blades. Even half asleep and dealing with his wife's unglamorous morning ritual, he managed to be exactly what I needed.

"This is so romantic," I gasped between waves of sickness, my voice echoing off the bathroom tiles. "I bet this is exactly how you pictured married life."

"Actually," Jack said, his voice rough with sleep but gentle with understanding, "it's exactly what I imagined."

Despite feeling like death warmed over, I managed a weak laugh. "Your optimism is inspiring."

"It's realistic," he corrected, helping me to my feet when the worst had passed. "This won't last forever. And once it's over, we get a baby out of the deal."

After dry toast that tasted like cardboard and weak tea that barely qualified as flavored water, plus a hot shower that finally made me feel human again, we were ready to face whatever the day had in store. The drive to the sheriff's office was peaceful in the way that only early mornings could be, with mist rising from the Potomac like the breath of sleeping giants and the countryside painted in soft watercolors by the growing light.

We'd spent breakfast planning our strategy over Jack's coffee and my tea. Richard Blackwood and Margaret Randolph topped our interview list—they were the ones who'd directly threatened Thomas Whitman according to Patricia. But we also needed to approach the current generations of the Morton, Hughes, and Mills families to see if they could think of a reason their ancestors' graves would have been marked in relation to a murder.

The King George County Sheriff's Office occupied a brick building across from the courthouse in the Towne Square. The lobby was all polished linoleum and harsh fluorescent lighting, with community safety announcements and wanted posters covering a bulletin board that looked like it hadn't been updated for the last decade.

Jack parked in his designated spot, and we went in the side door instead of going through the front. Jack typed in his code and we passed through the security door into the heart of the operation. The bullpen was already humming with the controlled chaos of a shift change, phones ringing and coffee brewing while detectives and deputies prepared for another day of keeping King George County safe from itself.

"Well, look what the cat dragged in," Cole drawled teasingly. "And here are me and Martinez, up all night looking through surveillance footage."

"That's why we make the big bucks," Martinez said, grinning and putting his feet up on his desk.

"I thought you were looking a little worn around the edges, Martinez," Jack said good-naturedly. "Not often I see creases in those fancy shirts. I thought you were having woman trouble."

"Ahh, well, there'd have to be time for a woman to have woman trouble," Martinez said, dramatically clutching his heart. "We've been a little busy lately."

"No rest for the wicked," Cole said, sadly.

Martinez and Cole both had dark shadows under their eyes, but there was still an alertness there that belied years of experience in pushing through personal discomfort in the name of justice.

Jack went to the coffeepot and looked at the black sludge sitting inside and decided to start over by making a new pot. I detoured into his office where he kept a Keurig and I made a cup of tea for myself, needing the stronger kick now that the nausea had passed.

When I came back out of Jack's office some of the morning crowd had thinned out—deputies leaving to go out on patrol or answer calls—and the morning chatter had died down to a low buzz.

Jack was sitting on the corner of Cole's desk, and I took up residence in Sergeant Holt's ergonomic chair that he had specially requested because he had back trouble. It was pretty comfortable, and I rolled closer so I could hear the conversation.

"Give me an update," Jack said, blowing on his coffee.

"We were able to get security footage from the

gas station across the street," Cole said. "It's not great, but we were able to get a partial view of the vehicle and a partial of the front license plate. Dark sedan—not sure of the make and model since the video quality isn't great—is recorded pulling up around eleven the night of the murder."

"That tracks with what Al told us about the time he went to check the gates," Jack said.

"Vehicle is recorded as leaving in the opposite direction about fifteen minutes later," Cole continued. "The inside of the gas station closes at midnight, but the pumps stay open twenty-four seven. There's a few cars that came through between midnight and three, but around two forty-five the dark sedan pulls back up and parks in the same place. Still can't see the full body of the vehicle or the license plate, and no sign of anyone entering or exiting the vehicle from our camera angle."

"Maybe someone told them exactly where to park," Martinez said.

"Maybe," Jack agreed, a crease forming between his brows as he thought it through.

"There are houses in the direction the vehicle left," Cole said. "We're going to knock on doors and see if anyone has cameras that might have gotten a shot of the car as it drove down the street."

"Any hits on the partial plates?" Jack asked.

"We've got two visible letters," Martinez said. "J

and *F*. And when we run it through ALPR we get four hundred and sixty-seven potential matches in the tristate area. When we cull that down to sedans we get two hundred and two matches. I've got Riley going through the list to eliminate by color and then prioritize as far as location and where the vehicle is registered."

From our location in the bullpen, we had full visual access to the front of the station where Sergeant Hill guarded the inner sanctum like the walrus-mustached veteran cop he was. He sat behind a thick partition and directed people to the right department. So we saw the courier come up and say he had a delivery for Sheriff Lawson.

"Go ahead and sign for it," Jack told Sergeant Hill. "I'm expecting some information from Patricia Whitman."

"That's who it's from," Hill said, signing the courier's electronic pad. "I'll take it at the side door."

Hill crept off his stool with the careful consideration of someone who was no longer able to chase down suspects, and he ambled over to the locked door that led into the bullpen and let the courier inside with a large box.

"Just put it here," Jack said, motioning to the top of Cole's desk.

The courier was sweating under the strain, and seemed happy to dump the box onto Cole's desk before he hurried back out and Hill locked the door behind him.

"Jaye and I started a murder board in my office last night when we got back from meeting Al. We've done preliminary research on all of the families who had marked graves around Whitman's body, but I don't want to take a chance on anything happening to all of Whitman's research. Let's move everything to conference room A and let's keep it locked down tight. Someone contact Derby and have him transfer everything from my home office to the system here so we're all on the same page."

Jack lifted the box with ease and started toward the hallway that led to conference room A. I was slower to follow since the hot tea and coziness of the chair had made me uncharacteristically lethargic. I felt like I could have slept for days.

I was just a few steps behind the guys when I caught movement out of the corner of my eye. Jenkins and Riley were escorting a big brute of a man who'd been partially slumped over through the door that led to the holding cell area when all hell broke loose.

Before I knew what was happening Jenkins rammed into the wall like a rag doll, and Riley let out a yell as the perp's rock-solid head made contact with his nose. There was blood and shouts and chaos in a matter of seconds.

The man looked like he'd been constructed from spare linebacker parts and steroids—easily six-foot four and dense with muscle that strained against a torn T-shirt advertising some long-defunct motorcycle rally—and he was definitely on something as his eyes had the wild look of someone who lived in a different reality.

Prison tattoos covered every visible inch of skin that wasn't already hidden by grime and old scars. His arms were thick as fence posts, his neck disappeared into shoulders that belonged on a professional wrestler, and his hands—securely cuffed behind his back—were the size of dinner plates.

Jack, Cole, and Martinez didn't hesitate to jump into the fray, and I winced as Martinez grunted as the guy kicked out and made contact with Martinez's thigh. An inch or so north and Martinez would have been singing in a boys' choir. Cole was able to move in behind him and get an arm around his meaty neck in a chokehold, but it was like trying to hold on to a bucking bronco.

"You pigs don't got nothing on me!" the guy roared, his voice echoing off the cinderblock walls like thunder in a canyon. Without warning, he snapped his head backward, trying to catch Cole in the face with a skull-crushing headbutt that would have done some serious damage to that pretty face of his, but Cole let go of his neck and ducked just in time.

The big man pivoted, using his momentum to launch a vicious kick toward Jack, but Jack had been expecting it and grabbed hold of his leg and rammed him backward.

By this point cops had come running from all directions, but the guy was twisting like a dervish and feverish with rage.

Jenkin tried to jump back into the fray but the suspect's shoulder caught him in the solar plexus, driving the air from his lungs in a sharp gasp.

That's when Jack moved. He stepped around Martinez with the fluid precision of someone who'd learned violence as both an art and a science, timing his approach for the exact moment when the suspect was off-balance and focused on the others.

Jack's right cross came from his shoulder with years of training and experience behind it, every ounce of his weight and momentum focused into his fist as it connected with the suspect's jaw. The sound was like a baseball bat hitting a watermelon—sharp, final, and somehow deeply satisfying.

The suspect's eyes rolled back in his head, showing nothing but white, and his massive frame collapsed like a controlled demolition. All that phar-maceutical rage and enhanced strength meant nothing against the basic physics of a perfectly timed punch.

The sudden silence in the bullpen was deafening after the chaos of the fight. Everyone stood frozen for a moment, staring at the unconscious mountain of muscle sprawled across the linoleum like a fallen statue.

"Well," Martinez said finally, straightening his tie and trying to restore some dignity to his appearance. A thin line of sweat traced down his temple, and his breathing was still elevated from the struggle. "That was educational."

Riley was a bloody mess and he pushed himself up from the floor. It looked like no one had escaped completely unscathed.

"Sheriff, don't take this the wrong way," Martinez said, limping back and forth to try and stretch out his sore muscles. "But I might resign today."

"Why don't you go home and sleep on it a couple of hours and then get back to me," Jack said, looking down at the bruised knuckles on his hand. "Someone get EMTs over here to check out Riley. Anyone else need attention?"

"Nothing an ice pack and a beer can't handle," Cole said.

"Jenkins, get those ribs checked out," Jack said. "Paperwork can wait. Get this guy into holding before he wakes up again."

A group of the cops who'd been standing around moved in and hefted the unconscious man up under the arms and moved him toward the holding cells.

The aftermath of violence always left its own signature in the air—the metallic taste of adrenaline, the sharp scent of sweat and fear, the electric tension that took time to dissipate. Papers were scattered across the floor like confetti, a computer monitor flickered with a spiderweb crack across its screen, and someone's coffee mug had exploded against the wall in a brown starburst that would probably stain the paint permanently.

Jack turned to look at me and said, "You okay?"

"Just another day at the office," I said, my voice steady. My hands shook slightly and I was more shaken than I'd realized. Things could have been a lot worse than they had been.

Jack rubbed his bruised knuckles and surveyed the chaos around us. "This is going to take a while to sort out. Incident reports, internal affairs review, medical evaluations." He looked at me with tired eyes. "Give me a couple of hours to deal with this mess before we go talk to Blackwood and Randolph. I don't want to be interrupted halfway through an interrogation because someone needs paperwork signed."

"That's fine," I said, relieved to have some time to let my adrenaline settle. "I'll go check on things at the funeral home. Make sure everything's ready for the day."

Jack leaned over and pressed a quick kiss to my forehead, mindful of the audience around us. "Call me if you need anything. And Jaye? Try to eat something that isn't toast or crackers."

"I'll see what Emmy Lu has in the kitchen," I promised, gathering my purse and jacket.

The drive to the funeral home gave me time to decompress from the morning's violence. My hands had stopped shaking from the adrenaline by the time I pulled under the portico, though I could still taste the metallic tang of it on my tongue.

I let myself in through the side door, expecting to hear Emmy Lu's usual morning routine—the soft murmur of the radio, the gentle clatter of coffee cups. Instead, the building felt unusually quiet.

"Emmy Lu?" I called out, hanging my jacket on the hook in the mudroom.

"I'm coming," came her voice from her office, but there was an edge to it that wasn't normally there. "I was just about to put on the coffee."

She bustled in, staring at her phone with a worried frown, and immediately went to the coffeepot, her distraction palpable. According to everyone, I made terrible coffee so I was banned from the machine. Her light brown hair was pulled back in its usual messy bun, but it looked like she'd brushed it with an eggbeater—a sure sign of stress.

"What's wrong?" I asked, settling onto one of the barstools.

"Sheldon didn't come in this morning," she said, setting her phone down. "His mother called about an hour ago. Said his bed wasn't slept in and she's worried sick."

That got my attention. Sheldon was nothing if not punctual. "Have you tried calling him?"

"Goes straight to voicemail," Emmy Lu said, tapping her fingers on the counter. "I keep telling myself he's probably just fallen asleep at that creepy girl's place, but it's not like him. Even when he first started dating Leena, he always made it home at a decent hour."

The sound of the side door opening interrupted us, and we both turned to see Sheldon shuffling in.

"Good Lord, Sheldon," Emmy Lu said. "What happened to you?"

Even on a good day, Sheldon was one of those people who never quite looked put together. Something was always out of alignment or a little bit wrinkled. But today he looked like a disaster. He was disheveled—his shirt wrinkled and stained, his hair sticking up at odd angles, his glasses crooked on his pale face.

"Sorry," he mumbled. "I...lost track of time. I need coffee."

I caught a whiff of something strange clinging to his clothes—woodsmoke and something herbal that made my nose wrinkle. "What's that smell?"

He sniffed the sleeve of his shirt. "Must be the bonfire."

Emmy Lu crossed her arms. "I thought you were allergic to woodsmoke."

"I think it's just an intolerance," he said. "Did you know smoke from certain trees like the eucalyptus or cedar tree can cause a person to temporarily sing with natural vibrato?"

"I'll remember that next time I feel like bursting into song out on the campground," I said.

Sheldon sank onto the barstool next to me and Emmy Lu put a cup of coffee in front of both of us. "I think Leena might be out of my league. She's actually a really nice girl, but she's pretty intense. And she's got a good sense of humor, but sometimes she gets this look in her eyes that scares me. Ever since that guy got murdered she's gone kind of cuckoo. I thought it might be PMS and I told her so, but she threw a butter knife at my head so I'm guessing I was off the mark there."

"A classic sign," Emmy Lu said. "My ex-husband had the bad fortune to leave me when I had PMS and I tried to back over him with my car. I would have got him too except he hid behind a dumpster."

I'd known Emmy Lu's ex-husband and if there was anyone who deserved to be backed over it was him.

"Why's she so interested in the murder?" I asked.

Sheldon shrugged. "I don't know. But she's totally obsessed with Bridget Ashworth. She believes in reincarnation and stuff and she says she knew Bridget in a past life and they were good friends."

"You believe her?" Emmy Lu asked, brow arched.

"I'm Episcopalian," he said, as if that explained everything.

"So how'd you end up at a bonfire?" I asked.

"Leena said Bridget has been trying to communicate with her, but she's not very good at communing with the dead yet. So we went to see Madame Evangeline."

"A psychic?" Emmy Lu asked.

"Something like that," Sheldon said. "She lives in this old house out by the river. Leena said she could communicate with spirits so we drove out to see her."

My grip tightened around my coffee cup. "And this woman claimed she could channel Bridget's spirit?"

"Yeah, Leena says she's been taking lessons from her."

"Private necromancy lessons," Emmy Lu said, clucking her tongue. "Can you imagine? The only lessons I ever had growing up were for piano."

"Do you remember where her house was?" I asked.

"It's all kind of blurred," Sheldon said. "Leena was smoking, and it made my brain fuzzy. She said it's for medicinal purposes."

"Mmhmm," I said. "Then what did you do?"

"We got to Madame Evangeline's cabin and there was already this big bonfire laid out next to the river. Then she made me sit down on a pillow, and she took off my glasses and blindfolded me. Then she lit the bonfire and things got really weird. The fire was hot for just a couple of minutes and then things got really cold. She started talking in this low voice and then I felt like I was floating. Like a dream."

"Sounds like a nightmare to me," Emmy Lu said. "I hate being blindfolded.

"What did she say?"

Sheldon pushed his glasses up his nose. "She said justice had been denied for too long. That the first stone had been cast but more blood needed to be spilled to balance the scales. She said there are families with bad blood. I don't remember all the names she said. Blackwood I think. Hill or Mill. Do you know what that means?"

My heart started racing, but I looked straight at Sheldon. "I'm going to be straight with you, Sheldon. That all sounds like a lot of hooey to me disguised with smoke and mirrors. But it does sound like she knows something. We've not released any information about what was inscribed on those gravestones or whose graves they were."

"You think she could be in on it?" Emmy Lu asked.

"I think she's worth talking to," I said. "And Leena too."

Emmy Lu turned back to Sheldon. "Where is Leena? And did you sleep in the woods? You've got twigs in your hair."

"I slept in Leena's car. I don't remember a lot after the smoke and the séance, but I think we ended up at the cemetery to keep watch. There were cop cars blocking the entrance, but she had some night-vision binoculars. They were pretty cool, but my glasses kept getting in the way. Then she smoked some more and I fell asleep. When I woke up this morning she was gone."

"Gone where?" I asked.

He shrugged. "No clue, but she left a note that said Bridget was counting on her and she needed to meditate." He pulled a crumpled piece of paper out of his pocket and handed it to me. "But she left the keys in the ignition so I drove straight here. Now that I think about it, maybe I should go home. That smoky smell is really giving me a headache."

"I'm going to text Jack what you told me," I said, grabbing my phone. "Do you know anything else about the woman besides her first name?"

"Am I in trouble?" Sheldon asked.

"No," I said. "You're just a poor judge of character. We'll work on that."

"Oh good," he said. "I'm afraid of prison. I don't look good in orange."

"I'd think that would be the least of your problems in prison, darling," Emmy Lu said.

Sheldon let out a defeated sigh and said, "I remember we passed Portobago Trail and took a left toward the marshes. We stopped the car when the road ended and then walked the rest of the way to her cabin. I don't know her last name. She just told me to call her Evangeline."

"What'd she look like? Give me a description."

He seemed to remember he had coffee in his hands and took a hasty sip. "Oh, uh, she was old. Lots of wrinkles. Mixed race I think. Dreadlocks that looked like the steel wool my mother uses after she makes a pot of chili. Wore a lot of jangly bracelets."

"Well, that ought to narrow it down," Emmy Lu

said, squeezing Sheldon on the shoulder. "Go home and get some sleep. But maybe shower first. And if your head starts spinning around and you vomit pea soup make sure you call us. I've always wanted to see an exorcism in person."

CHAPTER TEN

THE SOUND OF JACK'S TAHOE PULLING UNDER THE portico was a welcome relief from the morning's revelations. Through the window, I watched him climb out, his movements sharp with the kind of focused energy that meant he'd shifted into full investigation mode. The bruises on his knuckles from the morning's altercation were already darkening, a reminder of how quickly things could turn violent.

I met him at the side door, grateful to escape the funeral home's suddenly oppressive atmosphere. The spring air was crisp against my skin, carrying the scent of fresh grass and the distant promise of rain. Storm clouds were building on the horizon, turning the sky a moody gray that matched my growing unease about this case.

"Sounds like you had an interesting morning," Jack said, taking my bag and holding the door of his Tahoe open for me.

"Just another avenue to check out," I said. "Maybe we can find more about Evangeline from Leena."

He closed the door and then came around and got into the driver's side. "I've got to say, I can't wait to meet the mysterious Leena. Maybe we can put the fear of God into her because it sounds like she's taking advantage of Sheldon."

"My hero," I said, buckling my seat belt. "I was thinking the same thing. You've never met Leena? I see her every time I go to Lady Jane's."

Jack's mouth quirked as he gave me an incredulous look and he said, "It might be hard to believe, but I've never actually been to Lady Jane's for donuts."

"What? How can that be? I see cops there every morning."

"Because they're weak," he said, shaking his head. "If I ate donuts every morning I'd start to look like Sergeant Hill. And then I'd either die on the job because my heart couldn't take the ups and downs of adrenaline rushes or you'd leave me for someone who didn't eat donuts every day."

"I eat donuts every day," I said, narrowing my eyes at him.

"Doesn't count," he said, grinning. "You're pregnant. And you've got those French genes that allow you to eat bread and cheese all day and never gain weight."

"I'm about to gain a whole bunch of weight," I said, trying not to think about my French genes. I'd been literally cut from my mother's womb and stolen by the woman I'd always thought had been my mother. I hadn't really had the desire to do a deep dive into that side of my childhood trauma yet, so I did what I always do when things like that arose and shoved it down.

"Yes, and I can't wait to explore every bit of more you," he said genially. "How did we end up talking about this?"

"You were rubbing it in about how your body is a temple and you don't contaminate it with donuts."

"I'm almost positive that wasn't the conversation at all," he said.

I shrugged, feeling like my body was completely detached from my brain. And after all the talk about donuts, I really wanted a donut. I decided the best course of action was to change the conversation. "So how's Riley?"

"Broken nose and a concussion. EMTs took him to the hospital." Jack's jaw tightened. Being the man in charge came with its own kind of headaches. "Jenkins has a sprained knee and he's too stubborn to admit it's bothering him, but the EMT hinted that she might be interested in going out for a drink with him as long as his knee was okay, so he slapped an ice pack on it and stopped complaining. Cole took a good shot to the ribs but they're not cracked. He's going to be moving slow for a bit though. And Martinez got lucky—just some bruising on his leg where he got kicked and sore knuckles."

"And you sent Cole and Martinez home to sleep?"

"Had to practically order them off the premises. They'll crash hard after that burst of adrenaline. They'll be more useful to the case after a few hours of rest than stumbling around half dead."

"Did you put any ice on your knuckles?" I asked. "Or are you waiting for the cute EMT to invite you for drinks first?"

He grinned and then winced as he flexed his hand. "I figured I could get my wife to kiss them and make it better."

I took his hand gently and kissed the bruised and raw knuckles softly. "The guy had a head like a cinder block. You still need ice."

"The kiss will hold me over."

I breathed in the familiar scent of Jack's after-shave mixed with the leather interior. It was comforting in a way that made my chest tight—this small, normal thing in the middle of chaos.

"I found something in the box of papers Patricia

had couriered over," Jack said, pulling a leather-bound datebook from his jacket pocket. The cover was worn smooth from handling, edges softened with age. "Thomas's appointment book."

I took it from him, the leather warm from being against his body. The pages were filled with Thomas's careful handwriting—meetings, research appointments, site visits. I flipped to the day he died, finding the entry I was looking for.

"'Dinner, seven thirty, JMH,'" I read aloud. "Just initials."

"Could be anyone," Jack said, pulling out of the funeral home's driveway. "But given what we know about the old families he was researching we should reference it against those names. Maybe he was trying to approach current family members directly, get their perspectives and any family records before going public with his findings."

The drive into town gave me time to study the datebook more closely. Thomas's entries painted a picture of a man consumed with his research—meetings with historical society members, visits to various archives, appointments with genealogists, weeks at a time spent at dig sites. The pattern became clearer as I read backward through the months. After his initial presentation to the historical society, his appointments became more secretive, with initials instead of full names, meeting locations moved from public places to private homes and restaurants.

"He's got consistent meetings with someone with the initials of GW," I said. "Mostly Tuesday mornings, but others are scattered throughout. Other common initials are BD and MA."

"Same days and times?"

"No rhyme or reason that I can see. The meetings with BD started back mid-January and are at least twice a month. MA started on February thirteenth and seems to be at least once per week except when he had trips scheduled. Not much in the grand scheme of things I guess. Looks like he made frequent trips to Williamsburg, Jamestown, and Roanoke.

"Before the fall semester started he was using full names. Looks like the GW could be George Wentworth." I took a minute to do a quick search for the name. "George Wentworth is the dean of the history department."

"Any kind of research funding would have to be approved by him," Jack added. "Plus I'd assume they'd have regular department meetings, so that checks out. But something made him paranoid enough to start being secretive in what he was doing."

"And then someone killed him," I added.

The King George Business Park sat on what had

once been prime farmland, converted in the eighties into a collection of glass-and-brick buildings that housed everything from insurance offices to consulting firms. It was the kind of place where successful people went to make other successful people more money, all wrapped in the veneer of corporate respectability that small towns used to prove they were keeping up with the times.

Blackwood Consulting occupied the top floor of the tallest building, which wasn't saying much since nothing in King George County was allowed to exceed three stories thanks to historical preservation ordinances. Still, the location gave Richard Blackwood a commanding view of the countryside his ancestors had helped shape, and I suspected that wasn't coincidental.

The elevator carried us up in silence that felt heavier than it should have, the kind of quiet that came before difficult conversations. When the doors opened, we stepped into a reception area that screamed expensive without quite crossing into tasteless.

The walls were a warm cream color that complemented dark hardwood floors polished to a mirror shine. Original oil paintings—landscapes of Virginia countryside that looked like they belonged in a museum—hung in heavy gilt frames. The furniture was all leather and brass, the kind that lasted for generations and got better with age.

Behind a mahogany desk that could have doubled as a small aircraft carrier sat a receptionist who looked like she'd stepped out of a corporate magazine. Mid-thirties, perfectly highlighted blond hair swept into a chignon, wearing a navy suit that probably cost more than most people made in a month. Her smile was professional but warm as she looked up from her computer screen.

"Good morning," she said, her voice carrying just a hint of a Richmond accent that had been carefully refined. "How may I help you?"

Jack showed his badge, and I watched her expression shift from polite interest to carefully controlled concern. "I'm Sheriff Lawson, this is Dr. Graves. We need to speak with Mr. Blackwood about a police matter."

"Of course." She reached for her phone with manicured fingers. "Let me see if he's available. May I tell him what this is regarding?"

"Just tell him it's official police business," Jack said, his tone leaving no room for negotiation.

She nodded and picked up the phone. "Mr. Blackwood? Sheriff Lawson and Dr. Graves are here to see you about official police business." A pause. "Yes, sir. I'll send them right in."

She hung up and gestured toward a set of double

doors that looked like they'd been salvaged from a nineteenth-century mansion. "Right through there. Can I offer you coffee or tea?"

"We're fine, thank you," Jack said, though I could have used another cup of tea. The morning's revelations had left me feeling unsteady, and the baby wasn't helping matters by making my stomach do little flips every time I thought too hard about what we might find.

Richard Blackwood's office was exactly what I'd expected from a man who spent his life trading on his family name. The room was large enough to hold a small dinner party, with floor-to-ceiling windows that showcased the rolling Virginia countryside in all its spring glory, though the view today was gray and dreary. More oil paintings covered the walls—these depicting what I assumed were Blackwood ancestors in various poses of Colonial importance.

The man himself stood behind a desk that looked like it had been carved from a single piece of walnut, his hands spread flat on its surface as if he were claiming territory. Richard Blackwood was in his late fifties, tall and still handsome in the way that money and good breeding could maintain. His silver hair was perfectly styled, his navy suit impeccably tailored, and his pale blue eyes held the kind of cold intelligence that made successful businessmen and dangerous enemies.

But there was something else there too—a tension in his shoulders, a tightness around his eyes that suggested our visit wasn't entirely unexpected.

"Sheriff Lawson," he said, and then he paused and said, "Jack," as if they were old friends. "How's your family?"

If Jack was surprised by the question he didn't show it. Jack's family had a long history in King George, just like Blackwood's, so it made sense that the families would know each other.

"They stay busy," Jack said vaguely.

"Please, have a seat."

Richard gestured to two leather chairs positioned in front of his desk, and I noticed he remained standing—a power play designed to keep us literally looking up at him. Jack settled into one of the chairs with the easy confidence of someone who couldn't be intimidated by furniture arrangements, and I followed suit.

"We appreciate you taking the time to speak with us," Jack said, his tone professionally neutral. "We're investigating the murder of Thomas Whitman."

"Terrible business," Blackwood said, finally taking his own seat. "Thomas was a respected member of the academic community. He was pretty well known around this area. Like a modern-day Indiana Jones. I can't imagine who would want to harm him."

The lie came so smoothly it was almost believable, but I caught the slight tension in his voice when he said Thomas's name. This was a man who'd had time to prepare for this conversation.

"We understand you had some disagreements with Mr. Whitman recently," Jack continued. "Particularly regarding his research into Colonial land grants."

Blackwood's expression didn't change, but I saw his hands tighten almost imperceptibly on the arms of his chair. "I wouldn't call them disagreements. More like concerns about methodology and the potential for academic sensationalism."

"Sensationalism?" I asked, leaning forward slightly. "How so?"

"Thomas was a good archaeologist, but he had a tendency toward dramatic conclusions that weren't always supported by the evidence." Blackwood's voice carried the dismissive tone of someone discussing a persistent annoyance. "His presentation to the historical society was filled with wild theories about land theft and murder conspiracies. The kind of thing that makes for exciting television but doesn't hold up to scholarly scrutiny."

"What specifically concerned you about his theories?" Jack asked.

"He was making accusations against some of the founding families of this county—families who built this community, who contributed to its growth and prosperity for centuries. He was suggesting they were murderers and thieves based on circumstantial evidence and speculative connections." Blackwood's voice was rising slightly, his carefully controlled demeanor beginning to crack. His pale eyes fixed on Jack with calculating intensity. "He was even trying to drag respected families like yours into it, Sheriff, claiming William Lawson's death was connected to the conspiracy. Do you have any idea what that kind of publicity could do to reputations, to property values, to the tourism industry that depends on our Colonial heritage?"

There it was—not scholarly concern, but economic worry. Thomas's research threatened more than just historical narratives; it threatened money.

"And that's why you threatened him?" Jack's voice remained calm, but I could hear the steel underneath.

"I never threatened anyone." Blackwood's denial came too quickly, too forcefully. "I simply pointed out the potential consequences of publishing unsubstantiated theories. I suggested he might want to be more careful about his conclusions before going public."

"According to witnesses, you told him he'd face lawsuits for libel and academic misconduct," I said. "That sounds like a threat to me."

"It was good advice," Blackwood shot back. "Thomas was putting his career at risk with shoddy research. I was trying to save him from himself."

Jack leaned back in his chair, studying Blackwood with the patient intensity of a predator sizing up prey. "Where were you Monday night between 11 p.m. and 3 a.m.?"

"I was at home with my wife," Blackwood said without hesitation. "We had dinner, watched the news, went to bed around ten thirty. You can ask her if you need confirmation."

"We will," Jack said mildly. "Do you know anyone with the initials JMH?"

For the first time since we'd entered his office, Blackwood looked genuinely confused. "JMH? Not off the top of my head. Why?"

Either he was an exceptional actor, or those initials meant nothing to him.

"We're trying to understand what Thomas was researching and why someone might have wanted to stop him," Jack explained reasonably.

Blackwood was quiet for a moment, apparently weighing his options. "The families you mentioned still own significant portions of their original grants. Including mine. The Blackwood property is worth several million dollars in current market value, and my brothers and I were fortunate to inherit the land, and we're all fortunate to be able to pass it to our own children. But that doesn't prove anything except that our ancestors were successful farmers and businessmen."

"Thank you for your time, Mr. Blackwood," Jack said, rising from his chair. "We may have more questions later."

"Of course," Blackwood said, though his tone suggested otherwise. "I hope you find whoever did this terrible thing to Thomas."

As we walked back through the reception area, I caught the blond woman watching us with barely concealed curiosity. She looked away quickly when she realized I'd noticed, but not before I saw something that looked like fear flicker across her carefully composed features.

The elevator ride down was silent, but I could feel Jack's tension like electricity in the air. It wasn't until we were back in the Tahoe that he finally spoke.

"He's hiding something," Jack said, starting the engine with more force than necessary.

"Definitely. But is he hiding knowledge of a three-hundred-year-old conspiracy, or did he kill Thomas Whitman?" I buckled my seat belt and settled back against the leather seat. "Or both?"

"His alibi with the wife isn't worth much," Jack said, pulling out of the business park and heading toward the university. "Spouses lie for each other all the time, especially when there's money involved."

"Speaking of money," I said, "Did you notice how quickly he went from scholarly concerns to economic impact? He's not worried about historical accuracy—he's worried about property values and tourism dollars."

"Makes you wonder what else he's willing to do to protect those interests," Jack said grimly.

The drive to the university gave me time to process what we'd learned. Blackwood was definitely a person of interest, but something about the interview bothered me. His reaction to the initials JMH had seemed genuine, and his anger when we'd questioned his family's integrity had felt real rather than calculated.

King George University spread across a series of rolling hills about twenty minutes from town, a collection of red-brick buildings connected by tree-lined walkways that looked like something from a college brochure. The campus had the vacant, tired feel that came with the end of the semester—students already packing up their dorms to head home, others making their way to final exams, professors walking with the slightly distracted air of people whose minds were already on summer vacation.

The humanities building was one of the older structures on campus, its ivy-covered walls and tall windows speaking to an era when higher education was seen as a noble calling rather than a business enterprise. Inside, the hallways smelled of old books and chalk dust, with bulletin boards covered in announcements for lectures, conferences, and student activities.

Margaret Randolph's office was on the third floor, in a prime corner location with tall windows that overlooked the main campus quad. The nameplate on the door read *Dr. Margaret Randolph, Professor of American Studies*, and below that, in smaller text, *Office Hours: Tuesday/Thursday 2–4 p.m.*

Jack knocked, and a voice called out for us to enter.

If Richard Blackwood's office had been designed to impress, Margaret Randolph's was designed for serious scholarship. Every available surface was covered with books, papers, and research materials. Bookshelves lined three walls from floor to ceiling, packed so tightly that some volumes were stacked horizontally on top of others. Her desk was buried under towers of student papers, historical documents in protective sleeves, and what appeared to be several archaeological catalogs.

Margaret herself commanded the space behind her desk with the confident bearing of someone accustomed to being taken seriously. She was an attractive woman in her mid-thirties, with shoulder-length auburn hair that caught the light from her windows and intelligent green eyes that assessed us with calculating intensity. Her sleeveless black blouse revealed toned, athletic arms that spoke of someone who spent time in the field as well as the library, and she wore dark slacks that looked both professional and practical.

This was no ivory tower academic who'd never gotten her hands dirty. Everything about her suggested competence, physical capability, and the kind of sharp intelligence that didn't suffer fools gladly.

But it was her hands that caught my attention— long, elegant fingers stained with what looked like ink from documents, the nails cut short and practical. These were hands that spent their time carefully handling historical artifacts and turning the pages of ancient books.

"You look like cops," she said sardonically. "Can I assume you're here about Thomas?"

"Sheriff Lawson," Jack said, introducing himself. "And Dr. Graves. She's the coroner for the county."

Margaret nodded. "I can't say I haven't been expecting you."

"Have you?" Jack asked, settling into one of the two student chairs that faced her desk. I took the other, noting how the springs were worn and the upholstery had faded to an indeterminate beige.

"Of course. Thomas's murder is the talk of the

entire history department. We're colleagues and friends. We sit on boards together and have done research together. And our departments compete for grants and funding, so we're rivals as well. I assumed as soon as you spoke to his wife that I'd be the next person on your list." She resumed her seat, her hands folding neatly on her desk. "Thomas was a brilliant researcher, but a terrible communicator. And his interpersonal skills weren't that great either."

"We were told you threatened him at the historical society meeting," I said.

Margaret's composed expression didn't change, but I saw her hands tighten slightly. "I wouldn't characterize it as a threat. I was concerned about the implications of his research. And like I said, Thomas's interpersonal skills lacked at times."

"Were you concerned enough to follow him to the parking lot and tell him terrible accidents happen to people who dig in the wrong places?" Jack's voice was deceptively mild.

"I won't deny I was angry. And I may have been... overly emphatic in expressing my concerns," Margaret admitted, her academic precision making each word sound carefully weighed. "But Thomas wasn't acting like himself. He was more distracted than usual. More driven, more focused. To the point he was rude and evasive. Nothing mattered but his research, and he didn't give a damn who he steam-rolled in the process. He was talking about publishing theories that could destroy innocent people's lives based on incomplete evidence."

"What kind of incomplete evidence?" I asked.

Margaret leaned back in her chair, studying us through her wire-rimmed glasses. "Thomas was an excellent field archaeologist, but he wasn't trained in documentary analysis. He found some unmarked graves and immediately jumped to conclusions about murder and conspiracy. But there are dozens of perfectly innocent explanations for unmarked burials in Colonial America."

"Such as?"

"Poverty, illness, religious differences, family disputes." She ticked off the possibilities on her stained fingers. "Colonial record-keeping was sporadic at best, especially during times of conflict or disease. The absence of official records doesn't neces-sarily indicate criminal activity."

"But you'd reviewed his evidence yourself?" Jack asked.

"Thomas shared some of his findings with me, yes. We'd collaborated on several projects over the years." Something flickered across her face—an emotion I couldn't quite read. "He valued my exper-tise in Colonial documentation."

"And what did you think of what he'd found?"

Margaret was quiet for a long moment, her gaze studying something beyond our shoulders. When she finally spoke, her voice was softer, more thoughtful.

"I thought Thomas had stumbled onto something significant, but not necessarily something criminal. The discrepancies in the land grant records are real—I verified that myself. But Colonial property law was incredibly complex, and there were legal mechanisms for transferring land that might seem suspicious to modern eyes but were perfectly legitimate at the time."

"Legal mechanisms like what?" I asked.

"Debt settlements, marriage contracts, military service grants, royal pardons." She was warming to her subject now, the way academics did when they got to discuss their area of expertise. "When Bridget Ashworth was executed for witchcraft, her property would have been subject to forfeiture to the Crown, even though she had a husband and a daughter.

"Legend says that Bridget knew her time was coming to an end and she had her husband sneak away in the night with her daughter and head north to save their lives. There is no record of them after that date, so we can only assume that names were changed and they started life over. Once the Ashworth property was forfeited to the Crown, it would have then been distributed to other colonists.

So that doesn't necessarily mean theft. It could have been entirely legal under Colonial law."

"But Thomas didn't think so," Jack said.

"No, he didn't." Margaret's voice carried a note of sadness. "Thomas was convinced there was a conspiracy, that Bridget Ashworth had been deliberately targeted for her land. He'd found what he believed was evidence of coordinated testimony against her, witnesses who all had financial incentives to see her convicted."

"What kind of evidence?"

"Depositions, witness statements, property assessments." Margaret reached into a filing cabinet and pulled out a folder that looked like it had seen better days. "He shared copies of some documents with me, asked for my opinion on their authenticity."

She spread several photocopied pages across her desk, and I leaned forward to study them. The writing was in the careful script of Colonial clerks, but the ink had faded to brown with age and some sections were barely legible.

"These are depositions from Bridget Ashworth's trial," Margaret explained, pointing to one of the documents. "Thomas found them in the courthouse archives, misfiled in a box of tax records. What caught his attention was the pattern of testimony."

"Pattern?" Jack asked.

"Every single witness who testified against

Bridget Ashworth either owned property adjacent to hers or had recently applied for land grants that would be more valuable if her property were available for distribution." Margaret's finger traced across the faded names. "Jonathan Blackwood, Ezekiel Morton, Joseph Hughes, Rachel Mills—they all stood to gain financially from her death."

I felt a chill run down my spine as she named the same families whose graves had been marked around Thomas's body. Except there was one name missing. The Lawson name wasn't part of Thomas's research, even though Richard Blackwood had said it was.

"And they all testified against her?" I asked.

"They all claimed to have witnessed her practicing witchcraft. Cursing livestock, flying through the air, consorting with the devil." Margaret's voice carried the skepticism of someone who'd spent years studying the realities of Colonial life. "The testimony reads like a coordinated effort to build a case for conviction."

"You think Thomas was right?" I asked. "That Bridget Ashworth was murdered for her land?"

"It's impossible to know for sure," she said. "But I think Thomas was asking the right questions. But he didn't have the hard evidence to publish in academic circles. At least as far as I know."

"You warned him off the research," Jack said. "Threatened him. Told him to leave it alone."

"Because I was scared," Margaret admitted, her academic composure finally cracking. "Not of the historical implications, but of the current ones. If Thomas was right, if there really was a coordinated conspiracy to steal Bridget Ashworth's land, then the families who benefited are still living on that stolen property. Still profiting from it. And people will kill to protect that kind of wealth."

The admission hung in the air between us like smoke from a funeral pyre. Margaret had just confirmed what we'd suspected—Thomas's murder was connected to his research, and the stakes were higher than just historical reputation.

"We came across Thomas's appointment book," I said. "In the past ten months or so, he went from writing everything down in the book meticulously, names, dates, details, to only using initials."

"Yes, he mentioned a couple of times that he thought someone had gone through his office, and he said once that he felt like someone was following him. He got more and more paranoid over these last couple of months. I just chalked it up to being over-worked, stress, marital problems, funding prob-lems...you name it and Thomas was dealing with it."

"Marital problems?" Jack asked.

"Sure," Margaret said, shrugging. "Thomas was a

brilliant man. Charismatic, charming, ruggedly handsome, adventurous. But he was a horndog."

I raised a brow at how she said it. "Are you the MA that's listed in his appointment book?"

Her cheeks flushed with color, but she met the question without flinching. "Yes. Thomas and I had a physical relationship. On and off. Mostly off these past weeks."

"When did it start?"

She blew out a breath. "Oh, gosh. It's hard to explain. If you want to get technical I guess it started about fifteen years ago when I was his TA at William & Mary. Thomas was a visiting professor there for a semester, and I was finishing my master's degree. Then he went back to his digs and his life here, and I went on to get my doctorate at UVA. Thomas had a short attention span, so it would last for a few months and then he'd go off on a dig and it might be more than a year or two before I'd hear from him again. So I threw myself into my studies and my doctoral research, and when he came back into town I'd make time for him in my schedule if I wasn't in another relationship."

She paused and then smiled slyly, like a cat that ate the canary. "And then three years ago I got the position here at King George University, and I think he wasn't pleased about that. Thomas was very competitive and I'm very good at my job. Not just the teaching side, but the research and funding side of things. He was no longer the golden boy on campus, and some of his budget was diverted to my department."

"How'd he handle that?" I asked.

"He was angry," she said, smiling. "Very angry. He stormed into my office and yelled at me. Threw a paperweight at my chalkboard. And then he seduced me right on the desk. Best sex of my life." She cleared her throat and looked down at her joined hands. "But the pattern of our sexual relationship stayed the same. Except that early last year I met a man I was serious about. Thomas wasn't happy I wasn't there to scratch his itch, but I'm sure he found someone else. He always did. But we still worked close together on research, especially when he started digging into this stuff with Bridget Ashworth. He was like a dog with a bone.

"And then my boyfriend dumped me just before Valentine's Day," she said, bitterly. "Spent a year of my life with the guy and he decided that was the best time to end things. Darren is a business professor here on campus. It just so happened Thomas was in the vicinity. Darren broke things off and one thing led to another. Again."

"Did Patricia know about your relationship with her husband?" Jack asked.

"I'm sure she did," Margaret said. "Thomas never

rubbed his lovers in her face, and I certainly never acted inappropriately when she was with him. But not all of his enthusiasts were so subtle, especially the grad students."

"There were other frequent initials in his appointment book over the past few weeks," Jack continued. "Know anyone with the initials BD? Appointment was always during the day."

"Brian Dunlowe," she said immediately. "He's the provost for the university, and he has a lot of sway when it comes to funding. I know Thomas had been meeting with him, and that he didn't want me to know about it. I'm sure Thomas was giving him a preview of this sensationalized witch hunt. Pardon the pun. And I'm sure in the end Thomas would have gotten his money. He was very persuasive."

"How about JMH?" I asked. "Does that ring a bell?"

Margaret narrowed her eyes in thought, but shook her head. "No, that doesn't ring a bell."

"He met with someone with those initials the night he died," Jack said. "There was an appointment for dinner at seven thirty. It'd be nice to see if he made that dinner date. To be able to trace his last hours of life."

"I understand," she said. "If I think of someone it could be I'll let you know."

"Dr. Randolph," Jack said, "we need to know

where you were Monday night between 10 p.m. and 3 a.m."

She seemed surprised by the question, but regrouped quickly. "At home grading term papers," she said. "It's finals so I haven't had time for a social life. I live alone, but I can show you the papers—they're all time-stamped in the online grading system." She turned toward her computer. "I submitted the last batch of grades at one forty-seven. The system keeps records of everything."

It wasn't a perfect alibi—she could have graded papers earlier and submitted them later to create a false timeline—but it was something we could verify.

"Thank you for your time, Dr. Randolph," Jack said, rising from his chair. "We may have more questions later."

"Of course. And Sheriff?" Margaret's voice caught. "I hope you find whoever did this. Thomas had his faults, but he was a good man. And a great historian."

As we left her office, I found myself thinking about the complexity of human relationships—how love and guilt and fear could tangle together into patterns that led to tragedy.

"Let's take a quick look at Thomas's office while we're here," Jack said as we walked down the hallway.

"Maybe there will be something to point us to JMH," I said.

Thomas Whitman's office was on the ground floor in the archaeology department, tucked away in a corridor that smelled of earth and old stone. Unlike Margaret's cluttered academic nest, Thomas's workspace was meticulously organized. His desk was clean except for a few carefully arranged stacks of papers, his bookshelves were arranged by subject and author, and even his computer monitor was positioned at the perfect ergonomic angle.

He had two white-paned windows that needed a good cleaning, and the walls were covered with photographs from his various dig sites—images of excavated foundations, carefully catalogued artifacts, and students learning the painstaking work of archaeological recovery. But it was the map that caught my attention—a large, detailed survey of King George County that covered one entire wall, marked with colored pins that corresponded to various research sites.

"Look at this," I said, moving closer to study the map. Red pins marked the locations where Thomas had found the unmarked graves, while blue pins indicated officially documented historical sites. The pattern was striking—almost all of the red pins were clustered around areas that had originally belonged to Bridget Ashworth's property grant.

Jack joined me at the map, his eyes tracing the pattern of markers. "He was systematic about it. Every unmarked burial corresponds to property that was transferred after Bridget Ashworth's execution."

I counted the red pins. "Seventeen unmarked graves? Patricia said they'd found burial sites, but she didn't mention this many."

Jack's jaw tightened as he traced his finger across the map. "Either she didn't know the full extent, or she was holding back."

Seventeen people. The number sat like lead in my stomach. "That's not a few random burials—that's systematic elimination. If Thomas was right about this…"

"If Thomas was right about the conspiracy," Jack said. "That's a lot of people who would have had to disappear to make room for the land grab."

We spent the next thirty minutes going through Thomas's files, looking for any reference to JMH. His research was extensive and carefully documented, with cross-references and supporting evidence that painted a picture of a man obsessed with uncovering the truth. But there was nothing that pointed to who he might have had dinner with on the night he died.

"Nothing," I said, closing the last folder and rubbing my tired eyes. "If JMH exists, Thomas was being very careful about keeping that connection private."

Jack leaned back in Thomas's desk chair, surveying the organized chaos of the office. "Could be someone he was trying to protect. If he was meeting with a family member who was willing to share information about their ancestor's involvement, he might not have wanted to create a paper trail that could expose them."

As we locked up Thomas's office and headed back toward the parking garage, the weight of what we'd learned settled over me like a heavy blanket. Thomas's extracurricular activities shed new light on a few things.

"We need to take a deeper look at Patricia Whitman," I said, voicing what we were both thinking. "The grieving widow act seems a little thick now that we know her husband had a tendency to stray."

"One of the oldest motives in the book," Jack agreed. "Maybe the setup was just window dressing."

The storm clouds that had been threatening finally opened up as we reached the Tahoe, fat raindrops hitting the pavement with the violence of accusation. By the time we were inside the vehicle, the drops had turned into a steady downpour that drummed against the roof and turned the campus walkways into rivers.

"The question is what to do next," Jack said as he navigated through the streaming rain. "We need to verify Margaret's alibi with the online grading system, and we need to have another conversation with Patricia Whitman."

"The one where we ask her if it bothered her to share her husband's affections," I said, watching the windshield wipers fight their losing battle against the deluge.

"That's going to be a fun conversation," Jack said grimly. "But first, how do you feel about stopping for a donut?"

"I was just thinking I could use a snack."

The rain was coming down harder now, turning the Virginia countryside into a watercolor painting where the edges of everything blurred together. It seemed fitting, somehow, for a case where nothing was quite what it appeared to be, and the truth was as elusive as shadows dancing in the mist.

CHAPTER ELEVEN

The rain had finally stopped by the time we pulled into one of the angled parking spaces that surrounded King George's historic Towne Square, though pewter clouds still threatened overhead like a storm that couldn't make up its mind. It was one of those picture-perfect spaces filled with reminders of a different era—cobblestone streets, American flags, gas streetlamps, and antique hitching posts.

But today, something felt off. Maybe it was the way the Spanish moss hung too still in the humid air, or how the usual foot traffic seemed sparse for a weekday afternoon. Even the cheerful pink-and-white-striped awning of Lady Jane's Donuts, nestled between a women's clothing boutique and an art gallery in the middle of the block, looked somehow garish against the brooding sky.

"The baby wants a donut," I announced. "And then tacos for lunch."

Jack's mouth quirked in that way that meant he was fighting a smile. "The baby's pretty opinionated for someone who doesn't have a job."

I snorted out a laugh and Jack opened the door for me to Lady Jane's. The bell chimed with false cheer as we entered, the sound somehow too bright for the heaviness that had been following us all morning. The interior was a deliberate throwback to simpler times—white subway tiles, vintage cake stands displaying the day's offerings, and mason jar light fixtures that cast a warm glow over everything. The sugar-scented comfort of yeast and glaze bombarded my senses and I inhaled deeply and closed my eyes.

Behind the counter stood Jane herself—a woman in her early forties who looked like she'd stepped out of a 1950s magazine and never quite found her way back to the present. Her dark hair was styled in perfect victory rolls, her red lipstick was flawless, and she wore a fitted blue dress with white bobby socks and saddle shoes. A frilly apron tied around her waist completed the look, though I'd always suspected the vintage aesthetic was carefully calculated to charm the steady stream of male customers who kept her business thriving.

She looked up as we entered, and her face immediately lit up with recognition—though her gaze lingered on Jack a beat too long for my comfort.

"Well, well," Jane said, her professional smile not quite reaching her eyes. "Sheriff Lawson and Dr. Graves. I saw that awful business at the cemetery on the news. Must've been terrible finding that poor man like that." She smoothed her apron with careful hands. "I don't think I've ever seen you in here before, Sheriff."

"I'm usually too busy to stop in," Jack said, his tone professionally neutral.

"That's a shame," Jane said, her smile sharpening just slightly. "Your deputies certainly find time. They keep me in business."

"As long as they can run down a criminal then what they eat is between them and their sugar dealer," Jack said smoothly.

"Oh, they stay in shape," she said, her smile knowing in a way that made me wonder how many of Jack's men she was keeping physical fitness tabs on. "And after seeing the top cop for the county in the flesh I can see why the standard is so high."

I cleared my throat and Jane's unrepentant gaze turned my direction.

"What can I get you? Your usual?"

"We're here on business," I said. "Is Leena working today?"

"Called in sick," she said, the aggravation thick in

her voice. "Third time this week. If you ask me, she's either pregnant or on drugs."

"We need to speak with her," Jack said. "In an official capacity. Do you have her address?"

"Is she in trouble?" Jane asked, looking more curious than concerned.

"We just need to ask her some questions," Jack said, his tone carefully neutral. "Her address?"

"Sure, sure." Jane pulled out her phone and started scrolling. "Leena Cross. Lives at 47 Mockingbird Lane in the Willows Apartment Complex. Not a great area of town."

"We appreciate it," Jack said. "And I'll take that donut you mentioned. Can't let good hospitality go to waste."

I was weighing whether or not I'd lost my appetite after watching Jane's calculated interest in my husband, but by the time I'd made the decision I had a bag of fresh pastries in my hand and Jack was ushering me back outside.

As we walked back toward the Tahoe, I felt eyes on us from every direction. The few people moving around the square seemed to be watching without watching, their gazes sliding away just a second too late. Even the windows of the shops felt like they were staring.

"That was weird," I said.

"I appreciate your restraint in not clawing her eyes out."

"I really wanted a donut," I said. "I figured that might put a damper on things. But just in case, it's probably best you don't go there again. She seems aggressive."

"That's the talk around the bullpen. That place is like a cop's kryptonite. There's a pool going to see who ends up with her." He hesitated for a second. Long enough to let me know he was thinking twice about saying something.

"What?" I asked.

He was silent as he navigated the narrow streets and headed out of downtown. And then he said, "My guess would have been Cole. She had her hooks in him pretty good, and she wanted a ring out of the deal. I thought for a time he was going to cave."

"You're kidding," I said, shocked at that bit of news. "Surely a guy like Cole would know to stay far away from a woman like that."

Jack laughed. "A woman like that screams trouble, and that's exactly the kind of woman that most cops are attracted to. When you add in sex then even an experienced pro like Cole can be wrangled. Maybe it's the adrenaline rush. Who knows. But cops tend to make terrible decisions when it comes to their personal lives. I think it's because they always have to make the right decisions in their professional lives."

"And you?"

"I'm different," he said, giving me a wink. "I made all my stupid decisions about women when I was younger. I've gotten smarter as I've aged. Marrying you was the best decision I've ever made. And you still give me the adrenaline rush. I haven't completely recovered from seeing you tied to a chair and that bastard hitting you."

"Just another day at the office," I said.

"Which is weird since I'm the cop and out on the streets and you're the one who's supposed to be safe in your lab."

"Here, have a donut." I shoved one of the eclairs under his nose. "You'll feel better."

Twenty minutes later, we were pulling into the Willows Apartment Complex, and the feeling of being watched hadn't left me. This was a run-down area of King George, close to the county line, just before you crossed the Rappahannock River.

The buildings were generic brick rectangles that squatted like sleeping beasts under the threatening sky, surrounded by patchy grass that looked more dead than alive. Everything about the place screamed temporary—a way station for people who didn't plan to stay long enough to care.

Building C sat at the back of the complex like it

was trying to hide, its entrance marked by concrete steps that had crumbled at the edges. The hallway inside smelled like industrial carpet cleaner and something else—something organic and unpleasant that made me breathe through my mouth.

Apartment 47 was on the second floor, behind a door that had been painted institutional beige so many times the handle looked like it was drowning in layers of paint. Jack knocked, the sound echoing off the narrow hallway walls with hollow finality.

Silence.

He knocked again, harder this time. "Leena Cross?"

The door across the hall cracked open before the echo died, revealing a slice of face belonging to a woman with gray hair and eyes that held the kind of sharp intelligence that came from watching neighbors and filing away their secrets.

"She ain't been home since yesterday," the woman said without being asked. "Heard her leave around six last night with that strange boy who's been hanging around—the one with the thick glasses. Then they came back around midnight, making all kinds of racket. Then she left again, alone this time. Haven't seen her since."

The woman's eyes fixed on me with uncomfortable intensity. "You're that coroner, aren't you? The one who found the dead man. I seen you on the news."

"Did you see what she was driving?" Jack asked, steering the conversation back on track.

"That ugly black car of hers. Looks like a hearse." The woman's gaze never left my face. "There was someone in the car with her. She was making so much noise I kept an eye on her until she left. Just to make sure nothing hinky was going on."

"Good thinking," Jack said, but the woman snapped the door shut with the finality of a coffin lid.

"Friendly place," I said. "I'm guessing the guy in the car was Sheldon. He's mostly drawing a blank from what happened, but maybe he's heard from her."

"Good idea," Jack said. His phone erupted into sound, the ringtone cutting through the oppressive quiet like a scream. He answered on the first ring. "Lawson."

I could hear Cole's voice through the speaker—urgent, clipped. Jack's face went through a series of micro-expressions as he listened, each one grimmer than the last.

"When?" Jack asked, and the single word carried the weight of someone who already knew the answer would be terrible. "Are you sure about the registration?"

Jack was already walking down the hallway and toward the stairs, so I followed after him.

"We'll be right there," he said, hanging up.

"What now?" I asked

"Cole and Martinez ran the partial plate from the surveillance footage."

"And?"

"It's registered to Dr. Victoria Mills."

"Ahh," I said. "We're back to the long-lost ancestors. I'm guessing she's connected to Rachel Mills?" I searched my memory, trying to remember what had been significant about her grave. "Didn't she have the stone circle placed around her grave?

"That's the one," Jack said.

"If Thomas's cardiac arrest was medically induced then Dr. Mills would certainly have access."

"Why don't we pay her a visit and ask her why her car was seen near the crime scene at the time of the murder?"

"It's a workday," I said. "Let's check her office first. She might have a perfectly reasonable explanation."

"We need to ask," Jack said, starting the engine with more force than necessary.

The drive through King George County should have been peaceful—rolling hills painted in every shade of spring green, dogwood blossoms scattered like confetti against the darker backdrop of ancient oaks. But today the countryside felt watchful, as if the very trees were holding secrets behind their budding branches.

"Jack," I said, watching storm clouds gather on the horizon, "What if this isn't about historical justice at all? What if someone's using the witch trial story as camouflage for something happening right now?"

His hands tightened on the steering wheel. "Like what?"

"I don't know yet. But three hundred years is a long time to hold a grudge. Modern money, modern secrets, modern revenge—those feel more immediate."

"Current wealth built on old blood," Jack said, his voice carrying the grim recognition of someone who'd seen how far people would go to protect their fortunes.

The King George Family Medicine office sat in the shadow of towering magnolias, their waxy leaves dripping from the morning's rain. The converted Victorian should have looked welcoming with its pale yellow clapboard siding and wraparound porch, but something felt wrong. The building seemed to hunker down against the approaching storm, windows dark and lifeless.

"Office hours say they should be open," Jack said, checking his watch as we climbed the front steps.

The boards creaked under our weight, a sound that seemed too loud in the unnatural quiet.

I pressed my face to the front window, cupping my hands against the glass. The waiting room looked frozen in time—magazines fanned neatly on side tables, chairs positioned in perfect rows—but empty of any human presence.

Jack tried the door handle. It turned, but the door was locked from the inside.

"That's not normal for a Wednesday afternoon," I murmured, that familiar itch between my shoulder blades that meant danger was close.

"Let's see what the neighbors know."

Mason & Associates Insurance occupied the adjacent building, and the moment we walked through the door, a woman behind the reception desk looked up with the eager expression of someone starved for conversation. She was probably in her mid-sixties, with steel-gray hair teased into a style that hadn't changed since 1985 and reading glasses hanging from a beaded chain around her neck.

"Well, hello there," she said, her voice carrying the melodic cadence of Virginia born and bred. "Y'all aren't here about insurance, are you? You've got that official look about you."

Jack showed his badge. "Sheriff Lawson. We're looking for Dr. Mills next door. Her office appears to be closed."

The woman—her nameplate read *Dolores Hutchins*—leaned forward conspiratorially, her eyes bright with the thrill of being part of something important. "Oh honey, she's been gone since day before yesterday. Just up and left like the devil himself was chasing her."

"Can you tell us what you saw?" I asked, settling into the chair across from her desk. Sometimes the best way to get information was to make people comfortable, let them tell their story.

"Well now," Dolores said, adjusting her glasses and settling in for what was clearly going to be a detailed recounting. "I was just finishing up the Jones policy renewal—Myra Jones lives out on Tobacco Road with all those cats." She said it all in one breath and I thought the woman must have incredible lung capacity. "That's when I heard Dr. Mills's car start up. Must've been around five thirty, maybe quarter to six."

She paused for effect, making sure she had our full attention.

"Now, I wouldn't normally pay it much mind, but she was loading a suitcase into her trunk. A big one, the kind you take on vacation. And Dr. Mills, bless her heart, hasn't taken a vacation in the three years I've been working here. Woman's married to that practice."

Jack leaned forward slightly. "Did she seem upset? In a hurry?"

"Oh, she was rattled all right. Kept looking over her shoulder like she expected someone to jump out of the bushes. Her hands were shaking so bad she dropped her keys twice before she got the car started." Dolores's voice dropped to a whisper. "And she had her medical bag with her, which struck me as odd if she was going on a trip."

My pulse quickened. A doctor's bag could contain all sorts of interesting things—including drugs that could stop a heart.

"Has anyone else been asking about Dr. Mills?" I asked.

Dolores's eyes lit up. "Well, now that you mention it, I did see someone poking around her office earlier this morning. Tried the door, looked in the windows. When they saw me watching, they waved and walked off toward the parking lot."

"Can you describe them?" Jack asked.

"Not really, honey. I wasn't paying that much attention until they started acting suspicious. Average build, I'd say. Could've been a man or woman—they were wearing one of those baseball caps pulled down low."

"What kind of vehicle were they driving?"

"Didn't see one. They must've parked somewhere

else and walked over. By the time I got curious enough to get a better look, they were already gone."

We thanked Dolores and stepped back outside, where the air had grown heavy with the promise of rain. Thunder rumbled in the distance, and the first fat drops began to splatter against the pavement.

"She ran," Jack said, his voice carrying the grim certainty of a man who'd seen too many suspects flee. "Packed a bag, took her medical supplies, and disappeared right after we found her car on our surveillance footage. That's not the behavior of an innocent witness."

"Could be she's scared of whoever killed Thomas," I said, pulling my jacket tighter as the wind picked up. "Or could be she killed him herself and realized we were closing in."

Jack was already pulling out his phone. "Either way, I'm putting out a BOLO on Mills and her vehicle. And I want a deputy to check her home address immediately."

The storm was moving in fast now, turning the afternoon prematurely dark. Lightning flickered in the distance as Jack finished his calls, coordinating the search for a woman who might be a killer or might be the next victim.

As we drove away from the empty medical office, I couldn't shake the feeling that we were already too late. Somewhere in King George County, the truth was waiting—and so was death.

CHAPTER TWELVE

THE VIRGINIA COUNTRYSIDE BLURRED PAST IN SHADES of storm-gray and emerald as we headed toward Newcastle, but the peaceful scenery did nothing to calm the knot of unease growing in my stomach. Something about this case felt like standing on the edge of a cliff in the dark—one wrong step and everything would come crashing down.

Jack's phone shattered the tense silence, Cole's name flashing on the display like a warning.

"Talk to me," Jack said, his voice carrying the controlled tension of a man bracing for bad news.

Cole's words crackled through the speaker, each one hitting like a physical blow. "That deputy you sent to check Mills's house just called it in. Jack, you need to know—the front door was standing wide open like an invitation to hell. Chen and I are heading over there now."

My blood chilled. "What did you find?"

"House looks like a tornado hit it. Every drawer dumped, furniture overturned, papers scattered everywhere. Someone was looking for something specific, and they weren't being careful about it." Cole's voice dropped. "There's blood in the kitchen. Not a lot, but enough to paint a story nobody wants to read."

Jack's knuckles went white against the steering wheel. "How much blood are we talking about?"

"Enough to know someone got hurt. Not enough to know if they walked away." The sound of voices and activity filtered through the phone. "I've got Potts and the CSI team processing everything, but whoever did this had time to be thorough."

The line went quiet except for the static of an active crime scene, and I could picture Cole standing in the middle of chaos, trying to piece together a puzzle painted in violence.

"Any sign of Mills?"

"Gone. But her purse is still sitting on the counter with two hundred dollars cash and all her credit cards. This wasn't about money, Jack. This was personal."

Jack's expression darkened. "Cole, we've got Mills's car on surveillance footage at the cemetery the night of Thomas's murder. If her house was ransacked and she's missing…"

"Someone could have taken her car that night," Cole finished. "Used it to get to the cemetery, then brought it back. Mills might not have been involved at all."

"Or she was there willingly and someone silenced her afterward," I said grimly. "Either way, she's connected to this."

As Jack ended the call, the weight of what we were facing settled over me like a shroud. Two crime scenes, one dead professor, and now a missing doctor whose house had been torn apart by someone desperate enough to risk everything.

"We need to continue to Morton's," Jack said, his jaw set in the hard line that meant he was thinking three steps ahead. "If Mills found something threatening enough to get her house ransacked, Morton's historical documents could put him in the same danger."

"And he might know something about why his family's involved," I added, watching the storm clouds gather overhead. "Judge Morton's spent his whole career dealing with facts and evidence. If anyone can help us understand what happened in 1725, it's him."

The drive to Judge Morton's house took us through the kind of Virginia countryside that made people fall in love with the state. Rolling hills dotted with horse farms, stone walls that had probably been built before the Revolution, and ancient oaks that created natural cathedrals over winding roads. It was the sort of landscape that belonged on postcards, all pastoral beauty and timeless grace.

Morton's place sat at the end of a tree-lined drive that could have been featured in *Southern Living*—a stately brick Georgian that managed to look both impressive and welcoming. The gardens were beautifully maintained but not aggressively manicured, with boxwood hedges that had been allowed to grow into their natural shapes and flower beds that looked like they'd been planted by someone who actually enjoyed getting dirt under their fingernails. A wooden swing hung from an enormous oak tree, its ropes worn smooth by decades of use. Jack parked behind a newer model Tesla.

Judge Harold Morton answered the door before we'd finished climbing the front steps, as if he'd been watching for us through the front windows. He was a man in his early sixties with the kind of face that belonged on a Norman Rockwell painting—kind eyes behind wire-rimmed glasses, silver hair that needed cutting, and the rumpled appearance of someone who'd been reading by the fire rather than worrying about appearances.

"Jack," he said warmly, extending his hand. "And your lovely wife. We've never had the pleasure."

"No, sir," I said, shaking his hand warmly. "It's a pleasure to meet you."

"Come in, come in," he said, ushering us inside. "I'm assuming this isn't a social call. You both look very official."

"Unfortunately, it's not," Jack replied. "But my mother said next time I see you to tell you not to be a stranger and to accept her invitation for dinner."

"Your mother is a rare treasure," he said. "Are she and Rich doing well? I heard he was thinking of semi-retiring."

"I'll believe that when I see it," Jack said as we followed him into the heart of the home. "Dad has a fear of missing out. He likes to keep a toe dipped into everything from the farm to his businesses."

"Smart man," Morton said. "I've found the older you get the more your brain needs to stay engaged in something scintillating."

The furniture was quality without being showy, books were stacked on every available surface with the comfortable chaos of someone who actually read them, and family photographs covered the mantel-piece in genuine clusters rather than formal arrangements.

"I heard through the grapevine that you had an extra surprise after you found Thomas Whitman on

Bridget Ashworth's grave. Something about carvings in founding family gravestones."

"No one gossips like cops do," Jack said with an aggravated sigh.

"If it makes you feel better," Morton said. "I don't think your secret is out in the public. I've found in my line of work sometimes it's good to have a contact or two on the inside. My first year on the bench a bomb was found under my car. A guy I'd put away when I was a young prosecutor had done his thirty years, and I was the first person he thought of when he got out."

"You must be a memorable man," I said.

He chuckled and said, "I don't like surprises. So I do my best to keep my ears to the ground. Have a seat and let me get us some coffee. My housekeeper just made a fresh pot. I live on the stuff."

"I'd appreciate it," I said, thinking that our trip to Lady Jane's seemed like a lifetime ago.

"I knew Thomas Whitman a little," he said as he got out proper cups and saucers and the sugar and milk caddies. "I met him a time or two at founders' events. His parents were more involved in those things."

"What were your impressions?" Jack asked.

"He was a man who seemed always ready to pick up and leave," Judge Morton said immediately. "Had trouble settling. Even at something as mundane as a fundraiser or party. He married an outsider if I remember right. His mother was a bit distraught over that, but it's been close to two decades so I'm not sure of her feelings now. Last I heard his mother was moved into memory care after his father passed away. Thomas was nice enough, but his mind was always on his work. Tragic what happened to him though. And being found the way he was it seems someone was trying to send a message of some kind."

"That's our thought too," Jack said.

Judge Morton brought the coffee tray over to the little breakfast table where Jack and I sat. I found myself relaxing for the first time all day. There was something inherently trustworthy about this man.

"Now," he said. "Considering the graves I was told were marked, you're wondering about Ezekiel Morton and how he was connected to Bridget Ashworth."

"What can you tell us about him?" Jack asked, accepting the coffee with the appreciation of someone who'd been running on adrenaline and determination.

Morton sat on the bench seat across from us and wrapped his hands around his cup. "I can tell you quite a bit actually. I have been blessed with ancestors who saw the importance in both education and legacy. I come from generations of attorneys and judges, and I have original documents—letters, court papers, journals. Many of the documents are in museums, but I have copies of everything."

"That's incredible," I said.

"Indeed," he said. "And lately there's been quite a bit of renewed interest in this particular historical period. Just last Sunday, Dr. Victoria Mills stopped by asking about the same families and time period you're investigating."

Jack and I exchanged glances. "Dr. Mills was here?"

"Oh yes. She said Thomas Whitman's recent presentation to the historical society had prompted her to look into her own family's medical history, particularly interested in Rachel Mills and the other founding families. She seemed worried about what Thomas might publish. Very knowledgeable woman —we had tea and talked for over an hour about Colonial medical practices and the witch trials."

"What specifically was she interested in?" I asked, feeling that familiar tingle that came when pieces of a puzzle started clicking together.

"She wanted to know about the property transfers after Bridget Ashworth's execution, and whether any of the original land grants were still intact." Morton's expression grew thoughtful. "She seemed particularly concerned about whether her family had been among the victims or the perpetrators. She kept asking if being descended from someone involved in the conspiracy could have modern legal implications. Said she'd been doing genealogical research and found some disturbing connections."

My pulse quickened. "What kind of connections?"

"Well, she asked what would happen legally if it could be proven that land had been stolen rather than legally transferred. Whether current property ownership could be challenged if historical fraud was discovered." Morton paused, stirring his coffee slowly. "She seemed quite worried about what she might find."

"Did she mention anyone else asking about her research?" Jack asked. "Or seem concerned about being followed?"

Morton's brow furrowed. "Now that you mention it, she did seem nervous. Kept checking her phone, looked over her shoulder a few times when we were sitting by the window. She asked if I'd told anyone else about our conversation, and when I said no, she seemed relieved."

"What did you tell her about the property transfers?"

"The truth. That if sufficient historical evidence existed to prove fraud in the original transfers, it could potentially create legal complications for current landowners, especially if the property was valuable." Morton set down his coffee cup with care. "She seemed quite troubled by that possibility."

Jack leaned forward. "Did she ask to see the original documents?"

"She asked, but I explained I don't show the originals to anyone—too fragile and valuable. However, I did show her some photocopies from Ezekiel's journals." Morton's face grew troubled. "She was particularly interested in the entries about pressure being applied to ensure Bridget's conviction.

"Ezekiel Morton was appointed as Justice of the Peace to preside over several trials in the early Colonial period, including Bridget Ashworth's," Morton continued, rising to retrieve a thick spiral-bound album from a side table. "According to his journals, he was deeply troubled by that particular case."

"Troubled how?"

"He didn't believe that Bridget Ashworth was a witch." Morton opened the album to reveal photocopied pages covered in careful Colonial script. "As judge, he was duty bound to listen to all the testimony against the accused. But the testimony against Bridget Ashworth was very coordinated, too convenient. Every witness seemed to have the same story, told in nearly identical language. People said she'd been sacrificing their animals and witnesses would corroborate—blood appearing on their doorposts and things like that. Whole families would say she cursed them when they all came down with an illness. Others accused her of murder if someone died. Of course, illness and death were not uncommon in those times. There were entire families wiped out from influenza, smallpox, typhoid..."

Morton pushed the thick folder across the table to us. "But more than that, Ezekiel documented pressure from other prominent men to ensure a guilty verdict."

"What kind of pressure?"

"Threats, bribes, promises of political advancement if he cooperated and social and financial ruin if he didn't." Morton's voice carried the weight of generations of family shame. "According to his journals, Jonathan Blackwood and Jasper Hughes visited him privately the night before the verdict. Jasper was the husband of Rebecca, and she was one of the primary witnesses against Bridget. These men made it clear that acquitting Bridget Ashworth would be seen as treason against the colony's interests. They threatened his wife and children."

"That's a hard place for anyone to be in," Jack said.

Judge Morton nodded. "I'd like to think if I were in his place that I'd stand for justice and I'd protect what was mine at the same time, no matter the cost, but when it comes down to it, not all men are created to go to war. Sometimes you have to think of other ways to protect what you love most. I can't fault Ezekiel for the choice he made. I wouldn't be here otherwise."

"What happened to him?" I asked.

"It's documented in his journals," he said. "He was weighed down with shame and guilt over Bridget's death. He became ill, losing weight and sleep until he'd wasted away to nothing. He wrote in his journal that he felt it was a just punishment for his sins. And then he died less than a year later. His sons were old enough to steward the property and provide for the family, so our line and the inheritance of this land passed on through generations."

"Judge Morton," I said carefully, "Dr. Mills is missing. Her medical practice was closed yesterday, and this morning we found her house had been ransacked. There were signs of a struggle."

The color drained from Morton's face. "Missing? Good God. You think someone took her because of what she was researching?"

"We're not sure yet," Jack said. "But we're concerned about anyone who has knowledge of these historical documents. Have you had any other unusual visitors or phone calls recently?

Morton was quiet for a moment, clearly thinking. "There was one odd phone call, about two weeks ago. Right around the time Thomas Whitman made his presentation to the historical society, now that I think about it. Someone asking about Ezekiel's journals, claiming to be doing genealogical research. But the questions were very specific—about property boundaries and land transfers. And there was something strange about the voice."

"Strange how?"

"It sounded electronically distorted, like someone was deliberately disguising it. They knew details about the journals that aren't in any published accounts. You can understand that there are some aspects of my family history that aren't open for public consumption and opinion."

Jack leaned forward, his expression growing more serious. "Judge Morton, between Dr. Mills's visit last week, this suspicious phone call, and now Thomas's murder, I think you need to consider that you might be in danger too."

"You really think so?" Morton asked, though his voice suggested he'd already been wondering the same thing.

"Someone is eliminating people who have knowledge of this historical conspiracy," I said. "And you have more documented evidence than anyone."

Morton was quiet for a moment, clearly weighing the implications.

"Do you mind if we take these with us?" Jack asked, indicating the photocopied journals.

"Of course. I had the letters published several

years ago, so I have books of them. I have a sister in Richmond," Morton said, understanding the gravity of the situation. "I can drive down there this evening."

"Good. And Judge? If anyone else calls or visits asking about those journals, you contact me immediately."

As we drove away from Judge Morton's house, I found myself mentally cataloging the pieces of a puzzle that was finally starting to make sense. This wasn't about historical justice or supernatural revenge.

This was about secrets. Deadly secrets that someone was willing to kill to protect.

"Jack," I said, watching the Virginia countryside roll past, "What if Dr. Mills discovered she was connected to this conspiracy? Either as a descendant of the victims or the perpetrators?"

"Then she became a liability," Jack said with the matter-of-fact tone he used when analyzing criminal behavior. "Someone who knew too much about the past and might expose the truth."

"The question is, who else knows enough about this conspiracy to be considered a threat?" I said.

"We need to get these documents digitized and secure," Jack said, patting the folder Morton had given us. "And we need to find out exactly what Mills discovered before someone decided she was too dangerous to live."

As we headed back toward town, I felt the familiar satisfaction that came when a case started clicking into place. Three centuries ago, a group of men had conspired to steal land and eliminate anyone who threatened their plan.

Now someone was playing the same deadly game, silencing anyone who might expose the truth.

The killer was cleaning house, eliminating anyone who knew too much about a three-hundred-year-old conspiracy. But they'd made a mistake— they'd left a trail of bodies and ransacked homes that told their own story.

We still didn't know who JMH was, the person Thomas had dinner with the night he died. That meeting might have sealed his fate. But we were closing in, and the killer had to know it.

The question was whether we could stop them before they finished what they'd started.

CHAPTER THIRTEEN

THE VIRGINIA COUNTRYSIDE UNFURLED BEFORE US LIKE a watercolor painting left in the rain, all bleeding greens and soft edges that should have been soothing but somehow felt ominous instead. Jack's hands were steady on the wheel, but I could read the tension in the set of his shoulders, the way his jaw tightened whenever he glanced at the folder on the back seat that held three centuries of buried secrets.

"You know what's eating at me?" I said, watching a red-tailed hawk circle lazily over a tobacco field that probably hadn't changed much since Bridget Ashworth's time.

"The fact that someone's been planning this for a long time," Jack said without hesitation. "The voice distortion, the specific questions about property boundaries—that's not casual curiosity. That's reconnaissance."

"Exactly." I shifted in my seat. "Someone's been watching, waiting, gathering information. The question is how long they've been at it."

Our house rose from the pine-covered cliff like something out of an architectural magazine. It was supposed to be our sanctuary, a place where the ugliness of our work couldn't follow us. But tonight, even home didn't feel entirely safe.

The office that had once been Jack's private retreat now looked like a war room, with Morton's documents spread across every surface like battle plans. The late afternoon sun slanted through the floor-to-ceiling windows, casting long shadows that seemed to dance with secrets of their own.

"Time for a briefing with the team," Jack said, already reaching for his phone. "How do you feel about pizza?"

I thought about it for a few seconds. "I can do pizza. Maybe. It's all coming up in the morning anyway."

"You've got to think positive," he said, leaning back in his chair. "Maybe you won't be sick."

"I'll remind you you said that when you're holding my hair back in the morning. We'll see how positive you feel."

While Jack made calls, I found myself studying

the photocopied pages of Ezekiel Morton's journal, trying to imagine the man who'd written these words. His handwriting was careful, precise—the work of someone who understood that his words might be read long after he was gone. But between the lines, I could read the weight of a terrible decision, the slow erosion of a man's soul under the pressure of keeping a deadly secret.

I must have been lost in his journal longer than I thought because the sound of gravel crunching under tires caught me by surprise. Through the window, I watched Cole unfold himself from his pickup truck with the easy grace of a man who'd spent his life moving with purpose. He was moving a little slower than he normally did, and I could see he was favoring his ribs some from the altercation at the station that morning.

"Heck of a thing," he said by way of greeting. "Makes you wonder what other skeletons are rattling around in these old family closets."

Martinez arrived moments later. Where Cole was all rough edges and cowboy pragmatism, Martinez was polish and precision. But beneath the expensive veneer was a sharp mind and a relentless pursuit of justice that made him one of the best detectives I'd ever worked with.

"This feels like something out of a Gothic novel," Martinez said, picking up one of Morton's journal pages with the careful reverence of someone who understood the weight of history. "Conspiracy, murder, stolen land—all we need is a mysterious woman in white wandering the moors."

"Don't give anyone ideas," Jack muttered.

The third arrival was Deputy Potts, and watching her climb out of her county vehicle was like observing a study in controlled efficiency. She moved with the precise economy of someone who'd learned that wasted motion could mean missed evidence, her dark hair pulled back in a ponytail that somehow managed to look both professional and severe.

"Sheriff," she said, her voice carrying that neutral tone that good cops learned to use when they wanted to keep their thoughts private. "Nice house."

"We like it," he said. "Come on in. The office is through there. Pizza should be here soon."

"Now you're speaking my language," she said, nodding casually to Cole and Martinez. "I've got preliminary findings from the Mills scene."

She carried her tablet and camera like extensions of herself, tools that had become as natural as breathing. Potts was the kind of CSI who saw patterns where others saw chaos, who could read a crime scene like a novel written in blood and fiber evidence. But there was something else there too— an intensity that went beyond professional dedication into something more personal.

"Hold your horses, Deputy Do-Right," Cole said. "Pizza isn't even here yet. We're gonna need fuel for the brain."

"My brain is always fueled," she said, deadpan. "But I'm a little concerned now knowing yours isn't."

Cole grinned and crossed his arms lazily across his broad chest. "Oh, there's always something rattling around up here. That's why I make the big bucks."

Potts widened her eyes comically. "I was wondering what that sound was. I thought someone had a pack of Tic Tacs in their pocket."

Martinez snorted out a laugh and gave Potts a knuckle bump. "Welcome to the team."

The doorbell rang again and Cole said, "That's probably Lily. I just told her to meet us here. We're like ships passing in the night with our schedules."

"See," I told him. "It's like you're married already."

Cole grimaced and said, "That's what I keep telling her. I think I'm wearing her down."

"Golly, Cole," I said. "You're such a romantic. Just what every girl wants. To be worn down."

"If y'all are going to gang up on me all night I'm going to go off duty and switch to beer."

Lily came into the room with an oversize backpack and eyes only for Cole. Lily was the kind of beautiful that smacked you right in the face, even though she was wearing one of Cole's police academy hoodies and a pair of loose black shorts. Her long dark hair rained straight down her back and her face was free of makeup. She looked younger than her twenty-three years, and I could tell by the look on Cole's face he still wasn't completely comfortable with the seventeen-year difference in their ages.

She gave him a quick kiss and settled cross-legged on the floor near Cole's chair with the unconscious flexibility of youth. "Three more days and finals are done. I am not sorry to see the end of organic chemistry."

The doorbell rang again. "That must be the pizza," I said, but when I opened the door Sheldon was standing on my doorstep.

"Sheldon?"

"Did you check your Ring Camera?" he asked. "Burglaries are reduced by as much as fifty-five percent for those who use them."

"Are you going to rob me?" I asked, confused.

He stared at me like I'd lost my mind. "Of course not. Your gate was open. Can I stay with you? I brought my overnight bag. I think someone is watching me at my house. Maybe Leena. Or Evangeline. Or maybe they drugged me and I'm having hallucinations. Things have been a blur since last night and I can't put all the pieces together."

He looked pretty forlorn standing on my front porch with his Dungeons and Dragons backpack.

"I'll run it by Jack, but I'm sure it'll be fine." I ushered him inside and then saw the pizza delivery guy pull up.

Our house felt like Grand Central Station. This is what happened when your circle of friends kept growing. I'd never had that as a kid. My parents had been solitary people—understandably so—and I'd kept my circle of friends small and never expanded it. Marriage had changed things for me in more ways than one, and I moved slow when it came to relationships. I didn't trust easily and I was always a bit skeptical of people, but I'd slowly adjusted to these new friendships over the past couple of years.

I took the pizzas and then turned to find everyone had come out of the office and was heading toward the kitchen.

"Nice backpack," Jack told Sheldon.

"Thanks. I only brought clothes for a couple of days. That's all that would fit."

Jack looked at me and raised his eyebrows and I shrugged. "He said he only has a couple of days of clothes. That's promising."

With the exception of Potts, everyone had been in our home enough that they knew where plates and drinks and anything else they wanted was located. Cops tended to make themselves at home as long as they were in the safety of other cops. I guess it's encouraging that they feel that way at our place.

"Sheldon thinks someone has been watching him," I said to the group at large, and then I snagged a couple of pieces of pizza before they all disappeared.

"I know someone has been watching," he corrected, wiping the sweat off his upper lip before he took a bite. "The name Durkus was feared for generations in Poland. It's said our lineage descends directly from the Baba Yaga. I think that's why Leena was interested in me in the first place. She could feel my magical properties."

Everyone froze where they were and stared at Sheldon. The silence wasn't a comfortable one, so I felt obligated to fill the space.

"Have you heard from Leena?" I asked.

"She called a few hours ago," he said. "I hate when pizza burns the roof of my mouth. Did you know that seventy percent of the population has experienced palate burns?"

"Focus, Sheldon," I said. "What did Leena want?"

"I'm not really sure," he said shrugging. "She hasn't really been acting like herself. She's pretty obsessed with Bridget Ashworth, especially since Thomas Whitman's body showed up. She asked if I could take her down to the lab and show her. She wanted to see if he had any leftover energy or something."

"You can't do that," I told him, just to make sure he wasn't planning a nighttime heist into the lab.

"Oh, I know," he said. "I think I need to break up with her. I hate breaking up with women."

"You've had to break up with women a lot?" Cole asked.

"Oh, sure," Sheldon said. "I'm not ready to settle down yet, and women get attached to me pretty quickly."

"Huh," Cole said.

"Has Leena asked any questions about the investigation?" Jack asked. "Tried to get information from you about suspects or anyone we've talked to?"

"Not so much that," he said, chewing thoughtfully. "But she told me about markings on other graves, and about how she wanted to see the engravings because Bridget might be sending a message and only another witch can read it."

"Sounds like we've got a leak in the department," Martinez said, scowling.

"Leena hears from the other world," Sheldon said. "It's kind of creepy. But sexy too."

"Did she hear from Bridget?" Lily asked, curious.

"No, that's why we went to see Evangeline," Sheldon explained like we were all simpletons.

"Bridget has a supernatural force field around her, so an apprentice witch like Leena can't get through."

Cole nodded with all the seriousness in the world. "That's a job for a professional witch."

"Exactly," Sheldon said. "But Leena told me that Bridget had been betrayed by the very people she trusted, and then she said that those bloodlines needed to be cleansed."

Cole leaned forward, narrowing his eyes. "Cleansed how?"

"I don't know," Sheldon said, his voice shrinking to a whisper. "She said she'd call me later and hung up. And then I looked out my bedroom window and there was this car sitting across from my house. It was raining so it was kind of hard to see, but I could tell someone was looking straight at me."

"What'd the car look like?" Jack asked.

"It was a nice car," Sheldon said. "Black sedan, looked expensive. Mercedes, I think. The one with the silver emblem on the front."

Martinez got out his phone and pulled up the DMV records. "Victoria Mills drives a black Mercedes E-Class. That what you saw?"

"Yeah, that's it," Sheldon said, nodding. "I remember thinking it was too nice a car to be sitting in my neighborhood."

"No hits on the BOLO?" Jack asked.

"Nothing," Cole said.

"What time did you see the car?" Jack asked Sheldon.

"Well, after I got sent home from work I went home and took a shower and a nap. And then I got up at one and had some SpaghettiOs. The kind with the little wieners in it. And then I went back to my room and turned on that new documentary about that funeral home that was embalming people while they were still alive. *Preserved in Silence.*"

"Oh, yeah," Lily said. "I watched that. Very creepy. I'm going to get cremated when it's my time."

"What made you go to the window?" Jack asked, his patience everlasting.

"I had a feeling," he said. "I think the Baba Yaga warns me about things sometimes. And there was this crazy-loud thunder and a lightning strike that was so bright it lit up my room. I went to the window to see if anything had been barbecued."

"Baba Yaga," I said.

"Call in Sheldon's address," Jack told Martinez. "Let's see if we can get footage from stoplights and see what direction the car went. That was only a few hours ago."

Something was bothering me about Victoria Mills, and I didn't have a good feeling. "Seems strange for a woman to pack her bags to get out of town and then drive around the town you're escaping from, skulking about at gas stations and people's houses."

"Yeah," Jack said. "That's just one of the many issues with this case. Let's send someone to pick up Leena."

"Good luck with that," Sheldon said. "She's like smoke—here one minute, gone the next. And then you wake up naked in her car."

"You didn't tell me you were naked," I said.

Sheldon's cheeks turned pink. "It didn't seem relevant at the time."

"I'll have a couple of deputies go by her apartment," Cole said. "Maybe we'll get lucky. Even witches need to get something to eat and take a shower."

We cleaned up the kitchen and then ambled back into the office, taking seats around the conference table. Lily grabbed her backpack and settled in one of the overstuffed chairs by the fireplace.

Potts pulled out her iPad and said, "I hear you've got state-of-the-art technology here. Can I connect? I've got the photos and evidence documentation from the Mills house. CSI finished processing the scene about an hour ago."

"Absolutely," Jack said, moving to activate the wall-mounted display system. "What've you got for us?"

The large screen came to life, and Potts began

swiping through crime-scene photos with the methodical precision that made her so good at her job. "Dr. Mills's house tells a story of interrupted escape. Her bedroom shows she was packing in a hurry—drawers opened, clothes missing, closets' contents reduced. But then there are clear signs of a struggle in the living room and kitchen."

"So she was trying to leave when someone surprised her?" Martinez asked.

"That's what it looks like," Potts said, pulling up photos of Mills's home office. "She was gathering important documents when her attacker arrived. Her desk was partially cleaned out, and I found indentations on a notepad that show she wrote down a phone number."

She displayed an enhanced image showing faint impressions on paper. "Lab enhanced this. The number traces to a burner phone purchased two weeks ago with cash at a Walmart in Richmond."

"Untraceable," Cole said. "Someone who knows how to stay off the grid."

"There's more," Potts continued. "I found additional blood evidence in her garage. This was inside, where her car should have been parked."

"Could belong to her or the attacker," I said.

"Still waiting on DNA confirmation, but the spatter pattern suggests someone was injured in her garage. Could be where the attack started before moving into the house."

Martinez was taking notes. "Any security cameras in the area?"

"Checking on that. Most of these older neighborhoods don't have much coverage, but there's an intersection camera about two blocks away that might have caught something."

Cole stretched in his chair, wincing slightly as his ribs protested. "So we've got Mills on the run, but we still don't know if she's running from someone or running because she's guilty."

"All solid possibilities," I said. "But we're missing something. The timeline doesn't quite work."

Potts looked up from her tablet. "How so?"

"Thomas died from cardiac arrest, but his appointment book shows he was supposed to meet someone with the initials JMH for dinner the night he died. But according to the woman at the insurance office we interviewed, she saw Victoria leaving her medical practice next door around five thirty in a hurry. Said she was loading some bags in her trunk and then she took off."

Jack nodded, picking up the thread. "Here's what doesn't add up," he said. "The neighbor at the insurance office said she saw Mills loading bags into her trunk at five thirty, looking scared. But what if Mills never made it out of town? What if someone intercepted her at her house, staged it to look like she'd fled, then used her car for Thomas's murder?"

"That would explain the blood in the garage," Potts said. "Someone attacks her there, forces her into her own vehicle."

"Or into the trunk," I added, feeling sick at the thought.

"But we also know Victoria's vehicle was caught on camera at the gas station that night on two separate occasions. The most damning being around the time Thomas Whitman was murdered and laid out at the cemetery."

"So by those pieces of information," I said. "We can assume Victoria was actually the first one to be attacked."

Jack continued. "But what we don't know is where Thomas was taken from or where he died. All we know is someone took the time to lay him out on Bridget Ashworth's grave and move those heavy stones. We also don't know where Victoria would have been during that time. Was she being held somewhere? Was she already dead? Still in the trunk?"

"That would have been a crowded trunk," Cole said. "Maybe Mercedes should think about that for a new slogan—*Trunks big enough you can fit two bodies.*"

"It sounds like we need to find JMH," Martinez said.

The room fell quiet as we all considered the implications. If our killer was working through a list, we needed to figure out who else might be targeted.

"We should run those initials against everyone we've interviewed," Jack said. "All the family names, current and historical."

"Good idea," I said. "There has to be a connection we're missing."

"I'll start tonight," Martinez said, pulling out his laptop. "DMV records, voter registration, university directories. Someone with those initials had dinner with Thomas, and they might be the last person to see him alive."

"Check the historical society membership too," I suggested. "Thomas was connected to all those circles."

Potts was packing up her equipment with her usual efficiency. "I'll have the DNA results on that garage blood evidence by tomorrow morning. Should help us figure out what happened there."

Jack's phone rang, cutting through the quiet of the evening. The caller ID showed dispatch, and the room went silent.

"Lawson," he answered. His face went stone cold as he listened. "Female? What's the condition?" A pause. "God. Yes, secure the scene. We're on our way."

He hung up and looked around the room. "Body

dumped at Rappahannock River boat launch. Female victim, signs of violence."

"Mills?" I asked, though my gut already knew this case was about to get worse.

"They can't make a visual ID. The face is..." He paused, choosing his words carefully. "Damaged."

We all started gathering our things. Lily looked up from her textbooks. "I'll stay here with Sheldon," she said. "Someone should keep an eye on him."

"Good thinking," I said, looking over at Sheldon. He'd fallen asleep on the couch sometime during our briefing. "Don't let him leave. And just in case, don't answer the door for anyone. We'll lock the front gate and be back as soon as we can."

CHAPTER FOURTEEN

THE DRIVE TO RAPPAHANNOCK RIVER STATE PARK FELT endless despite being only twenty minutes from our house. The darkness beyond the Tahoe's headlights seemed to press against the windows like something alive, and the humid night air carried the promise of more rain. I found myself gripping the door handle as Jack navigated the winding park roads, my mind racing through possibilities I didn't want to consider.

"Daniels is already on scene," Jack said, checking his phone at a red light. "Full CSI team deployed. Whatever we're walking into, it's not going to be pretty."

The boat launch area was lit up like a movie set when we arrived, portable floodlights casting harsh white pools of illumination across the graveled parking area and wooden dock that stretched into the Rappahannock. The familiar controlled chaos of a major crime scene was already in full swing—yellow tape stretched between orange cones, CSI techs moving with practiced efficiency, the low murmur of professional voices cutting through the night sounds of water lapping against the shore.

Lieutenant Daniels stood near the body like a conductor orchestrating a symphony of evidence collection. The recent blond additions to her braids caught the portable lights, and despite the late hour and grim circumstances, she radiated the kind of calm competence that made everyone around her work better. Daniels was the best CSI supervisor in the state, a stickler for details who somehow managed to combine absolute professionalism with genuine compassion for victims.

"Sheriff," she said, turning as we approached. Her beautiful tawny eyes were serious but warm, and I felt that familiar comfort that came from working with someone you trusted completely. "Doc. Got a messy one here."

"Run it down for me," Jack said, pulling on latex gloves. I followed suit.

"Female victim, appears to be in her forties. Found by a jogger around seven thirty this evening." Daniels consulted her tablet with the methodical precision that made her team the best in the business. "Jogger is Robert Peterson, local resident, regular evening runner. He's clean—no connection to the victim that we can find."

Cole and Martinez had arrived right behind us, pulling up in Martinez's sedan. Cole immediately headed toward the jogger who was waiting near a park bench, while Martinez approached the CSI tech who was setting up to photograph tire impressions in the muddy area near the boat launch. Even in the harsh artificial light, I could see the grim set of their faces, the way they moved with the careful deliberation that came when a case turned personal.

"Anything unusual about positioning?" I asked. In reality, I was hoping there would be some similarities to the first body to help us narrow down the identity on the victim.

"Nothing that stands out," Daniels said, leading us toward where the body lay under the portable lights, her steps careful not to disturb any potential evidence. "Someone dumped her in a hurry."

The smell hit me first—the metallic tang of blood mixed with the organic decay that came from being near the river, plus something else I couldn't immediately identify. The woman lay crumpled near the water's edge, her body showing the unmistakable signs of having been discarded rather than carefully positioned. Her face was so badly beaten that identification would be difficult, but I could see she wore medical scrubs.

"Could be our missing doctor," I said, studying the scrubs.

The light blue fabric was stained dark in several places, and I could see immediately that she'd fought for her life. Her hands bore defensive wounds, knuckles scraped raw, fingernails broken and bloody. Someone had beaten her badly before putting a bullet in her chest.

"Between the medical scrubs and the timeline, this has to be Victoria Mills," I said, studying the body more closely. "We'll need dental records or DNA for official confirmation, but everything points to our missing doctor." I knelt carefully beside the body. "She suffered."

The woman's face was a mass of bruises and swelling, her features distorted beyond easy recognition. Dark hair matted with blood stuck to her scalp in clumps, and defensive wounds covered her hands and forearms—evidence of a desperate fight for life. The scrubs she wore were torn and stained dark with blood that had dried to a rusty brown.

I began my preliminary examination with the methodical precision that years of training had ingrained in me. Starting with external observation, I noted the positioning of the limbs, the condition of her clothing, any obvious trauma. My hands moved carefully over her body, checking for injuries while being mindful not to disturb potential evidence.

"Single gunshot wound to the chest," I said, studying the entry point. "Close range based on the powder burns and stippling around the wound. Looks like a small caliber, probably a .22."

The bullet had entered just left of center mass, and the lack of an obvious exit wound suggested it was still lodged inside her chest cavity. I'd know more once I got her back to the lab.

But as I continued my examination, something else caught my attention that made my blood run cold.

"Look at this," I said, carefully moving aside the torn fabric of her scrubs to reveal markings carved into the skin just below her collarbone.

The symbol was crude but unmistakable—scales of justice, roughly the same design we'd seen etched into Rachel Mills's headstone at the cemetery. The cuts were precise and deliberate, made with something sharp like a knife or scalpel.

"Postmortem," I said, studying the edges of the wounds that showed no bleeding or inflammatory response. "Someone took time to send a message after she was already dead."

"Same symbol from the cemetery," Jack said grimly. "Someone's completing their historical revenge list."

"But this is an escalation," I said. "The cemetery

markings were on stone. This is carved into flesh. The killer's getting more personal, more violent."

"Or more desperate to send their message," Jack said.

I photographed the symbol from multiple angles before continuing my examination. The defensive wounds on her hands and arms told the story of someone who'd fought back with everything she had. Broken fingernails, scraped knuckles, bruising on her forearms where she'd tried to block blows—this woman hadn't gone quietly.

"She fought hard," I said, carefully examining her hands for trace evidence. "There's material under her fingernails—looks like fabric fibers, possibly skin cells. She got a piece of her attacker."

Using small evidence bags, I carefully collected samples from under each fingernail, documenting everything with photographs and detailed notes.

"Left shoe missing," I noted, looking around the immediate area. "And her right shoe has a torn sole."

"Found the missing shoe down by the water," Potts said, appearing beside us with an evidence bag. Even under Daniels's watchful supervision, she maintained her usual professional competence.

Cole approached from where he'd been interviewing the jogger, his expression grim but determined. "Peterson's clean. Regular evening runner, lives about two miles from here. Says he saw a dark sedan leaving the area when he pulled into the park entrance. Around six o'clock. He said the car stood out because there isn't much traffic at this time in the evening, but also because the driver almost hit the gate leaving the park. Said he was driving kind of erratically."

"He's sure the driver was male?" I asked.

"No," Cole said. "He couldn't confirm that. He said he just seemed male because of the way he drove."

"That's helpful," Daniels said.

"That's the timeline we'll work with," Jack said. "Victim was killed elsewhere and dumped here around six. Body was discovered ninety minutes later."

"Wait," Martinez said, frowning. "If Mills was dumped here at six, who was driving her car at Sheldon's house just a few hours ago?"

"Our killer," Jack said grimly. "They've been using her vehicle to move around undetected. Bold move, considering we have a BOLO out on it."

"Or desperate," I added. "The killer's timeline is accelerating."

Jack pulled out his phone, checking for updates. "Still no hits on the BOLO for Mills's Mercedes. How does a car that distinctive just vanish?"

"It doesn't," I said. "That car has been all over King George the last two days—the cemetery, Sheldon's house. Someone's using it, but they're being smart about where they park it."

"I'd like to know the answer to that as well," Jack said.

"Car might still be AWOL," Martinez said, joining our group. "But we found her cell phone." He held up an evidence bag containing what looked like the shattered remains of a smartphone. "Someone really didn't want us seeing her call history."

"I want every available unit looking for that Mercedes," Jack said, pulling out his phone. "Roadblocks, checkpoints, BOLO alerts to surrounding counties. I want it found."

Daniels took the bag, examining the damaged phone under the portable lights with the kind of thoroughness that made her legendary. "Might be able to recover data even with this level of damage. Maybe Lieutenant Derby could take a look."

"The contrast between the murders is striking," I said. "Thomas Whitman's death was almost clinical—cardiac arrest, careful staging. But this? This is rage. Personal."

"The killer's deteriorating," Jack said. "Or Mills fought back and forced them to get messy."

"Either way, they're not as in control as they were three days ago," I said.

The night air carried the sound of Martinez's voice

as he coordinated with the park maintenance worker who'd seen the dark sedan. Everything felt surreal under the harsh portable lights—the way shadows danced between the trees, the constant hum of generators powering the crime-scene equipment, the methodical click of cameras documenting every detail.

Cole made the call to Derby while we continued processing the scene. Twenty minutes later, his unmarked sedan pulled into the parking area, and I watched the tall, thin man unfold himself from behind the wheel.

His blond hair was already staging its usual rebellion against whatever product he'd used to try to tame it this morning, and he pushed his glasses up his pointed nose as he surveyed the crime scene with sharp intelligence.

"Got something," Derby called out from where he'd set up his laptop and specialized recovery equipment near Daniels's vehicle. "Memory card is intact. I can see recent call activity."

We gathered around his setup, watching as he navigated through recovered data with the kind of technical expertise that made him invaluable to investigations like this.

"Last outgoing call was yesterday at 5:47 p.m.," he said, scrolling through the call log. "Number's listed in her contacts under the initials JMH."

"JMH?" I asked, perking up at the mention of those familiar initials

"That's our connection," Jack said, his voice carrying the satisfaction of a puzzle piece finally clicking into place. "JMH. is the link between both murders."

"Can you get me a name for that number?" Daniels asked.

Derby typed rapidly, running the number through various databases. "It's a landline registered to Judith Marie Hughes. Address is 1247 River Road."

"Hughes," I said. "That's one of the families whose ancestors testified against Bridget Ashworth."

"Now we need to figure out if she's the killer or the next victim," Jack said. "Let's head over to River Road and see what we find."

"I'll get EMTs to transport the body," I said.

Since the jogger had called 911 it was automatic that the ambulance arrived on the scene, which was nice considering I was shorthanded with Lily and Sheldon both being out. It would be a while until the scene was cleared so I'd have time to go with Jack to River Road.

Somewhere in this river, Colonial ships had once carried tobacco to market, their holds filled with the wealth that had built the great plantation houses of King George County. Now those same waters reflected the lights of a modern crime scene, witness to murders that spanned three centuries.

The drive back through the Virginia countryside felt different this time—less ominous, more determined. We had a name, an address, a concrete lead to follow. But as we passed the darkened fields and sleeping farmhouses that dotted the landscape, I couldn't shake the feeling that we were racing against time.

Somewhere in King George County, Judith Marie Hughes was either in mortal danger or planning her next murder. And somewhere in the shadows of history and revenge, a killer was waiting to complete their three-hundred-year-old mission of blood and justice.

CHAPTER FIFTEEN

THE DRIVE TO RIVER ROAD STRETCHED BEFORE US LIKE a descent into something darker than mere night. Our headlights carved narrow tunnels through the Virginia darkness, illuminating ancient oaks that twisted overhead like arthritic fingers reaching across the asphalt. Spanish moss hung from their branches in ghostly curtains, swaying in the humid breeze with an almost hypnotic rhythm that made my skin crawl.

"Do we know anything about Judith Hughes?" Cole asked over the radio from Martinez's car, his voice cutting through the oppressive silence that had settled over us since leaving the crime scene. "What are we walking into?"

"Her name came up initially when we did the cursory background checks on ancestors we were able to trace from the names of the marked graves," I said, scrolling through my phone. "I'm pulling up the file now. We'd placed her down on the list because her current address is listed outside of King George. She's a grad student at Georgetown. Twenty-four years old. Both parents deceased when she was nineteen. Her father to cancer and then her mother six months later when she and a couple of friends were robbed at gunpoint outside of Ford's Theater. Took a bullet to the chest when she tried to push the attacker away."

"Losing both parents in a short amount of time could make a person a sociopath and go on a killing spree," Martinez said, his voice thin through the receiver.

I opened Jack's portable laptop that was attached to the dash in his Tahoe, an idea forming. It took less than two minutes to find what I was looking for.

"Judith Hughes purchased a Walther P22 from a shop in Richmond in December of last year."

"That's why I never believe in coincidences," Cole said. "I guess we need to ask her if she's recently shot anyone with it."

The deeper we drove into the plantation district, the more the landscape seemed to change around us. Modern subdivisions and strip malls gave way to vast stretches of farmland punctuated by the skeletal remains of old tobacco barns. Massive houses set far back from the road loomed in the darkness like sleeping giants, their windows dark and unwelcoming.

"There," I said, pointing to a rusted mailbox that leaned at a drunken angle beside a crumbling stone pillar. "1247."

The driveway was little more than a dirt track that wound through an avenue of live oaks so old they might have witnessed the original land grants being signed. Their branches formed a canopy so thick that even our headlights seemed to dim, and I found myself holding my breath as we navigated the narrow path.

Then the house appeared, and my heart sank.

The Hughes mansion had once been magnificent —a perfect example of antebellum architecture with its soaring columns and wraparound veranda. But neglect had taken its toll. Paint peeled from the shutters in long strips, several porch boards had rotted through completely, and ivy covered half the structure in a green shroud that made it look more like a mausoleum than a home.

"Looks like she didn't keep things up after her parents died," Jack said. "It'd be hard for a kid to even know where to start with a place like this."

"You'd think she'd have sold it," I said.

"Family legacy is a weird thing sometimes," Jack said. "The blood of her ancestors is soaked into the dirt of those fields. And the stories those walls could tell might be the only thing she has left of her family to hold on to."

Jack parked behind an old pickup truck that sat in the circular drive like a monument to better times. No lights showed in any of the windows, and the only sound was the wind moaning through the broken shutters and the rhythmic creak of a loose board somewhere on the porch.

Cole and Martinez parked on the other side of the circular drive so we could all get out easy in case of an emergency.

"Maybe you should stay in the car," Jack said, his hand on his holster. "She could be dangerous."

"You go, I go," I said, reaching in my bag for my Beretta and sticking it in the small of my back.

The truth was I was always armed. There'd been a time when I'd stared into the eyes of my killer and had nothing to fight back with but weakness. I thought I'd breathed my last breath, and don't remember anything until I'd woken up in the hospital attached to machines. That was over two years ago, when Jeremy Mooney had nearly strangled me to death.

I'd been driven to arm myself first out of fear, but then I'd seen it as a necessity for the kind of work I'd been called to. I wouldn't be a weak link for Jack or any of the team. If I went with them on a call they deserved to have someone to watch their backs. Not someone who needed saving. So I'd trained and worked until the fear was gone and I wasn't a liability to anyone.

Jack looked at me and nodded. I knew he was thinking of the baby. I was too. But the baby needed a father and I trusted Jack with both of our lives.

"Guess we don't need a warrant," Cole said, pointing to the open front door and drawing his weapon.

We approached the house, our footsteps echoing off the warped porch boards. The smell hit me as we reached the entrance—something stale and wrong, like flowers left too long in stagnant water.

"Ms. Hughes?" Jack called out, his voice swallowed by the darkness inside. "King George County Sheriff's Department. We need to speak with you."

Silence answered us. Even the wind and land hushed.

"We'll circle around back," Cole said, and he and Martinez split off in different directions.

Jack pushed the front door open a little wider and the hinges creaked. My flashlight beam revealed a scene of elegant decay—crystal chandeliers thick with dust, furniture covered in white sheets like ghosts waiting for resurrection, and family portraits hanging at odd angles as if the house itself was slowly sliding sideways.

But it was the living room that told the real story. Overturned chairs, scattered papers, and dark stains on the Oriental rug that might have been wine or might have been something much worse.

"Someone was here," Jack said, noting the coffee cup still sitting on a side table, its contents long cold but the ring still visible on the wood beneath it. It was untouched by dust or time.

I picked my way carefully through the debris, my flashlight beam playing across family photographs that had been scattered across the floor. In several of them, faces had been scratched out with something sharp, leaving only gouged holes where eyes and mouths should have been.

"Jack," I whispered, crouching down near the fireplace. "Look at this."

My light had caught something that made my pulse quicken—tiny droplets of what looked suspiciously like blood, barely visible against the dark wood of the floor. They formed an irregular pattern leading from the overturned furniture toward the back of the house.

"Blood trail," Jack confirmed, kneeling beside me. "Not completely dry. Could be from this afternoon or evening."

We followed the scattered drops through the formal dining room, past the kitchen, and out through a back door that stood wide open to the night. The trail continued across an overgrown garden where weeds grew waist-high and the remains of what had once been elegant landscaping now resembled something from a fairy tale gone wrong.

Our flashlight beams converged on a massive structure that loomed against the star-filled sky—a barn that belonged to the plantation's working past, easily twice the size of most modern houses. Its weathered siding had turned silver-gray with age, and one of its doors hung partially open.

Cole and Martinez came met us where we stood and I shined the flashlight on the drops of blood leading toward the barn.

"Should we call for backup?" Martinez asked, his hand resting on his weapon.

"Let's see what we're dealing with first," Jack said. "But stay sharp. Someone was hurt here, and whoever did it might still be around.

"Wasn't it Hansel and Gretel that followed the trail of candy?" Cole asked. "Why am I feeling that right now?"

"I don't know," Martinez said. "But I think they get shoved in an oven once they reach the end of the trail, so maybe think of a different fairy tale."

"No time like the present," Jack said, taking the lead.

As soon as we started walking it's like the earth

could breathe again and inhaled deeply. The barn seemed to pulse as we approached, its metal roof expanding and contracting with temperature changes that created an irregular rhythm of pops and groans. Wind whistled through gaps in the siding, creating a sound like distant voices whispering secrets we weren't meant to hear.

Cole and Martinez used their own flashlights, adding to the harsh pool of illumination that only seemed to make the shadows deeper and more threatening.

The barn doors opened with high-pitched squeals that set my nerves on edge and made the flesh on my arms pebble. They revealed an interior that was a maze of agricultural equipment from decades past. Hay bales stacked to the rafters created narrow corridors between towering walls of moldering straw, and ancient farm machinery cast twisted shadows that seemed to move independently of our flashlight beams.

The smell inside was overwhelming—decades of hay and manure, mixed with something fresher and more disturbing. The metallic tang of blood, and underneath it all, the sour scent of human fear.

"Spread out," Jack ordered in a whisper. "Watch your corners."

I followed the blood trail deeper into the barn, my light playing across the rough-hewn beams overhead. The drops were becoming more frequent now, forming an almost continuous line that led toward the back of the structure where a series of horse stalls had been built against the far wall.

My heart was hammering so hard I was sure everyone could hear it. Every shadow seemed to hide a threat, every sound—the settling of old wood, the scurrying of mice, the distant hoot of an owl. But I couldn't ignore the evidence. Someone had been hurt, and that someone had come here looking for safety.

The stall doors were all standing open except for one near the back corner. I motioned for Jack and he stepped in front of me, his flashlight and his weapon following the blood into a stall, where fresh straw had been scattered over what must have been decades of accumulated debris.

Jack pushed open the stall door, our flashlight beams sweeping across the interior, and that's when I heard it—the faintest sound of labored breathing coming from behind a pile of feed sacks stacked against the back wall.

"Jack," I whispered, nodding to the hiding spot.

We approached carefully and shined our lights behind the feed bags. A woman looked back at us, and my lungs froze with fear and my heart stuttered.

Behind the feed sacks, a young woman was huddled against the wall, her knees drawn up to her chest. Blood seeped through a makeshift bandage on her left arm, and her face was pale with shock. When our lights hit her, she flinched back, raising her good arm to shield her eyes.

"Please," she whispered, her voice cracking. "Don't let them find me."

"Judith Hughes?" Jack asked, lowering his weapon but keeping it ready.

She nodded, tears cutting tracks through the dirt on her face. "They tried to kill me," she said. "Just like the others. But I got away."

CHAPTER SIXTEEN

THE TRANSITION FROM THE CHAOS AT THE HUGHES plantation to the sterile quiet of my lab felt like stepping between worlds.

Jack had dropped me at the funeral home to meet the ambulance while he accompanied Judith Hughes to the hospital. The woman we'd found cowering in that barn had been beyond hysterical, her terror so profound it seemed to emanate from her very bones. But it was her words that haunted me as I descended into the secure basement, echoing in the antiseptic silence like an ancient curse refusing to be silenced.

Bridget Ashworth...she's still here...the curse isn't finished...

The memory of Judith's voice made me shiver despite the lab's controlled temperature. Blood had streaked her face in ritual-like patterns, and her eyes had held the glassy stare of someone who'd seen beyond the veil of normal reality. When she'd grabbed my wrist with fingers slick from her own wounds, her grip had been surprisingly strong.

She told me...Bridget told me...they're all going to die.

I shook off the recollection and pulled on fresh gloves. Whatever game someone was playing with historical symbols and terrified witnesses, our Jane Doe deserved the dignity of a thorough scientific examination. The dead spoke to me through evidence, not manufactured hysteria.

The security monitors mounted along the upper walls flickered between exterior camera feeds, showing empty parking areas and the tree line that bordered the funeral home. Wind bent the ancient oaks into tortured shapes, their branches scraping against the building's brick façade with sounds like fingernails on slate. A storm was building—I could feel the pressure change even in this sealed environment.

Our victim lay beneath the harsh examination lights, her injuries stark against pale skin. Someone had beaten her savagely before ending her life with a single bullet. Without an identity, I couldn't make assumptions about connections to our other cases, though the brutality suggested this wasn't random violence.

I began with photographs, documenting every angle and detail before moving to fingerprint collection. The digital scanner would give us answers—a name to match the battered face, a connection that might tie this murder to Thomas Whitman's case or prove it was something else entirely.

Focus, I told myself. *Science, not superstition.*

The external examination revealed the full extent of the violence. Defensive wounds painted a clear picture of her final moments—torn fingernails, bruised knuckles, deep scratches along her forearms. She'd fought like a wildcat against her attacker. Under my magnifying lens, I found fabric fibers embedded in her abraded knuckles, dark threads that might help identify her killer's clothing.

But it was the carved symbol below her collarbone that made me pause. Unlike the crude markings on the cemetery headstones, this had been created with surgical precision. The scales of justice were perfectly proportioned, each line deliberate and measured. Whoever had done this possessed both artistic skill and intimate knowledge of anatomy.

I photographed the symbol from multiple angles, noting how the cuts had been made postmortem with something extremely sharp—a scalpel, perhaps, or a razor blade. There was something ritualistic about the placement and execution that made my skin crawl.

The external examination took forty minutes, each injury catalogued and photographed. When I finally made the Y-incision, my hands were steady despite the growing unease that seemed to emanate from the very walls around me.

The bullet had done exactly what small-caliber rounds were designed to do—penetrate deeply without leaving an exit wound. It had tumbled through her chest cavity, shredding her heart and major vessels before lodging against her spine. Death would have been quick, a mercy after the prolonged beating she'd endured.

I extracted the bullet with careful precision, dropping it into an evidence container with a metallic *ping* that seemed unnaturally loud. .22 caliber, just as I'd suspected. The lab's ballistics database would compare it to any weapon recovered, though finding the gun was Cole and Martinez's job.

They're all going to die.

The memory of Judith's voice made me glance at the security monitors again. The exterior cameras showed nothing but wind-tossed vegetation and empty parking areas, but something felt wrong. A shadow that didn't quite match the swaying trees, a movement too purposeful to be natural.

I returned to my work, taking tissue samples for

toxicology analysis. Our victim's blood would reveal whether she'd been drugged before the attack, and her stomach contents might provide clues about her final hours. The routine of scientific methodology grounded me, pushing back against the supernatural dread that seemed to seep from the building's bones.

The digital fingerprint scanner would confirm our victim's identity once the analysis completed. Her prints would be cross-referenced against medical license databases, driver's records, and criminal files until we had a name to go with the brutalized face on my examination table.

As I worked, the storm intensified. Rain began hammering the building in sheets, and the security cameras showed water streaming down their lenses like tears. One exterior feed flickered between clear and static, creating a strobe effect that made shadows dance across the monitors.

That's when I saw it.

A black cat sat motionless in the main camera's field of view, positioned directly under a security light. It stared straight at the lens with luminous eyes that seemed to glow against its dark fur. The animal was perfectly still despite the driving rain, as if it were immune to the storm's fury.

I watched the monitor for several minutes, waiting for the cat to move. It remained frozen in place like a statue, never blinking, never shifting position. When lightning illuminated the scene, its eyes reflected the flash with an otherworldly brilliance.

Don't be ridiculous, I told myself. *It's just a cat.*

But Judith's words echoed in my memory: *She's still here.*

I forced my attention back to our victim's body, completing the internal examination with methodical thoroughness. Her organs showed no signs of disease or toxicity, confirming that violence alone had ended her life. Someone had beaten her, shot her, and then taken time to carve a message into her flesh. The progression suggested ritual rather than simple murder.

The lab's climate control system cycled on with a mechanical sigh, and the sudden rush of air made the victim's hair flutter slightly. For one heart-stopping moment, it looked like she was trying to lift her head.

I jerked backward, my pulse spiking with primitive fear. *She's dead*, I reminded myself. *It's just air circulation.*

But my hands shook as I began suturing the incision closed. The familiar task should have been calming, yet every stitch felt like binding more than just flesh. The silence pressed against me, broken only by the storm's assault on the building and the steady hum of machinery.

When I glanced at the security monitors again, the black cat was gone.

I checked every camera feed, scanning the empty parking areas and tree lines for any sign of movement. Nothing. The animal had vanished as suddenly as it had appeared, leaving only wind-driven rain and dancing shadows.

The rational part of my mind insisted it had simply run for shelter when the storm worsened. Cats were smart that way—they didn't sit in downpours for hours just to unnerve forensic pathologists. But the primitive part of my brain, the part that remembered humanity's superstitious past, whispered different explanations.

I finished the autopsy after one in the morning, sealing the last evidence bag and updating my digital notes. Our Jane Doe had died violently, likely incapacitated by blunt force trauma to the head before being transported elsewhere. The defensive wounds told the story of someone who'd regained consciousness and fought back with everything she had—probably when her attacker opened a trunk or moved her to the final location. The skin cells and blood under her fingernails meant she'd wounded whoever killed her.

A single gunshot to the heart had ended her life, followed by the deliberate carving of a symbol into her flesh. Her killer was strong enough to overpower a fighting woman and organized enough to transport and dump her body where it would be discovered. But beyond those facts, the physical evidence couldn't tell me who or why.

Just as I was preparing to transfer the body to cold storage, the fingerprint scanner chimed with results. The match confirmed what we'd suspected.

Dr. Victoria Mills, age forty-seven. Licensed physician. King George County resident.

The missing doctor whose car had been spotted at the cemetery. The woman whose house had been ransacked. The descendant of Rachel Mills, whose grave had been marked with the stone circle.

I was gathering my things when the security system made a sound I'd never heard before—a low electronic whine that seemed to emanate from the steel door's locking mechanism. The LED panel flickered between green and red, as if the system couldn't decide whether the lab was secure or compromised.

On the monitors, I watched shadows move across the empty parking lot in patterns that didn't quite match the swaying trees. The motion was too fluid, too purposeful. Someone could be out there, circling the building with predatory patience.

The lock mechanism whined again, and this time the sound was accompanied by a soft *click* that made my pulse spike. In the sudden silence that followed, I could hear my own heartbeat hammering against my ribs.

I stared at the monitors, searching for whatever had triggered the security system. The cameras showed nothing but storm and darkness, yet something had approached the building. Something that didn't register clearly on visual surveillance but had somehow interfaced with our security network.

That's when I realized the steel door was opening.

A shadow filled the threshold—the silhouette of a man, tall and broad shouldered, backlit by the hallway lights above. Every instinct screamed at me to run, but there was nowhere to go. The lab that had always been my sanctuary had become a trap, and someone had just walked into it with me.

CHAPTER SEVENTEEN

"Jaye."

The sound of my name, spoken in that familiar baritone, dissolved the terror that had wrapped around me like ice. Jack materialized from the shadows beyond the doorway, and the sight of him—rumpled shirt, hair mussed from the rain, those steady blue eyes focused entirely on me—made something tight in my chest finally release.

"Thank God." My voice came out breathless, shaky. "You scared the daylights out of me."

"Sorry." He hurried down the stairs and crossed to me in three quick strides, kissing me on the top of the head. "The storm knocked out the main power grid for about thirty seconds. When it came back online, the security system had to run through its full reboot cycle before I could access the lower level."

The relief was so profound it left me dizzy. Of course. The electronic whining, those flashing lights—it had all been circuits and programming, not some otherworldly presence. My rational mind reasserted itself, embarrassed by how completely I'd let fear take control.

"I blame the pregnancy hormones," I said. "How's Judith?"

Jack's expression darkened. "She's heavily sedated now, but when she was lucid enough to talk, I managed to piece together fragments of what happened." He rubbed his face with both hands, the gesture of a man who'd heard too much human horror for one night. "Most of it was rambling, but certain words kept coming up—Bridget Ashworth, ancestors, land, trust."

"Someone came to her house?"

"That's what I gathered. She kept saying they knew things—her family history." Jack's voice dropped. "Then she said something about blood ties and revenge.

"From what I can piece together she managed to run into the woods behind the house, and lose the attacker there. When night came she moved to the barn and that's when we found her."

"My God." The pieces were starting to form a picture I didn't like. "So our killer isn't just targeting these family members randomly."

"She kept getting more hysterical the more she talked. Most of what she said doesn't make much sense—trauma and sedatives will do that. But she kept telling me they watch everything and they're always there but never seen."

"Who?" I asked.

"That's the million-dollar question," he said. "Could mean everything or nothing at all."

"Paranoia is common with that level of trauma," I said, though something cold traced down my spine.

"Maybe. But here's the thing that really bothers me—buried in all the rambling about bloodlines and justice, she mentioned details about our investigation that haven't been released to the public."

"What kind of details?"

"The symbols on the graves. The stones and positioning." Jack's expression was troubled. "Either she's involved somehow, or someone with access to our case files has been feeding her information."

The lab suddenly felt smaller, more confining. "We already know we have a leak. Judge Morton proved that."

Jack grunted in agreement. "I've got a deputy posted outside her room, but honestly? I'm not sure if he's there to protect her or to watch her. We can't rule out that she's involved somehow. Maybe she's just a really good actress."

"If she is she deserves an award," I said,

remember the pale, bloody face that had looked at me out of vacant eyes. I shuddered and shook it off, remembering the newest occupant of my refrigeration unit.

"I'm finished up here," I said. "I've got the ID confirmation on our victim from the fingerprint scanner. Victoria Mills."

"That's what I was afraid of. Before now those graves that had been marked were theory. Now it's as good as a murder list."

The drive home was quiet, both of us lost in our own thoughts as the Tahoe's headlights carved through the pre-dawn darkness. By the time we reached our house, exhaustion had settled into my bones like lead. Jack's arm around my waist as we climbed the stairs was the only thing keeping me upright.

"Few hours of sleep," he murmured against my hair as we collapsed into bed still wearing yesterday's clothes. "Then we tackle this fresh."

I was asleep before my head hit the pillow.

***

The smell of coffee drifted up from the kitchen, followed by something richer and more complex that made my stomach do a little flip. Not the good kind. I'd been dreaming of carved symbols and terrified eyes, but it was the scent of bacon hitting the air that dragged me fully awake.

"Oh no," I whispered, pressing a hand to my mouth as saliva flooded in that telltale way that meant trouble.

I barely made it to the bathroom before my stomach rebelled against whatever optimism I'd been feeling about this pregnancy getting easier. Jack's footsteps on the stairs told me he'd heard, and by the time the worst had passed, he was sitting on the bathroom floor beside me with a damp washcloth.

"So much for progress," I said weakly, accepting the cloth gratefully. "Every morning I think to myself that it'll be the last time. But then the next morning comes."

I leaned into him, letting his warmth anchor me while my stomach decided whether it was finished being dramatic. "I think it was the bacon."

"Hmm," he said. "You want oatmeal instead?"

"God, no," I said with a shudder. "Throwing up is bad enough. Why would you do that to me?

"You're right. Silly question. What about toast?"

The thought of any food sounded like a terrible idea, but I nodded because I knew he was just trying to help.

"Give me a minute to brush my teeth and I'll be down."

"Take your time. I'll turn off the bacon."

Twenty minutes later, I made it to the kitchen in fresh clothes and with a stomach that had settled into uneasy peace. Jack had indeed turned off the bacon, opened windows to air out the smell, and was sitting at our kitchen island with coffee and what looked like plain toast waiting for me.

"Better?" he asked, standing to pour hot water over a tea bag. Chamomile, I realized, not my usual morning blend. I hated chamomile, but to say so would be childish.

"Getting there." I accepted the mug, wrapping my hands around its warmth. The kitchen felt like a sanctuary—our sanctuary—with morning light streaming through the windows and the familiar sounds of our life together. The coffee maker's gentle burble, the house settling around us, the way Jack moved through the space with the unconscious grace of someone completely at home.

"If I drink all of these flowers can I have coffee?" I asked.

Jack's mouth twitched in a half smile. "I wondered how long you'd last before you mentioned the chamomile."

"I thought it was a long time considering," I said, taking a large gulp and burning my tongue. "I keep thinking about what Judith said. About bloodlines and justice. What if there's more to this than we're seeing?"

Jack's hand found mine across the counter, his thumb tracing circles over my knuckles in that absent way that meant he was thinking. "What if there isn't? What if someone's just using all this historical drama as cover for something more straightforward?"

"Like what?"

"Money. Revenge. Jealousy." He lifted his coffee mug, pausing before taking a sip. "Patricia Whitman's got motive, means, and opportunity. Her husband was cheating. And she's in good shape from being on digs. She's got the physical strength to move those stones, and she certainly knows enough about archaeology to stage that cemetery scene."

I nibbled at the toast, testing my stomach's tolerance. So far, so good. "But does she seem like someone who could plan something that elaborate? She was so controlled, so professional when we talked to her. Almost too composed for someone who'd just lost her husband."

"People can surprise you. Especially when they're pushed past their breaking point."

The quiet stretched between us, comfortable in the way that only came from years of sharing mornings like this. Even with everything happening around us—the murders, the investigation, the weight of secrets that reached back three centuries—this felt normal. Real. Like the rest of the world could wait a few more minutes.

"Jack," I said finally, "what if this baby changes everything? What if I can't do this job anymore once—"

"Stop." His hand tightened on mine. "Don't borrow trouble from tomorrow. We'll figure it out as we go. And yes, the baby will change everything. That's a good thing."

"But what if—"

"What if we have a healthy baby and you discover you're even better at your job because you're fighting for something bigger than just justice?" His eyes found mine, steady and sure. "What if everything works out exactly like it's supposed to?"

I wanted to argue, to list all the ways this could go wrong, but the look on his face stopped me. This man had loved me through transformations I'd never thought possible. He'd seen me broken and helped me rebuild. If he thought we could handle whatever came next, maybe I needed to trust that.

"What's the plan for today?" I asked instead, letting him redirect us back to solid ground.

"Patricia Whitman. Let's pay her a visit." Jack's voice carried the focused intensity that meant he was already three steps ahead. "I want to see her reaction when we bring up Thomas's affair with Margaret."

"You think confronting her about it will break her composure?"

"Margaret said Patricia knew, but knowing and having it thrown in your face during a murder investigation are two different things." Jack set down his coffee mug with deliberate precision. "I want to see how she reacts when we make it clear that her husband's affair is part of our investigation. People reveal themselves when they feel cornered."

Jack called Patricia from the truck while I finished my toast. When he reached her, she told him she was already out at a dig site and would be there most of the day if we needed to speak with her. Something in her voice—too eager to accommodate, too quick with the invitation—made Jack's eyes narrow as he hung up.

"She wants us to come to her," he said. "Could be she feels more comfortable on her own turf. Or could be she's got something to hide and wants the distraction of work around her."

An hour later, we were driving through King George County as it shook off the effects of the previous night's storm. The countryside looked freshly scrubbed, all bright greens and clean edges under a sky that couldn't decide whether to stay clear or threaten more rain. Puddles reflected the moving clouds, and the air that came through the vents smelled of earth and growing things.

"Storm seems fitting for this case," I observed, watching gray clouds gather on the horizon. "All this ugliness from the past finally breaking open."

Jack's hands tightened on the steering wheel. "Let's just hope we can weather it."

The GPS led us off the main road onto a series of increasingly narrow lanes that wound through farmland and forest. We passed a hand-painted sign that read *Ashworth Archaeological Survey—Historical Preservation in Progress* with an arrow pointing down a gravel track that disappeared into a stand of ancient oaks.

"Well, that's ironic," Jack said grimly.

The track ended in a clearing that had been transformed into an active dig site. Canvas tarps stretched between metal poles created shelter over several excavated areas, and folding tables held an array of tools, measuring devices, and artifact containers. A white pickup truck and a Jeep were parked near a trailer that looked like it served as a field office.

But it was the site itself that made my breath catch.

We were standing in what had once been a small settlement—the kind of place where Colonial families had carved out lives from the Virginia wilderness three centuries ago. Foundation stones marked the outlines of buildings, and carefully excavated fire pits showed where hearths had warmed long-dead families. The entire area was gridded with string and stakes, each section meticulously mapped and documented.

It should have felt peaceful, this glimpse into the past. Instead, something about the place made my skin crawl.

"There," Jack said, pointing toward the far end of the site.

Patricia Whitman was crouched near one of the excavated foundations, using a small pump to remove standing water that had collected despite the tarps stretched overhead. She wore field clothes—waterproof boots, mud-stained khaki pants, and a canvas vest over a long-sleeved shirt. Her hair was pulled back in a practical ponytail, and even from a distance, I could see the methodical efficiency of someone salvaging a dig site after storm damage.

The sound of our footsteps on gravel made her look up. Recognition flickered across her face, followed immediately by wariness.

"Sheriff. Dr. Graves." She climbed to her feet, brushing dirt from her hands. "I wasn't expecting company."

"Mrs. Whitman," Jack said, his tone professionally neutral. "We have some follow-up questions about Thomas's research."

"Of course." She gestured toward the trailer. "Would you prefer to talk inside? I can make coffee."

"Here's fine," Jack said, and I could hear the subtle shift in his voice that meant he wanted her to feel exposed, off-balance.

Patricia's eyes flicked between us, and I caught something that made my investigative instincts perk up—scratches along both her forearms, red and raw against her tanned skin.

"What happened to your arms?" I asked.

"Occupational hazard," she said, following my gaze. "You spend enough time digging in brambles and root systems, you're going to get scratched up." She turned her arms to show us more clearly. "This site's been overgrown for decades. Yesterday I was clearing vegetation from what looks like a well foundation."

The scratches looked fresh—maybe a day old, consistent with her story. But they also looked consistent with someone who'd been in a violent struggle.

"Mrs. Whitman," Jack said, "we need to ask you about Thomas's relationship with Dr. Margaret Randolph."

The change in Patricia's expression was immediate and dramatic. Her face went sheet white, then flushed deep red. Her hands clenched into fists at her sides, and for a moment I thought she might actually swing at one of us.

"That woman," she said, the words coming out like a physical blow. "I should have known she'd be involved in this somehow."

"Involved how?" I asked.

Patricia's expression shifted, but not to rage—more like weary resignation mixed with distaste. "Thomas and Margaret had an on-and-off relationship for years. She was different from his usual... diversions."

"Different how?" Jack asked.

"The others were just physical. Graduate students, conference flings, women who were impressed by his reputation." Patricia's voice was matter of fact, like she was discussing a chronic medical condition she'd learned to manage. "But Margaret was intellectual competition. She challenged his work, pushed back on his theories. Thomas thrived on that kind of conflict."

"That must have been difficult," Jack said carefully.

"It was what it was." Patricia shrugged, though I caught a flicker of old pain in her eyes. "Twenty-three years of marriage teaches you to pick your battles. Thomas was brilliant, charming, and completely incapable of monogamy. I knew that when I married him."

"But Margaret was different," I said.

"Margaret made him think. The others just made him feel good about himself." She straightened, brushing dirt from her hands. "If you're asking whether I killed my husband over his affairs, the answer is no. If I was going to murder him for infidelity, I would have done it years ago."

Jack studied her for a long moment. "In Thomas's appointment book, his last entry was dinner with someone with the initials JMH. Do you know who that might be?"

Patricia's brow furrowed in concentration. "JMH? No, that doesn't ring a bell. Thomas kept his research contacts pretty close to the vest lately. Said he didn't want word getting out before he could present his findings properly."

"Could it have been Judith Hughes?" I asked. "She's a graduate student at Georgetown, descendant of one of the families Thomas was researching."

"Hughes..." Patricia shook her head slowly. "The name's familiar from the historical records, but I don't recall Thomas mentioning anyone current from that family. Certainly not recently."

I watched her carefully as she spoke. Patricia Whitman was a strong woman—I could see it in the way she moved, in the defined muscles of her arms and shoulders. Years of archaeological work had given her the kind of physical capability that most people didn't possess. She could have overpowered Thomas if she'd surprised him, could have moved those stones at the cemetery.

But would she have had the emotional control to stage such an elaborate scene? The cemetery arrangement had required planning, patience, and attention to detail. This woman seemed pragmatic, direct—not someone who dealt in symbolic revenge.

"Mrs. Whitman," I said carefully, "We found DNA evidence under Victoria Mills's fingernails. She fought back against her attacker. We'd like to get a DNA sample from you to rule you out as a suspect."

Patricia's expression didn't change, but I caught the slight stiffening of her shoulders. "You think I killed Victoria Mills?"

"We're eliminating possibilities," Jack said evenly. "Standard procedure."

"I have a medical kit in the truck," I added. "Just a simple cheek swab. Takes thirty seconds."

Patricia looked around the dig site—at the careful excavations, the documented foundations, the painstaking work of uncovering the past. Her whole career was built on finding truth buried in the earth, on giving voice to people who'd been forgotten by history.

Now she was the one being examined, her life sifted through for evidence of guilt.

"Fine," she said quietly. "But I want this on record

—I'm cooperating voluntarily. I have nothing to hide."

As I retrieved my medical kit from Jack's Tahoe, I found myself wondering if we were looking at our killer. Patricia's scratches could be from archaeological work, or they could be from a desperate woman fighting for her life.

The storm clouds on the horizon were moving closer, and I had the uneasy feeling that we hadn't seen the worst of it yet.

CHAPTER EIGHTEEN

THE DRIVE BACK FROM PATRICIA'S DIG SITE FELT different than our arrival. The same Virginia countryside rolled past our windows, but now it seemed to watch us with calculating eyes. Every farmhouse tucked behind ancient oaks, every family cemetery glimpsed through breaks in the tree line, every weathered barn that had stood since Colonial times—all of it felt connected to the web of secrets we were trying to untangle.

"She's hiding something," I said, breaking the silence that had stretched between us since leaving the archaeological site.

Jack's hands shifted on the steering wheel, a subtle tell that meant he was working through possibilities. "Maybe. Or maybe she's just a woman who's learned to compartmentalize in twenty-three years of marriage to a serial cheater."

"The DNA will tell us if she fought with Victoria Mills." I pressed the sealed sample container in my lap, feeling its slight weight like evidence of guilt or innocence waiting to be revealed.

Jack slowed for a curve that wound through a stand of tulip poplars, their leaves creating a green tunnel that filtered the afternoon light into dancing patterns.

"She's definitely got motive," Jack said. "A woman scorned. She's got no alibi, and the scratches on her arms are pretty damning. But I don't know if she fits the profile. This killer thinks in symbols and rituals, plans elaborate scenes that tell stories. Patricia Whitman strikes me as someone who'd use a shovel if she wanted to kill someone, not stage a historical reenactment."

The observation was quintessentially Jack—cutting through emotion to reach the practical heart of human behavior. It was one of the things that made him such an effective sheriff, this ability to see past surface drama to the patterns underneath.

We drove back toward the Towne Square and the sheriff's office, but before Jack could pull into his parking spot Cole was flagging him down. I passed the DNA sample to him.

"From Patricia Whitman," I said. "We need to

expedite that. The lab already has Victoria Mills's sample. It should only take a couple of hours to determine whether Patricia is our killer."

"Got it," Cole said and looked at Jack. "Got a lead on your missing donut girl. Martinez tracked down the registered address for that Lincoln Town Car she drives. Turns out it belongs to someone named Evangeline Toscano, lives out on Marsh Creek Road near the wildlife preserve."

"The mysterious psychic," I said. "How far is that from here?"

"Thirty minutes if you take Route 218 through the bottomland. Fair warning though—it's pretty isolated out there. Cell service is spotty, and there's only one road in and out."

"We'll head there now," Jack said. "Have Martinez run a background check on this Evangeline Toscano. I want to know if she's got any connection to our victims' families."

"Already on it." Cole slapped the hood of the Tahoe and said, "Happy hunting."

Jack nodded and backed out, turning on his lights without sirens as we navigated through the traffic of downtown.

The drive to Marsh Creek Road took us deeper into the kind of Virginia wilderness that most tourists never saw. Here, the carefully manicured horse farms and historic mansions gave way to something older and more primal. Ancient cypress trees rose from brackish water, their knees creating a landscape that looked prehistoric. Spanish moss hung like tattered curtains, and the air that came through the vents carried the rich, organic smell of decomposition and new growth happening simultaneously.

"This place gives me the creeps," I admitted, watching a great blue heron lift off from a hidden creek and disappear into the canopy.

"It's beautiful," Jack said, but I could hear the wariness in his voice. "And isolated. Perfect place to hide if you don't want to be found."

The road narrowed until it was barely wide enough for one vehicle, with thick vegetation pressing in from both sides. Water glimmered between the trees—sometimes a narrow creek, sometimes a pond whose surface reflected the sky like black glass. We passed a few mailboxes attached to crooked posts, but no houses were visible from the road.

"There," Jack said, pointing to a hand-painted sign that read *Toscano* in faded letters. But instead of a driveway, there was only a dirt path that disappeared into the trees.

The road ended at a small clearing where the black Lincoln Town Car sat beside a weathered wooden post with a chain across what looked like an old logging trail. Jack parked behind the Lincoln, and we could see the path continued on foot toward the sound of moving water.

"Guess we walk from here," I said, noting how the trail wound through dense undergrowth toward the river.

The path was well worn but narrow, meandering through stands of ancient cypress and over wooden planks that bridged the wetter areas. Spanish moss draped from every branch like nature's curtains, and the sound of our footsteps was muffled by decades of accumulated leaves. The air grew thicker as we approached the water, heavy with the rich scent of river mud and blooming jasmine.

The cabin that emerged from the green tunnel was exactly what Sheldon had described—a rustic structure that seemed to grow from the landscape itself. Built of weathered cypress logs with a tin roof gone green with age, it sat on stilts above the marshy ground with a screened porch facing the slow-moving river. Wind chimes hung from the porch rafters, and what looked like herb gardens sprawled in seemingly random patterns around the raised foundation.

A small wooden dock extended into the dark water, and I could see where someone had cleared areas for what looked like ritual circles—bare patches of earth surrounded by carefully arranged stones. The whole place had an otherworldly quality, as if it existed in the space between the mundane world and something older, more mysterious.

"Definitely feels like the kind of place where people hold séances," I said.

We approached the cabin carefully, our footsteps muffled by the soft ground. The air was thick with humidity and the competing scents of jasmine, woodsmoke, and something earthy that might have been patchouli. Wind chimes created a gentle symphony, their tones ranging from deep metallic gongs to the crystalline tinkle of glass tubes.

The woman who answered our knock was not what I'd expected.

Evangeline Toscano stood barely five feet tall, with silver-streaked brown hair pulled back in a practical bun and intelligent dark eyes that assessed us with calm interest. She wore a simple cotton dress in deep blue, sensible sandals, and the kind of jewelry that suggested careful selection rather than random accumulation—a single silver pendant, small hoops in her ears, a watch that looked expensive but understated.

"You must be the sheriff," she said, extending a work-roughened hand to Jack. "And Dr. Graves. I've been wondering when you'd find your way out here."

"Ms. Toscano," Jack said. "We're looking for Leena Cross. We believe she might be here."

"She is. We've been expecting you." Evangeline

stepped back, gesturing for us to enter. "Leena's been quite concerned about young Sheldon. She wanted to speak with you about what happened the other night."

The interior of the house was a fascinating blend of the practical and the mystical. Bookshelves lined every wall, packed with volumes on everything from medicinal herbs to quantum physics. Crystals shared space with houseplants, and what looked like serious scientific equipment sat alongside candles and incense burners. The overall effect was of someone who approached the unknown with both open mind and healthy skepticism.

"Leena," Evangeline called toward the back of the house. "Your visitors are here."

The young woman who emerged from what looked like a kitchen was a study in contrasts to her older companion. Where Evangeline radiated calm competence, Leena fairly vibrated with nervous energy. Her black-dyed hair hung in uneven strands around a face that was pretty despite—or perhaps because of—the dramatic makeup that emphasized her dark eyes and pale skin. She wore layers of black clothing that managed to look both carefully constructed and carelessly thrown together.

"I didn't do anything wrong," she said immediately, her voice carrying the defensive edge of someone who'd been questioned by authority figures before. "Sheldon came with me willingly. I didn't hurt him."

"We need to ask you some questions about your connection to our investigation," I said carefully. "Sheldon mentioned you had specific knowledge about the marked graves at the cemetery, and we're trying to understand how you knew details that weren't released to the public."

Leena's expression shifted from defensive to uncomfortable. "I...Evangeline and I went to the cemetery after we heard about the murder. We could feel the energy there, the disturbance. When we saw the symbols, I recognized what they meant."

"You went to an active crime scene?" Jack's voice carried the sharp edge of authority. "The area was cordoned off."

"You don't feel energy like that every day," Leena said quickly. "And in that part of the cemetery it's easy to stay hidden, so no one saw us. Someone was using justice magic. The symbols almost glowed with power. You could see them even outside the perimeter."

"And you told Sheldon about them," I said.

"I was excited. I'd never seen real ritual magic being used before. I thought he'd be interested." She paused, seeming to realize how that sounded. "I didn't know it was connected to the actual murder until later."

Jack pulled out his phone, scrolling to crime-scene photos that showed the carved markings on the cemetery headstones. "Since you claim to understand what these mean, can you explain them to us?"

Leena studied the images with the focused attention of a scholar examining primary sources. Her fingers traced the air above Jack's phone screen, following the lines of the carved symbols with precision that suggested genuine expertise.

"These aren't random," she said finally. "Someone who understands ritual magic created these. The scales of justice represent divine judgment—the belief that cosmic forces will balance wrongs that human courts failed to address. But look at the way they're positioned."

She gestured to the image of Ezekiel Morton's headstone. "They're not centered on the stone. They're placed specifically to the left, which in ceremonial magic represents the path of severity, of punishment without mercy."

"What about these?" I asked, showing her the Roman numerals carved on Rebecca Hughes's grave.

"VI, XII, III," Leena read. "Six, twelve, three. Those aren't dates—they're a countdown. Six families were involved in the original injustice, twelve bloodlines were affected, three generations have passed. It's a way of saying the debt is coming due."

The hair on my arms stood up despite the warm

afternoon. "And the initials around William Lawson's headstone?"

"Binding circle," Leena said immediately. "The initials represent the conspirators, carved in a pattern that's designed to trap their spiritual essence. Someone believes these people need to be held accountable even in death."

Evangeline had been listening quietly, but now she moved to a bookshelf and retrieved a leather-bound volume that looked genuinely ancient. "The stone circle found around Rachel Mills's grave is more complex," she said, opening the book to reveal pages covered in hand-drawn diagrams. "It's called a justice circle, specifically designed to channel the energy of the wronged dead toward their persecutors."

"You're saying someone believes they're channeling the spirit of Bridget Ashworth?" Jack asked.

"I'm saying someone with significant knowledge of ceremonial magic is using these symbols to justify murder," Evangeline corrected. "Whether they believe Bridget's spirit is guiding them or they're simply using her story as psychological justification, the result is the same."

Leena was still studying the phone images, her dark eyes intense with concentration. "There's something else. The precision of these carvings, the specific positioning—this isn't someone who learned about ritual magic from books or internet forums. This is someone who was taught these symbols, who understands their traditional meanings and applications."

"Taught by whom?" I asked.

"Someone with access to genuine grimoires, old family traditions, or formal magical training," Leena said. "These symbols are very specific to justice magic, which isn't commonly practiced anymore. Most modern practitioners focus on healing or prosperity magic. Justice magic is considered dangerous because it's designed to cause harm."

"How dangerous?" Jack asked.

Evangeline closed her book carefully. "Dangerous enough that most responsible teachers won't pass on the knowledge. It requires absolute certainty about guilt and innocence, and humans are notoriously bad at that kind of judgment."

"But someone taught our killer," I said.

"Or they're part of a family tradition that's been passed down through generations," Leena added. "Some bloodlines maintain magical practices for centuries, especially if they believe their ancestors were wronged."

The implications of what they were telling us settled over me like a cold blanket. We weren't just looking for someone with access to historical records and crime-scene evidence. We were looking for someone who'd been trained in a specific, dangerous form of magic designed to punish the descendants of people who'd committed injustices centuries ago.

"Have either of you heard of anyone in King George County practicing justice magic?" Jack asked.

"No," Evangeline said immediately. "And I've lived here for forty years. I know most of the people who practice any form of alternative spirituality, and none of them would be involved in something like this."

"What about someone new to the area?" I pressed. "Someone who might have moved here specifically because of the Bridget Ashworth connection?"

Leena and Evangeline exchanged glances. "There have been a few people asking about local magical history lately," Leena admitted. "Someone called Evangeline a few weeks ago, wanting to know about sites connected to the witch trials. But they wouldn't give their name, and the number was blocked."

"What did they want to know specifically?" Jack asked.

"Locations where accused witches were buried, whether any of their possessions survived, if there were any living descendants," Evangeline said. "I told them I didn't have that information and suggested they contact the historical society. I don't give out details about burial sites to strangers."

"Smart policy," Jack said. "Did they call back?"

"No. But a few days later, someone broke into my greenhouse and stole several rare herbs. Plants that are used specifically in justice magic—belladonna, mandrake root, graveyard dirt that I collected from Bridget Ashworth's burial site years ago for research purposes."

My blood ran cold. "You have dirt from Bridget's grave?"

"Had," Evangeline corrected. "Along with herbs that can be used to induce cardiac arrest if someone knows the proper preparations."

Jack and I looked at each other, the pieces of our puzzle suddenly shifting into a new and terrifying pattern. Thomas Whitman had died of cardiac arrest with no obvious medical cause. If someone had used magical herbs to stop his heart, it would explain why the autopsy hadn't revealed a clear cause of death.

"Could those herbs cause the kind of cardiac arrest we saw in our victim?" I asked.

"Belladonna and mandrake, properly prepared and administered, can definitely cause fatal arrhythmias," Evangeline said. "They're extremely dangerous in the wrong hands."

"When exactly was your greenhouse broken into?" Jack asked.

"Three weeks ago. I reported it to the sheriff's office, but honestly, I wasn't sure anyone would take it seriously. People assume anything involving herbs and magic is just silly superstition."

Jack was already pulling out his phone. "I need to check our incident reports. If someone's been stealing your supplies and asking about Bridget Ashworth's descendants, we might have a pattern."

The afternoon light was fading as we prepared to leave, turning the marsh landscape into something that belonged in a fairy tale—beautiful but slightly ominous, full of hidden depths and secrets that whispered in the wind. Leena walked us to our vehicle, her nervous energy finally settling into something that looked like genuine concern.

"Sheriff," she said quietly, "whoever's doing this isn't just interested in historical justice. Someone with this level of magical knowledge, combined with access to your investigation—they're not going to stop until they've completed whatever ritual they've started."

"How do we stop them?" I asked.

"Figure out how many people are on their list," she said simply. "Because justice magic doesn't end until the practitioner believes perfect balance has been achieved. And given what happened three hundred years ago, that could mean a lot more people have to die."

The drive back to town felt like emerging from another world. Cell service returned gradually, and with it the familiar buzz of Jack's phone with updates from the investigation. But my mind kept circling back to what Leena and Evangeline had told us about justice magic and the herbs that had been stolen.

"We need to talk to Patricia again," I said as we reached the outskirts of King George Proper. "If someone's targeting descendants for a magical ritual, she might know details about the financial stakes that could help us understand the scope."

"Agreed. And I want to check that incident report about the greenhouse break-in. If we can narrow down the timeline, we might be able to figure out when our killer started planning this."

Jack's phone rang as we pulled into the parking lot of a roadside diner that advertised the best fried chicken in three counties. The caller ID showed Patricia Whitman's number.

"Sheriff Lawson," Jack answered, putting the phone on speaker.

"Sheriff, it's Patricia Whitman." Her voice sounded strained, tinged with an urgency that made me sit up straighter. "I've been thinking about our conversation this afternoon, about Thomas's research and who might want to stop it. There's something I didn't tell you—something about the financial implications of what he'd discovered."

"What kind of financial implications?" Jack asked.

"The land that was stolen from Bridget Ashworth—it's not just historically significant. If Thomas could prove the original transfers were fraudulent, it would affect current property ownership throughout King George County. We're talking about millions of dollars in prime riverfront land, some of the most valuable real estate in Virginia. The homestead and land that Bridget and her husband farmed was parceled out after she was tried for witchcraft, having deemed property ownership null and void due to her crimes."

"Let me guess," Jack said. "The land that was parceled out went to the families went to the families whose names were marked on those graves."

"Partially true," Patricia said. "The Whitmans, Mortons, and Hughes were adjacent to the property and divided it up equally. There are records that show the Mills family was given all the livestock, as the Ashworths had one of the largest farms in the area at the time. And there is a single handwritten receipt that Blackwood took payment for his troubles in overseeing the whole affair by helping himself to gold bars that Bridget's husband had been given by the king himself because he'd once saved the king's life."

"So the Ashworths were the wealthiest family on the block and the other colonists got greedy," Jack said, summing it up.

"Essentially," she said. "If these records held up in court some of the biggest landowners in the county could lose everything if an heir was found." Patricia's voice dropped to a whisper. "In the weeks before he died, Thomas became increasingly paranoid. He said he felt like someone was watching him, following him. He started keeping his research locked up, wouldn't even discuss it with me at home."

"Did he say why he was worried?" Jack asked.

"He said the implications of what he'd found were bigger than he'd realized. That proving the land fraud wouldn't just be an academic exercise—it would destroy some of the most powerful families in Virginia." A pause, filled with static and what sounded like traffic in the background. "Sheriff, I think someone killed my husband because his research threatened to expose the biggest land fraud in Virginia history. And I think they're going to keep killing until everyone who knows the truth is dead."

"Have you received any threats?" Jack asked.

"No," she said. "I have to go. I've got meetings."

The line went dead, leaving Jack and me staring

at each other across the Tahoe's interior. Outside, the ordinary world continued—people pumping gas, families eating dinner at picnic tables, teenagers texting on their phones. But inside our vehicle, the weight of what we'd learned pressed down like storm clouds.

"If she's the killer then this is an interesting strategy," I said.

"It's hard to know which direction is up with this case," Jack agreed.

"But Patricia is right. This isn't about historical justice or magical rituals. This is about money. Millions of dollars' worth of stolen land, and someone willing to commit murder to protect their claim to it."

Jack glanced toward the diner's neon sign, then at me with that look that meant he was about to go into protective husband mode. "When's the last time you ate something that wasn't toast or crackers?"

"I had tea this morning," I said, already knowing where this was headed.

"Tea isn't food." He was already climbing out of the Tahoe. "And before you argue, the baby needs actual nutrients, not just caffeine and wishful thinking."

"I wasn't going to argue," I said, though we both knew I absolutely was.

"Sure you weren't." He came around to open my

door, that half smile playing at the corners of his mouth. "Come on. Let's get some protein in you before you pass out and I have to explain to the paramedics why my wife fainted in a diner parking lot."

"You're very romantic when you're being practical," I said, taking his offered hand.

"That's because keeping you fed and healthy is my favorite hobby," he said, his thumb brushing over my knuckles. "Well, second favorite."

CHAPTER NINETEEN

THE AFTERNOON SKY HAD TURNED THE COLOR OF OLD pewter by the time we climbed back into the Tahoe, the threatening clouds from earlier finally making good on their promise. The first fat drops of rain splattered against the windshield as Jack started the engine, the temperature dropping enough that the air-conditioning felt suddenly unnecessary.

"We should check on Judith Hughes," I said, settling back into the leather seat. "See if the hospital will let us talk to her. She might be able to tell us more about what happened at her house, or about that dinner with Thomas."

"Agreed," Jack said, pulling out of the diner's gravel parking lot. "And I want another look at those crime-scene photos from the cemetery. Something's been bothering me about the way those symbols were carved."

The rain picked up as we drove, turning the world beyond our windows into an impressionist painting of blurred colors and shifting shapes. Jack had the radio turned low to the local news station, the announcer's voice mixing with the rhythmic sweep of the wipers.

"...storms expected to continue through the evening with possible flooding in low-lying areas..."

Jack was adjusting his rearview mirror when his phone rang—not the sharp electronic buzz of his official line, but the softer chime of his personal cell.

He glanced at the unknown number and answered with his usual efficiency. "Lawson."

The voice that emerged from the speaker was neither male nor female, distorted by electronic modulation that stripped away humanity and left only cold purpose. But the words themselves carried the cadence of another century, formal and archaic as a judge's pronouncement from the Colonial bench.

"Listen well, Sheriff—justice delayed shall not be denied. Where ancient wheels once ground the grain, you'll find one who bore false witness against the inno-cent. The serpent's tongue has been silenced. The sun sets soon, and with it falls another who spoke lies. Do not

delay, or you'll find only silence where false testimony once rang."

The line went dead, leaving us staring at the phone as if it might explain the chill that had settled between us like fog off the river.

"What was that?" I whispered, though even as I spoke, my mind was already parsing the archaic phrases, searching for meaning in the ritualistic language.

Jack's expression had sharpened to the focused calm I'd seen when he faced armed suspects. "A riddle. Or a threat. Maybe both." He was already pulling up maps on his phone. "Ancient wheels that grind grain—has to be talking about a mill."

"Hawthorne Mill," I said, the pieces clicking together with sickening clarity. "It's the only Colonial-era gristmill still standing in the county. Built in the 1720s, right in the heart of all this Bridget Ashworth business."

The mill had been one of the county's earliest industrial sites, powered by the Rappahannock when it ran swift and deep enough to turn massive stone wheels. Local legend claimed it had been built on land confiscated from accused witches, though historians debated whether that was fact or folklore designed to add Gothic atmosphere to tourist brochures.

Jack was already making a sharp U-turn, the

engine roaring with urgency that matched the dread building in my chest. "Serpent's tongue, false witness, false testimony—someone's been targeted for speaking against our killer."

"Margaret," I said, the name falling between us like a stone into still water. "She warned Thomas away from his research. She knew how dangerous it was getting, tried to make him see reason. If our killer sees that as betrayal..."

We accelerated through the rain with controlled urgency, Jack's training keeping us just within the bounds of safety while still pushing toward whatever fresh horror awaited us. The wipers struggled against the downpour, and I found myself gripping the door handle as we took a curve faster than comfortable.

"How long would it take to set up something like this?" I asked, trying to focus on the investigation rather than the dread building in my chest. "The staging at the cemetery took hours. If Margaret's already dead—"

"Then our killer's been planning this for a while," Jack finished. "The call was just to make sure we'd be the ones to find her." His jaw tightened. "They want us to see their work. Want us to understand what happens to people who interfere."

"The language," I said, replaying the electronic voice in my mind. "It wasn't just archaic—it was specific. Biblical cadences mixed with Colonial court proceedings. Whoever called us knows their history."

Jack's hands remained steady on the wheel, but I caught the slight tightening around his eyes that meant he was thinking three steps ahead. "Question is whether they're showing off their education or whether there's something deeper. Some families in this county have been nursing grudges since before the Revolution."

Hawthorne Mill appeared through the trees like something from a Gothic nightmare, its stone walls rising from earth that had drunk three centuries of Virginia rain. The mill wheel stood frozen with rust, wooden sluices rotted away to skeletal remains, but the building itself endured—a testament to the men who'd built it and the secrets they'd taken to their graves.

Jack parked behind a dark sedan that sat empty in the gravel clearing, its engine ticking as it cooled. No other vehicles were visible, but fresh tire tracks in the soft earth told a story of recent arrivals and departures.

"Someone's here," Jack said, his hand moving instinctively to his service weapon.

We approached the mill with the careful deliberation of professionals who'd learned that death rarely announced itself with fanfare. The afternoon air was thick with humidity and the competing scents of honeysuckle, river mud, and something else —something metallic and wrong that made my stomach clench with recognition.

The mill's entrance gaped before. Inside, shafts of sunlight slanted through gaps in the stone walls, illuminating motes of dust that danced like spirits reluctant to depart. Ancient machinery cast twisted shadows, and the grinding platform where generations of grain had been processed into flour now served a more sinister purpose.

The body lay twenty feet ahead, positioned on the old grinding platform like an offering to forgotten gods.

My steps slowed as details emerged from the gloom. Margaret Randolph had been arranged with the careful precision of a museum display—arms crossed over her chest in the manner of medieval tomb effigies, each finger deliberately positioned. Her dark hair had been brushed and arranged in a perfect halo around her pale face, every strand placed with obsessive attention. The killer had taken time here. Hours, maybe.

Leather-bound books formed a ritual circle around her body, their spines turned outward so the gold-embossed titles caught what little light filtered through the gaps in the stone. I recognized some of them even from this distance—her own published works on Colonial Virginia, her groundbreaking research on the witch trials, the academic achievements that had defined her career. Now they served as props in her death tableau, scholarship transformed into accusation.

Jack moved beside me, his hand hovering near his weapon, both of us approaching with the careful steps of people who knew death could still hold surprises.

That's when I saw her face.

My stomach clenched, bile rising in my throat despite all my years of examining the dead. Margaret's mouth gaped open in an eternal scream, the cavity dark with congealed blood that had pooled and dried in rusty brown streaks down her chin and neck. The killer hadn't just removed her tongue—they'd displayed its absence, propping her jaw open with something to ensure the mutilation would be the first thing anyone saw.

The precision of it made my skin crawl. Where the tongue should have been was only a ragged cavity, but the muscle had been severed cleanly at its base with surgical skill. No tearing, no hesitation marks. Someone had known exactly what they were doing.

"A tongue for her testimony," I murmured, my professional training overriding the visceral horror even as my hands trembled slightly. "She spoke against them, so they silenced her permanently."

The mill seemed to breathe around us, old wood creaking in the silence. Dust motes danced in the shafts of light, and somewhere water dripped with metronomic persistence. Every shadow could hide evidence. Every corner could conceal—

A sound from the shadows near the far wall—the scrape of shoe on stone.

Jack's hand snapped to his weapon with the speed of pure instinct, the Glock clearing leather before my eyes could track the movement. My own hand found the Beretta at my back, though I kept it holstered, watching Jack's reaction to gauge the threat level.

A figure emerged from behind a massive gear assembly, moving with the unsteady gait of exhaustion or shock. Richard Blackwood stepped into a shaft of light, and I barely recognized the usually polished businessman. His expensive suit was torn at the shoulder, the fabric stained with dirt and something darker that could have been blood. His silver hair stood at odd angles, and his pale eyes held the wild look of a trapped animal.

"It's not what it looks like."

CHAPTER TWENTY

It's not what it looks like.

"Step away from the body," Jack commanded, his Glock already in his hand with that fluid economy of motion that meant his brain had shifted into tactical mode. "Hands where I can see them. Now."

Blackwood's hands went up like he was surrendering to more than just Jack's weapon. "I didn't—she was already—someone called me. Last night at ten oh-seven. I know the exact time because I was watching the news and looked at the clock when my phone rang."

"Stop talking." Jack's voice carried that particular tone that made smart men shut their mouths and criminals confess just to avoid whatever was coming next.

"The voice was distorted," Blackwood rushed on

anyway, desperation overriding common sense. "Electronic. Like those voice-changer things. They said Margaret had found something—documents that could prove my family wasn't part of the conspiracy. That we tried to stop it." His voice cracked like expensive crystal under pressure. "Said she wanted to meet me here at two o'clock to share it before going to the police. When I got here five minutes ago, the door was open. I found her like... like that."

"Face the wall," Jack said. "Hands against it, feet spread."

While Jack controlled Blackwood, I kept my hand on the Beretta at my back, scanning the shadows for any other surprises. The mill felt alive around us, every creak of ancient wood making my nerves fire. The killer could still be here, watching us discover their handiwork.

"Call it in," Jack told me, never taking his eyes off Blackwood. "Full response. CSI, backup, the works."

My fingers were steady as I pulled out my phone, though my pulse hammered against my ribs. "This is Dr. Graves at Hawthorne Mill off River Road. We need immediate backup, CSI team, and the medical examiner. We have one deceased, one detained at scene."

"Copy that, Dr. Graves," the dispatcher responded. "Units are en route. ETA four minutes."

Jack patted Blackwood down, checking for weapons while I kept watch. "Your phone on you?"

"Right jacket pocket," Blackwood said.

Jack retrieved an iPhone in a leather case, handling it carefully to preserve any fingerprints. The screen showed numerous missed calls and texts, probably from Blackwood's wife wondering where he'd disappeared to this afternoon.

"The voice," Jack said. "Male or female?"

"I couldn't tell." Blackwood's words tumbled over each other in his desperation to explain. "They said Margaret had found documents in the courthouse archives that could protect my family. That she'd discovered who was really behind these murders and had proof that would stop us from being next. I was supposed to meet her here at two. When I arrived, the door was open. I went in and found her like...like that. I was checking to see if she was really dead when you arrived."

I studied Blackwood as he spoke, noting the details that would matter later. His torn jacket and disheveled appearance made sense now—he'd stumbled through the dark mill, maybe tripped over equipment in his shock at finding Margaret's body. The scrapes on his knuckles looked fresh, probably from catching himself when he fell.

The sound of sirens grew closer, and within minutes, the quiet mill became a hive of controlled chaos. Cole's pickup truck arrived first, followed by Martinez's sedan, then two patrol units. The rain had picked up again, drumming against the restored cedar shake roof that the historical society had painstakingly re-created using Colonial-era techniques. Despite the authentic restoration, water still found its way through the centuries-old stone walls where mortar had worn away—preservation could only do so much against time and weather.

"Quite a scene," Cole said, taking in Margaret's displayed corpse with the grim expression of someone who'd seen too much death. "Want me to take Blackwood?"

"We need to secure him as a witness," Jack said. "Cole, take Mr. Blackwood outside. Get a preliminary statement while we process the scene."

Cole nodded and approached Blackwood. "Mr. Blackwood, I need you to come with me. We'll need a full statement about what you're doing here and what you saw."

"I already told you—" Blackwood started.

"And you'll tell us again, in detail," Cole said, his tone firm but not hostile. "Right now you're a witness to a crime scene. Let's keep it that way."

Blackwood's shoulders sagged as Cole escorted him outside. Through the mill's entrance, I could see Cole guiding him through the rain to one of the patrol cars, opening the back door for him to sit inside, out of the downpour. Cole slid into the front seat, turning to take Blackwood's statement through the partition. Standard procedure—separate potential witnesses from the crime scene, get their story while it's fresh, then determine if there's probable cause for arrest.

The CSI van arrived next, and Lieutenant Daniels emerged with her usual calm efficiency, Potts right behind her carrying equipment cases. Even in the chaos of a crime scene, Daniels moved with the methodical precision of someone who'd processed hundreds of scenes and knew exactly what needed to be done.

"Sheriff, Doctor," Daniels said, pulling on latex gloves. "What do we have?"

"Margaret Randolph, professor at the university," Jack said. "Found her approximately twenty minutes ago after receiving a tip. Richard Blackwood was already on scene—claims he was lured here by a phone call."

Potts was already photographing the entrance, the whir and click of her camera adding to the soundscape. She moved with her characteristic precision, documenting every angle before anyone could contaminate the scene. There was something almost meditative about the way she worked, as if crime scenes were puzzles she was born to solve.

"The body's been staged," I said, leading them

toward Margaret. "Similar theatrical presentation to what we saw with Thomas Whitman."

As we approached Margaret's corpse, I watched Daniels's expression tighten. Even for seasoned professionals, the sight of that gaping mouth and missing tongue was jarring.

"We'll need extensive photography of the body positioning and the surrounding area," Daniels said, already directing her team. "Potts, start with overall shots, then move to details."

I pulled on fresh gloves and knelt beside Margaret's body, beginning my preliminary examination while the CSI team set up their equipment. The liver temperature probe would give us a more accurate time of death, but rigor mortis was already well established in the small muscle groups.

"Based on the degree of rigor and the temperature drop," I said, carefully inserting the probe, "I'd estimate death occurred between 10 p.m. and midnight last night."

The numbers on the digital thermometer confirmed my estimate. "Margaret has been dead for at least twelve hours, probably more. Which means if Blackwood's call came at ten oh-seven, Margaret could've still been alive when he received it."

"Or freshly dead," Jack said.

Potts was photographing the books arranged around Margaret's body, documenting each one's position and title. "These appear to be academic texts," she said, reading the spines for the evidence log. "All related to Colonial Virginia history. Should I bag them individually or as a set?"

"Individually," Daniels instructed. "We'll need to process each one for prints."

I continued my examination, documenting every detail. The tongue had been removed with surgical precision—one clean cut at the base with something incredibly sharp.

"No defensive wounds," I noted, examining her hands and arms. "She never fought back."

"Sheriff," Potts called from near the grinding wheel. "I've found something."

We gathered around as she photographed a dark button lying in the dust about three feet from Margaret's body. Using tweezers, she carefully lifted it for closer examination.

"Looks expensive," she said, turning it to catch the light. "Mother-of-pearl, maybe? With gold threading."

I glanced toward the entrance where we could see Blackwood in the back of Cole's patrol car. His suit jacket was expensive, certainly, but even from here I could see all his buttons were intact.

"Bag it," Daniels instructed. "We'll compare it to Blackwood's clothing and check for prints."

The team worked with methodical precision for

the next hour. Every inch of the mill was photographed, measured, documented. They found fresh tire tracks from only the two vehicles parked outside.

"Land Rover is registered to the victim," Martinez said. "The BMW belongs to Blackwood."

"Killer drove her to her execution in her own vehicle," I said. "How'd the killer get away?"

"Want to bet money that Victoria Mills's vehicle was parked somewhere down the road?" Jack asked.

"That's a sucker's bet," I said.

"Victim's purse was on the passenger seat," Martinez continued. "Wallet and credit cards intact. Her phone was missing."

"This is a bold killer," Jack said. "A true sociopath. They don't worry about being caught. That's something to think about. The killer took time in the cemetery. Staged the body. Moved each board and stone. Then they moved on to Victoria. But things didn't go as planned. The drugs didn't do what they should have, so there was fight and the killer resorted to a bullet instead of whatever had been planned."

"At least Victoria took some DNA with her into death," I said. "So at least we'll have that when we catch him."

Jack nodded and continued. "Then they moved on to Judith Hughes. But that didn't go as planned either. Maybe Victoria got some good licks in and the killer was weakened. Or maybe they just didn't plan on Judith running the way she did, but whatever the case, we have a living witness once she can get past the fear and start talking coherently."

"The killer spent time here too," I said. "Other than her tongue being removed and all the blood, look how clean she is. She's been deliberately placed here, almost reverently, like on an altar."

The rain outside had intensified, and despite the building's restored roof, water seeped through the ancient stone walls where centuries of freeze-thaw cycles had opened gaps between the carefully fitted rocks. The historical society had done remarkable work preserving the mill—the wheel mechanism had been rebuilt to working condition, the grinding stones restored, educational plaques installed—but no amount of preservation could completely seal a building that had stood since the 1720s. The team worked faster, protecting evidence from the encroaching moisture.

"Got something!" Potts announced from near the restored mill wheel mechanism. She was photographing something wedged between two massive stones. "Looks like paper."

We watched as she carefully extracted what appeared to be an aged piece of parchment, protected from the rain by the reconstructed wooden housing that sheltered the mill wheel—part of the historical society's efforts to show visitors how the mechanism would have originally functioned. The paper looked genuinely old, yellowed and brittle at the edges.

"It's wrapped in plastic," she observed, using tweezers to carefully unfold it. "Someone wanted to make sure we'd find this intact."

Even from where I stood, I could see elaborate script covering the page.

Daniels leaned in with a magnifying glass to photograph the text clearly.

"What does it say?" I asked, looking at Jack. I knew he was thinking about the call we'd received on our way here.

"It says," Daniels said. "The serpent had many heads. One has been severed, but others still speak with forked tongues. The scales of justice remain unbalanced. Those who built their fortunes on innocent blood must pay the debt in full." She looked up. "We'll need a document expert to analyze the paper and ink."

A chill ran down my spine that had nothing to do with the damp air. "That's three murders and another attempted murder in the last three days. That's rapid escalation."

"That's premeditated," Jack said. "Someone who planned out methods and places well ahead of time.

Someone who's done surveillance and knows they won't be seen at certain times of the day or night."

"And they're obviously not just killing descendants," I said. "They're killing anyone they see as complicit in the cover-up. Margaret knew about Thomas's research, tried to stop him from pursuing it."

I stood up from Margaret's body, my knees protesting after kneeling on the hard floor. Every muscle in my body felt tight with tension.

The Suburban arrived just as we were finishing our initial processing. Lily jumped out from the driver's side, her dark hair pulled back in a ponytail, wearing scrubs under her rain jacket. Sheldon emerged from the passenger side, somehow managing to look both professional and slightly disheveled despite his rain gear. His attempts at the emo look from yesterday were mostly gone, though I could still see traces of eyeliner he hadn't quite managed to remove.

"Another one?" Lily said, her expression grim as she took in the scene. Despite her exhaustion from finals, she was all business. "Sheldon, let's get the gurney."

They worked together, navigating the rain-slicked ground and ancient doorway. Lily's medical training showed in the careful way she helped position Margaret's body for transport, while Sheldon handled the technical aspects with surprising competence.

"Tongue's been removed," I told Lily quietly as we prepared to zip the body bag. "You can assist with this one. It'll be interesting."

"That's a perk to my week," she said. "I have one more final and then I'm going to sleep for seventy-two hours."

Cole returned from interviewing Blackwood. "His story checks out so far. Phone shows an incoming call from a blocked number at eleven forty-seven. Duration one minute twelve seconds. He says he got the call last night telling him to meet her here at 2 p.m. today. Just arrived about five minutes before you all showed up. Said he saw her and freaked out and fell down the stairs. That's why he's all banged up. Tore his clothes and palms of his hands."

Martinez piped in and said, "I've got Chen pulling footage from every traffic cam between Blackwood's house and here."

The scene was winding down, evidence catalogued and bagged. As we prepared to leave, I took one last look at the grinding platform where Margaret had been displayed. The CSI team had finished their documentation, evidence markers removed, but I could still see her there in my mind's eye—silenced forever for trying to protect someone she cared about. She wasn't part of the original bloodlines, but she'd gotten in the killer's way.

The rain followed us out of the mill, turning the world into a gray blur of water and shadow. The killer was playing a game with rules we didn't fully understand, moving pieces on a board we couldn't quite see.

The storm that had been building all day finally broke in earnest, thunder rattling the windows and lightning illuminating the Virginia countryside in stark, momentary revelations. It felt appropriate somehow—nature itself acknowledging that something dark had been unleashed in King George County.

CHAPTER TWENTY-ONE

Jack stayed behind at Hawthorne Mill to coordinate with the CSI team, so I rode back with Lily and Sheldon in the Suburban. The storm that had been threatening all day was finally delivering on its promise, turning the late afternoon into premature twilight. Lightning split the sky in jagged veins, each flash turning the world into a photographic negative—stark white followed by absolute darkness.

"I hate this weather," Lily said. "If Cole doesn't take me somewhere sunny and hot soon I can't be responsible for my actions."

"Did you know there's a fifteen percent decrease in work productivity when it rains more than thirty-six hours?" Sheldon offered from the back.

"How about the murder rate?" Lily asked.

"Because this rain makes me want to stab some people. Like this guy in front of me who won't go more than ten miles per hour and has his hazard lights on."

Lily pressed down on the horn and I sat still and wide eyed in the passenger seat, trying to remember back to my days of med school and how the pressure affected me. To be honest, I couldn't really remember a whole lot. It's just a lot of black space and panic when I try to think about it.

"Sheldon, you doing okay back there?" I asked, glancing over my shoulder.

"Fine," he said, sitting next to the gurney where Margaret Randolph's body lay sealed in black plastic. "When someone gets their tongue cut out how do we prepare the body for an open casket? I've never dealt with a missing tongue before. I like working with you because I get to add new things to my mortuary journal."

"Thank you?" I wasn't sure if it was really a compliment directed at me or if it was directed at the depravity and creativity of murdering Virginians.

"Anyway, a missing tongue is no big deal," I said. "If the shape of the mouth changes you just shove some cotton or putty in there to make it look normal, and then staple the mouth closed like normal."

"I thought there'd be more to it," Sheldon said, sounding disappointed.

"I had a guy once get the whole bottom half of his jaw blown off with a shotgun," I said. "And the family wanted an open casket. You want to talk about miracle work? I was pretty proud of that one. By the time I was done you couldn't even see he'd been in an accident."

Lily navigated the familiar roads with ease despite the downpour that turned the windshield into a waterfall. The wipers fought a losing battle, each sweep immediately erased by fresh sheets of rain.

The funeral home materialized through the rain like a ship through fog, its red-brick façade dark with moisture. We pulled under the portico, and the sudden absence of rain on the roof was almost disorienting. The silence that followed felt heavy, expectant, as if the building itself knew what we were bringing into its walls.

We moved in tandem—Sheldon wheeling the gurney while Lily held the door and I punched in the security code. The elevator descended with its familiar mechanical groan, taking us from the world of the living to the realm where death revealed its secrets. The temperature dropped ten degrees between floors, the building's climate control keeping the lower level cold enough to slow decomposition, cold enough to make me wish I'd grabbed my jacket.

In the lab, the fluorescent lights flickered to life with a harsh brilliance that banished every shadow, leaving nowhere for death's secrets to hide. The sterile white walls seemed to close in, creating a world separate from the storm raging above—a place where violence could be dissected and catalogued, where the dead finally gave up their truths.

Lily started photographing while I began the external examination, and Sheldon finished the paperwork with the methodical precision of someone who'd documented too many violent ends.

"Time for autopsy is 5:17 p.m.," I said into the recorder. "Subject is Dr. Margaret Randolph, age thirty-six."

"Look at her hair," Lily said, leaning closer with the camera. "Someone washed and styled it. That's a lot of effort postmortem."

"Same with the clothes," I added. "Everything's been adjusted, arranged. Our killer spent time with her after death. Check her hands, Lily—any defensive wounds?"

"Nothing. Not even a broken nail." Lily photographed each hand methodically. "She never fought back."

"Which means she was unconscious when taken," I said. "I've got something here. Black fibers caught in the finger creases."

"From gloves maybe?" Lily said, already adjusting her camera settings for a macro shot.

"Looks synthetic. Bag these for me while I check the oral cavity." I positioned the overhead light. "The tongue removal is interesting—one clean cut, very sharp instrument."

"Scalpel?" Lily suggested.

"Or surgical scissors. Something precise." I opened the oral cavity a little wider. "I'm going to bet that when we open her up cause of death will be drowning."

"You think she drowned in her own blood?" Lily asked. "That's a horrible way to die."

I agreed, it was a horrible way to die. They posed her so serenely. You'd never think she suffered by looking at her. But suffered she had.

"Wait," I said, bringing the magnifier down over her arm. "She's got a tiny puncture mark here. Injection site. So maybe she didn't know she was dying."

"Small favors," Lily said.

The internal examination revealed no surprises. Healthy organs, no signs of disease. Stomach contents showed a partially digested dinner of fish and rice.

"Tox screen shows she has a BAC of .09," Lily said.

"So she had dinner and a couple of glasses of wine," I said. "She was over the legal limit so her reaction time would've been slow. She might not have even known she was in danger until the needle went into her arm."

"I need to head upstairs," Sheldon said, sealing the last evidence bag. "Mrs. Patterson has called three times about her mother's viewing tomorrow, and if I don't call her back she'll show up here with that taxidermied cat again."

"Good luck with that," Lily said, not looking up from her notes.

After Sheldon left, Lily and I continued working through the internal examination.

My phone buzzed as I was suturing the Y-incision.

"It's Jack," I said, seeing his name on the screen. I put him on speaker since my hands were occupied.

"How's it going?" Jack's voice sounded tired.

"Just finishing up. Found injection site, and some strange fibers on her hands. You?"

"Blackwood's alibi is solid. Traffic cameras confirm he was home until he left for the mill. He got there a few minutes before we did. And Patricia Whitman's DNA doesn't match the blood at Victoria Mills's house."

"So we're back to square one?" I asked.

"Not quite. Judith Hughes is stable enough to talk. Can you meet me at the hospital?"

"Give me twenty minutes."

King George County Hospital squatted against the evening sky like a monument to human frailty, its windows glowing yellow against the pewter clouds. The parking lot had become a shallow lake, each lamppost reflected in the standing water like drowning suns. Jack waited in the lobby, water still dripping from his jacket, creating small puddles around his boots that the janitor eyed with weary resignation.

"Third floor," he said. "Psychiatric wing. They've got a deputy posted."

The elevator ride was silent except for the mechanical hum and the ghost of classical music piped through speakers that had given up on quality decades ago. When we reached room 312, Deputy Rodriguez nodded from his chair outside, a paperback novel folded open on his lap—one of those true crime books that always got the details wrong.

"She's awake. Pretty anxious though."

The room beyond the door felt smaller than it was, shadows pooling in corners despite the bedside lamp's valiant effort. Judith Hughes looked nothing like her photo—the confident grad student researching Colonial property transfers had been replaced by something hollow and haunted. She sat propped against pillows that seemed to swallow her, arms wrapped around herself as if she could hold her pieces together through will alone. Scratches covered her arms like desperate calligraphy, telling the story of her flight through woods that had hidden her but couldn't protect her.

"Ms. Hughes," Jack said gently. "I'm Sheriff Lawson. This is Dr. Graves. We found you in the barn."

Her eyes tracked to us, but they weren't quite focused—like she was seeing through us to something else entirely. "You found me," she whispered. "Or maybe you were meant to find me. I can't tell anymore what's real and what she wants me to see."

"Who?" Jack asked, leaning forward slightly.

"Bridget." The name came out like a prayer and a curse combined. "She's been in my dreams for weeks. Showing me things. The stones crying blood. The earth opening up beneath the courthouse. My ancestors' sins written in fire across the sky." She laughed, a broken sound that made my skin crawl. "But that's crazy, isn't it? That's what I kept telling myself. Even when things started moving in my apartment."

"Your apartment?" I asked gently, taking the chair near her bed.

"I haven't lived in the family house since..." Her voice cracked. "Since my parents died. But several weeks ago, I started getting letters. Old paper, like parchment. It reeked of herbs, like rosemary or something—so strong it made my head spin." Her fingers twisted in the hospital sheets. "It said the house was calling me home. That I needed to face what my family had done. I threw it away, but then I found it on my pillow that same night. Then in my car. Then under my coffee cup at work."

"How long did you get the letters?" he asked.

"Almost every day. There was one in my apartment on Monday night when I came home from class. I didn't even open it. I threw it away. They always said the same things."

"You had dinner with Thomas Whitman on Monday night?" Jack asked.

She turned her head slightly so she was looking out the single window in her hospital room, the rain pouring down the glass like tears.

"Professor Whitman was one of my undergrad professors at KGU, and he gave me a recommendation for the master's program at Georgetown. He was obsessed with the founding families in this area. He liked to talk about how his ancestors and mine had probably shared drinks at Dorothy Roy's Tavern in Port Royal. He always asked questions about my family, wanted to know if I remembered any history or had any records my parents had left me."

"So that wasn't the first time you'd met for dinner?" I asked her.

Her voice was sleepy and monotone, her eyes

barely blinking. "We'd get together on and off. Whenever the mood struck him or he'd found some thread in his research."

"You had a sexual relationship?" I pressed.

"Like I said, off and on."

"Walk me through Monday night when he came for dinner," Jack said.

"I...I don't remember much," she said. "My head hurts. It feels like my skull is being crushed.

"You had dinner?" I asked. "Did you cook or order takeout?"

"I cooked. Chicken and rice. We had some wine." She shrugged. "He wasn't the kind of guy who would normally stay the night, but when we finished dinner neither of us was feeling well. I'm not the greatest cook I guess. He left and I went to bed."

"What time was that?" Jack asked.

"It was before nine," she said. "I just remember everything being hazy and feeling kind of nauseated. I just wanted him to leave so I could be sick in peace. It was almost noon when I woke up the next day. And there was a letter on my nightstand." She shuddered visibly. "I tore it up and flushed it down the toilet. Then I turned on the TV and I heard about Thomas. I didn't understand any of it, but I knew it was somehow tied to the letters. To Bridget Ashworth. Thomas always asked about Bridget." Her voice got so soft I could barely hear her next word. "Obsessed."

"Did you call anyone? Go anywhere?"

"I was supposed to have a meeting with my advisory board about my thesis," she said. "I called my advisor and cancelled. Told him I was sick." She licked her lips, but it didn't seem to help with the dryness and I handed her the cup of water next to her bed with a straw so she could drink.

"When I came out of the shower there was another letter on my table. I could smell the scent of it before I even walked into the room. It said the same thing all the others did—that the house was calling me home and I had to face what my family had done."

Jack and I exchanged glances. "So you went to the house?"

"I had to." Her eyes filled with tears. "I was so tired of fighting it. Every night the dreams got worse. I'd wake up choking, feeling dirt in my mouth, stones on my chest. I could hear her voice—not in my ears but in my bones. She said if I didn't come home, she'd bring the house to me. And then yesterday morning, I woke up with graveyard dirt on my feet and dried herbs in my hair. I didn't remember how they got there."

The room seemed to grow colder as she spoke. I remembered Evangeline mentioning the stolen herbs—belladonna, mandrake root, graveyard dirt from Bridget's burial site.

"When I got to the house," she continued, "All the lights were on. Every single one. But I haven't been there in months. The front door was open, and there was a trail of rosemary and something else—the smell was strong again, like someone had poured a bottle of the scent across the threshold."

"What happened when you went in?" Jack's voice was steady, professional, but I could see the tension in his shoulders.

"The herbs led upstairs to my parents' room. Their things were arranged on the bed—my mother's jewelry, my father's watch, their wedding photo. And in the middle was another letter, surrounded by a circle of that graveyard dirt." She closed her eyes. "It said my blood could end this. That I could be the sacrifice that balanced the scales. That Bridget would accept me in place of the others."

"Did you see who left it?"

"I started to leave, but then I heard footsteps behind me. When I turned..." She shuddered. "The hallway was full of smoke. Not regular smoke—it was greenish, herbal. And in the smoke, I saw eyes. Red eyes, like coals. Dressed in black, face covered.

"I heard my mother's voice," Judith whispered. "She said she was disappointed in me. That I'd failed the family by not accepting my role. Then the voice changed—became something older, harder. Like stones grinding together. It said Bridget had been patient for three centuries, but patience has limits."

"How did you escape?" I asked.

"The rosemary smell—it was everywhere, so thick it made my eyes water. When Bridget grabbed me, we fought. I was terrified but I fought hard. Got my knee up, drove it into her ribs as hard as I could." She demonstrated the motion weakly from her hospital bed. "I heard something crack. She screamed and it made my blood run cold—I've never heard a sound like that."

"Then what happened?" Jack prompted.

"I was able to get loose and I ran. I could hear her behind me." Her voice got small and terrified, higher pitched as she relived the terror in her mind. "I made it to the woods and just kept running."

"Through the woods?" Jack asked.

"I knew those woods before I could walk. I could navigate them blind. But all night, I heard things. Whispers in voices I recognized—my parents, my grandmother. Telling me to come back. Telling me I was chosen." She looked at us with haunted eyes. "I'll never forget it. And in the dark, alone, terrified... I believed it. Part of me still believes it."

"Judith," I said carefully, "you were drugged. Whatever was in those herbs made you hallucinate. The things you thought you saw weren't real. Bridget

Ashworth has been dead three hundred years. The sheriff and I are hunting a real-life human who has killed three people."

"Not a ghost," she said, though the statement lacked conviction.

"Did you recognize anything else about the attacker?" Jack asked. "Height, build, anything?"

Her eyes went unfocused again, as if she was sliding back into that terror. "So strong. Their hands..." She touched her throat where bruises were starting to form. "Rough gloves. Black. Everything was black except the eyes. The red eyes in the smoke."

"Was it a man or woman?" Jack asked gently.

"I don't know. I don't know." Her voice rose with panic. "The voice kept changing. Sometimes my mother, sometimes something ancient. Sometimes..." She shook her head violently. "I can't tell what was real. I can still smell rosemary and dirt. I can't escape it."

She started rocking slightly, her arms wrapped around herself. Her hand shot out and grabbed my wrist with surprising strength, her nails digging in. "She's still coming. Bridget told me through the smoke. The debt isn't paid. The blood of the guilty must flow until the scales balance. Six families. Six deaths. She counted them on her fingers in the smoke."

Her eyes rolled back slightly, and she began to recite in a singsong voice that made my skin crawl: "Whitman, Mills, Hughes, Morton, Blackwood, Lawson, Randolph. Seven who bore witness. Seven who must fall."

Judith blinked, seeming to come back to herself. Jack and I stood frozen, neither of us sure what to say next.

A nurse appeared in the doorway. "She needs to rest now. It's going to take a while for those drugs to get out of her system."

In the parking lot, rain still fell in sheets that turned the world beyond the hospital into an impressionist painting—all blurred edges and uncertain shapes. Jack was already on his phone checking messages, the screen's blue glow making his face look carved from stone.

"She's traumatized," I said. "Half of what she said might be hallucination from the fear and whatever was in that smoke."

"Maybe," Jack said. "But she named seven families. Whitman's dead. Mills is dead. She was attacked. Morton went to his sister's. Blackwood we have in custody as a witness. That leaves—"

"Randolph, who's already dead. And Lawson." I looked at him. "Your family."

"Mom checked in earlier today," Jack said, already starting the engine. "I'll try calling them, but it's nine o'clock. They usually have their phones turned off this late."

Jack tried calling both of his parents, but true to form, both of their phones went straight to voicemail. "I can call the sheriff's office on Martha's Vineyard and ask them to do a welfare check."

Once he talked to the lieutenant in charge of night shift and the situation was explained, the lieutenant assured him they'd send someone out right away and he'd get back with Jack as soon as they had information.

"We still need to figure out what parts of Judith's testimony was hallucination and what part was reality," I said when he hung up.

The pieces were there, scattered like broken glass, but every time I tried to put them together, they shifted into a different pattern. Someone strong enough to overpower victims but small in stature. Someone who knew the family histories. Someone with access to Evangeline's stolen herbs. Someone who could stage elaborate scenes without being noticed.

The killer was close. Had been close all along. But in the storm-soaked darkness of King George County, shadows and truth had become indistinguishable.

And somewhere out there, someone was preparing for the next act of their twisted justice.

CHAPTER TWENTY-TWO

THE STORM HAD TURNED OUR DRIVEWAY INTO A RIVER by the time we made it home, water cascading down the slope toward the cliff edge where it disappeared into darkness. Jack killed the engine under the shelter of the garage, and we sat for a moment in the sudden quiet, just the sound of rain drumming on the roof and our own breathing.

"You okay?" he asked, his hand finding mine in the dark.

"Just thinking about Judith," I said. "All that terror, and she fought back. Drove her knee into the attacker's ribs and escaped."

"Strong woman," Jack agreed. "And lucky. If she hadn't known those woods..."

I sighed as I climbed out of the Tahoe. "I feel like I'm starting to mold with all this rain. Maybe we could ask Evangeline and Leena to do some kind of rain voodoo and get it to stop."

"I'd be good with never seeing either of them again," Jack said, ushering me toward the mudroom door. "All this witch stuff is freaky. We should go to church on Sunday."

"You afraid the witchy stuff rubbed off?" I asked, laughing.

"You can never be too careful in our line of work."

We made our way through the mudroom, peeling off soaked jackets and leaving wet shoes on the mat. The house felt empty at first—that particular quiet that usually meant we had it to ourselves. But as we headed toward the kitchen, I saw light spilling from Jack's office doorway.

"Doug's back," I said, unable to keep the smile out of my voice.

Sure enough, we found him in Jack's office, surrounded by what looked like the contents of our entire pantry. Empty bags of chips, three soda cans, a plate that had clearly held multiple sandwiches, and a mixing bowl with brownie batter remnants. Oscar was passed out at his feet, occasionally twitching in dreams that probably involved chasing squirrels.

Multiple monitors glowed with data, and I could hear Margot's familiar synthetic voice as we approached.

"—statistical analysis suggests a sixty-seven percent probability of precipitation continuing for the next four hours," she was saying.

"Nobody asked about the weather, Margot," Doug replied, spinning in his chair when we entered.

"I was merely providing contextual information that might affect your evening plans," Margot said with what sounded suspiciously like sniffiness. "Good evening, Jack and Jaye. You both appear to be experiencing elevated stress levels based on your vocal patterns and movement signatures."

"Hello, Margot," I said, unable to suppress a smile. "Keeping Doug company?"

"Someone has to ensure he maintains basic nutritional requirements," she replied. "He has consumed nothing but refined carbohydrates and caffeine for the past six hours."

Doug grabbed another handful of pretzels from the bag beside him. "What's up? Finals week was brutal, but I survived."

"How'd you do?" I asked, moving some of his debris to make room on the couch.

"Advanced Cryptography was a breeze," he said, trying to sound casual but unable to hide his pride. "Professor said my approach to the Byzantine Generals Problem was unconventional but brilliant. Turned in my master's thesis on quantum encryption this morning. I hate writing papers. Zeros and ones are so much more reliable than the English language."

"Great job, Doug," Jack said, though his eyes were already scanning the multiple monitors displaying what looked like genealogical databases and courthouse records.

"I'm pretty pumped," he said. "I've had about five hours of sleep all week, so I'm working off adrenaline. Missed you guys, but I needed some peace and quiet to study. Y'all have too much company over here and Mom is hardly ever home. I think I cramped her style though with her new boyfriend. She kept asking when I was going back to your house."

I tried to keep my face blank so my anger wouldn't show, but I glanced at Jack and saw the corners of his mouth tighten subtly. Doug's mom had never known what to do with a kid as special and unique as he was, and she'd been almost relieved when he'd gotten busted by the FBI for hacking into databases he had no business being in. Doug's Uncle Ben, who also happened to be Jack's best friend, had gotten the kid back on the straight and narrow. And Doug had come to live with us. I wouldn't trade it for anything.

"Speaking of company, did you know Sheldon's living in the room across from mine? I almost karate chopped him when I came in. He was just standing in the doorway like a weirdo. I think he ate all your food so I put in a grocery order."

"He's still upstairs now?" I asked, brows raised.

"Yep," Doug said. "He's looking paler that usual. I told him he looked like he'd seen a ghost, but he just blinked at me like he does and closed his bedroom door."

Jack pointed at the screens and said, "Do I want to know what you're doing?"

"Monitoring your investigation," Doug said, his expression shifting from casual to focused. "Margot's been helping me analyze data patterns. Someone's been accessing sealed Colonial records through the courthouse system for months."

"The access patterns are quite sophisticated," Margot interjected. "Whoever is conducting these searches demonstrates advanced knowledge of database architecture and historical record-keeping."

Jack's expression darkened. "Doug, please tell me you're not hacking into restricted courthouse systems."

"I'm not hacking," Doug said quickly. "I'm analyzing metadata patterns from legitimate access logs. Big difference."

"The difference being what, exactly?" Jack asked.

"Hacking implies unauthorized intrusion. I'm simply observing digital footprints that are technically visible to anyone with appropriate analytical software," Doug said.

"Your federal consulting agreement covers this?" I asked.

"Cybersecurity threat assessment," Doug confirmed. "Which this definitely qualifies as." His phone buzzed before Jack could respond. "Oh, and speaking of threats—Blackwood's lawyer just got him released. Traffic cameras confirmed his alibi."

Jack's jaw tightened. "Well, we knew that was coming."

"I need coffee," I said, heading for the little bar area. "Anyone else?"

"Always," Jack said. "But I'll make it. I don't want to be poisoned tonight."

"Can you toss me another soda from the fridge?" Doug asked. "I gotta keep the neurons snapping."

While Jack brewed coffee, he explained our timeline while Doug's fingers never stopped moving across his keyboards. Jack handed me a cup and I saw it was tea instead of coffee. I narrowed my eyes at the deception, but decided to let it pass. This time. I'd needed the coffee. I was falling asleep standing up.

"Let's walk through what we know," Jack said, settling into his chair with his coffee. "Three murders, one attempted. All connected to families from the 1725 witch trials."

"But not random descendants," I said, curling up on the couch with my tea. "Thomas Whitman was actively researching the land fraud. Victoria Mills was asking questions about her family's involvement. Margaret Randolph knew about Thomas's work and tried to warn him off."

"And Judith Hughes received those letters, was specifically targeted," Jack added.

Doug pulled up crime-scene photos on his largest monitor. "The staging is sophisticated. Whoever's doing this understands not just the history, but the symbolism. The positioning of Thomas's body, the carved messages, the books arranged around Margaret—it's theatrical."

"Someone who thinks in scenes," I said. "Someone who wants to tell a story."

"Or send a message," Jack said. "Three hundred years of injustice, and they're making sure everyone understands the connection."

Doug's fingers flew across the keyboard. "I've been analyzing the access logs for the courthouse database with Margot's help. Someone's been digging into these family records for six months."

"The search patterns indicate obsessive behavior," Margot added. "Always during off-hours, always from different terminals, but with consistent methodology and increasing frequency over time."

"Inside access?" Jack asked.

"Definitely," Doug said. "The queries were too specific, too sophisticated for a casual user."

"I have identified forty-seven individuals with both the technical knowledge and system access to conduct such searches," Margot said. "However, the behavioral patterns suggest someone with deep personal investment in the outcomes."

"Six months," I said. "That's a lot of planning."

"That's obsession," Jack corrected. "Someone who's been thinking about this for a long time."

Doug switched screens, showing a map of King George County with various locations marked. "Here's what bothers me about the crime scenes. Each one was chosen for maximum symbolic impact, but they're also practical. The cemetery—easy access after hours, secluded. The mill—isolated, historically significant. Dr. Mills dumped at the boat launch —convenient disposal, but also where she'd be found quickly."

"Our killer wants the bodies discovered," I said. "This isn't about hiding the crimes, it's about displaying them."

"But they're careful about evidence," Jack pointed out. "No fingerprints, no DNA until Victoria fought back, no witnesses."

"Professional," Doug said. "Someone who understands crime-scene processing."

That made me pause. "The herbs stolen from

Evangeline's greenhouse. Someone who knew exactly what they were taking and what it could be used for."

"Medical knowledge," Jack agreed. "Someone who understands how plant toxins work."

"Or just someone who did their research," I said. "It's not exactly classified information. You can find anything online these days."

Doug was pulling up incident reports now. "Let me check something." His fingers flew across the keyboard. "The greenhouse break-in three weeks ago—Chen was the responding officer." He paused, frowning at the screen. "But it says CSI was requested for processing."

Jack leaned forward. "Who processed it?"

"Doesn't say in the report. Just that evidence was collected." Doug looked up. "But Chen would remember."

Jack was already reaching for his phone. "Let me call her." He dialed and put it on speaker. "Chen? It's Jack. I've got you on speaker with Jaye and Doug."

"Sheriff." Chen's voice filled the office. "What can I do for you?"

"That greenhouse break-in three weeks ago at Evangeline Toscano's place—you responded to that, right?"

"Yeah, I remember. Weird one. Someone broke in but only took herbs and some dirt. Why?"

"We think those herbs might be connected to our current cases. Do you remember if CSI came out?"

"Oh sure, they processed it. Actually, Potts showed up pretty quick. I remember because she mentioned she'd been in the area finishing up another scene."

Jack and I exchanged glances. "Did she find anything?" Jack asked.

"Some partial footprints, but she said they were too degraded to be useful. No fingerprints either. She was thorough though—spent over an hour processing everything. Even took samples of the remaining herbs for comparison. Said she wanted to catalog exactly what was taken."

"That's helpful, Chen. Thanks."

"No problem, Sheriff."

Jack ended the call and tossed his phone on Doug's desk. "Chen said Potts processed the greenhouse scene. Thorough as always—spent over an hour cataloging everything, even took samples of what wasn't stolen."

"Professional," I said, settling back on the couch with my tea.

Jack nodded, then looked at Doug's screens. "The courthouse database access you found—six months of research into these families. That takes dedication."

"And knowledge," Doug said. "Margot's been helping me map the search patterns."

"The individual demonstrates sophisticated understanding of both historical research methodology and database architecture," Margot said. "They also show emotional investment patterns consistent with personal vendetta rather than academic inquiry."

"How can you tell?" I asked.

"The timing and frequency of searches correlate with emotional triggers," she explained. "Increased activity following news reports about local history, Colonial celebrations, and genealogical discoveries. This is not dispassionate research."

Doug pulled up more data. "The timeline bothers me too. Greenhouse break-in three weeks ago, voice-modulation software purchased three months ago, but database searches going back six months."

"Classic escalation pattern," Margot observed. "Planning phase, tool acquisition, action implementation. Very methodical."

"Someone with research experience," I said. "Academic background, maybe. Legal training."

"Or law enforcement," Jack added. "We're trained to dig through records, follow paper trails."

"I have been analyzing the voice modulation software purchase," Margot said. "High-end equipment, professional grade. Not consumer level."

Doug's fingers flew across the keyboard. "She's right—this stuff is expensive. Purchased locally with a credit card, King George County billing address."

"That narrows it significantly," Margot said. "Cross-referencing with the other parameters you've identified."

Jack leaned forward. "What parameters?"

"Doug has been feeding me data points throughout the investigation," Margot said. "Professional knowledge of crime-scene processing, access to courthouse databases, local residence, recent electronics purchases, and now genealogical connections to the 1725 events."

"Margot," Doug said suddenly, "run a full probability analysis. All county residents and employees, weighted for the factors we discussed."

"Processing," Margot said. "This may take a moment."

We sat in tense silence as data cascaded across the screens. I could almost hear Margot's electronic brain churning through thousands of variables.

"Analysis complete," she announced. "Results are...unexpected."

"Show us the top ten," Jack said.

The screen filled with names, photos, and probability percentages. My blood ran cold when I saw number three on the list.

Deputy Potts, Beverly A. - 73% probability match.

"That can't be right," I said automatically. "Check it again."

"My calculations are accurate," Margot said, and there was something almost apologetic in her synthetic tone. "Deputy Potts meets nearly all specified criteria."

Doug stared at the screen. "Her profile—Massachusetts background, forensic training, database access, recent local purchases including electronics."

"She has also been present at every crime scene this week," Margot added. "Often volunteering for assignments outside her scheduled duties."

Jack had gone very still. "Show me those duty rosters."

More data appeared on-screen. "Tuesday morning cemetery scene—Lieutenant Daniels assigned her standard CSI team, but Potts requested to be added even though she wasn't scheduled. Mills's scene at the boat launch—again, Potts volunteered for the call when she was supposed to be off duty. Margaret's scene at the mill—Potts asked Daniels if she could work overtime to help process the scene."

"She wanted to be there," Jack said quietly.

"At every single scene," Margot confirmed.

"According to department records, Deputy Potts has never before requested additional assignments or overtime for major crime scenes. This behavior pattern began only this week."

"She's been controlling the evidence from the start," I said, the implications making my stomach turn.

I set down my tea, my hands trembling slightly. "Margot, what can you tell us about her background? Family history?"

"Beverly Anne Potts, born Boston, Massachusetts, 1989," Margot recited. "Genealogical records trace back to Nathaniel Potter, executed for smuggling in Boston, 1748. Colonial court records show he was hanged for operating a large-scale smuggling operation during King George's War."

"Potter," I said, the name registering. "That's close to Potts."

"The connection becomes clear through the asset seizure records," Margot continued. "When Colonial authorities moved to confiscate Nathaniel Potter's smuggling profits, the court proceedings required him to document how he'd acquired his wealth. In his testimony, he revealed his true identity as Jedediah Ashworth. He explained that he'd fled Virginia in 1725 with his daughter after his wife Bridget was wrongly executed for witchcraft. He'd first changed their names to Ashford, then later to Potter when he began his smuggling operations."

"So the family name was Potter," Jack said. "But how does that connect to Potts?"

"Cross-referencing birth records," Margot said. "Nathaniel's daughter Mary Potter had a child out of wedlock in 1749, shortly after her father's execution. She changed her surname to Potts and claimed to be a widow to avoid social stigma. The genealogical trail from Mary Potts to Beverly Potts is direct and documented."

"She preserved the family story," I said quietly. "Passed it down through the generations along with the modified name."

"Statistical probability that this is coincidence: less than 0.3 percent," Margot concluded. "Deputy Potts is almost certainly a direct descendant of Bridget Ashworth."

The room fell silent except for the storm outside and the quiet hum of electronic equipment. We stared at the screens showing Potts's photo and genealogy, the weight of three centuries settling over us like a shroud.

"She's been planning this since she moved here," I said quietly. "However long that's been."

"Not just since she moved here," Margot corrected. "Based on the psychological profile and historical research patterns, she has been planning this her entire life. The Ashworth family story was likely passed down through generations, waiting for someone with the skills and opportunity to seek justice."

Doug was already pulling up more data, his fingers flying across the keyboard. "If Potts processed the greenhouse scene, she knew exactly what herbs were taken. Belladonna, mandrake—the same compounds that could cause cardiac arrest."

I remembered Thomas Whitman's mysterious heart failure. "She would have known exactly what they could be used for."

Jack moved to the murder board, studying our timeline with clinical precision. "She was at every scene, processed every piece of evidence. The DNA under Victoria's fingernails—that came back inconclusive."

"No match in the system," I said slowly. "But if Potts isn't in any database..."

"She wouldn't show up," Jack finished. "The DNA could be hers and we'd never know it."

Doug pulled up more purchase records on his screen. ""I found purchases of electronic components that could be assembled into voice modulation equipment," he said. "Bought separately over several months from different online retailers, paid with prepaid cards. Someone was being very careful.

"She's been accessing courthouse records, historical databases, even case files," Doug continued. "All legitimate for a CSI tech, but the pattern goes back months. She was researching these families before Thomas Whitman was killed."

Jack's expression didn't change, but I caught the slight tightening around his eyes. "The precision in Margaret's mutilation. Someone who's processed enough crime scenes to know anatomy, how to use a blade."

"She knew about the symbols at the cemetery," I added. "Pointed out the stone circle around Rachel Mills's grave. Said someone must have placed it after our initial processing."

"But she had access to place it herself," Jack said.

Jack was quiet for a moment. "Doug, I need you to run a full background check on Potts. Current address, vehicle information, duty schedule. But keep it quiet—I don't want this flagged in the system yet."

"On it," Doug said, his fingers flying across the keyboard.

Jack pulled out his phone. "Cole? It's Jack. I need you and Martinez mobile now. We've identified our suspect—it's Potts." He paused, listening to Cole's response. "She's Bridget Ashworth's descendant and she's been playing us from the beginning. Don't use radio. She may be monitoring. Doug will send coordinates once we have them."

He hung up and turned back to Doug. "What's her current status?"

Doug pulled up the duty roster. "CSI works regular eight-to-five unless called to scenes. She clocked out at five thirty today, about two hours ago."

"Vehicle?"

"Drives a personal sedan to work. 2019 Honda Civic, Virginia plates." Doug pulled up more information. "But she also has access to department vehicles when needed for scene processing."

Jack's expression darkened. "Check if she signed out a patrol unit today."

Doug's fingers flew across the keyboard. "She didn't sign out anything officially, but..." He pulled up another screen. "The fleet GPS shows one of our unmarked units moved from the impound lot twenty minutes ago. Unit 47."

"Can you track it?" Jack asked, his voice tight.

"Already on it." Doug's hands moved with lightning precision across multiple keyboards. "Margot, I need you to access the vehicle's dash cam footage. Pull everything from the last two hours."

"Accessing vehicle recorder," Margot replied. "Downloading dash cam files now."

The seconds stretched like hours. I could feel Jack's tension radiating across the room, a coiled energy that spoke of a predator sensing danger to his pack. Outside, the storm continued its relentless assault on the windows, each lightning flash illuminating the gravity etched on our faces.

"Got the files," Doug announced, fingers flying across the keyboard. "Fast-forwarding through the footage now...here, about forty minutes ago. She's making a traffic stop."

A window opened on the largest monitor, showing the dash cam's forward view. Rain streaked across the windshield, and through the downpour we could see another vehicle pulled over on the shoulder ahead. The time stamp showed the footage was from earlier that evening.

"She's approaching the vehicle," I said, watching the empty view as whoever was driving the patrol car —presumably Potts—got out to make contact.

Jack leaned forward, every muscle in his body coiled tight. "Doug, can you get the license plate on that car?"

"Working on it." Doug enhanced the image, zooming in through the rain and darkness. The luxury SUV sat with its hazard lights blinking, brake lights bright red in the storm. "Partial plate visible... running it now..."

The color drained from Jack's face before Doug even finished typing.

"That's my parents' Escalade."

CHAPTER TWENTY-THREE

"Keep it running," Jack said, his voice stripped of all emotion—the kind of flat, deadly calm that made seasoned criminals confess just to avoid whatever was building behind his eyes.

On the monitor, the dash cam footage continued. Jack's parents' Escalade sat motionless in the rain, hazard lights pulsing against the storm-darkened asphalt. The time stamp showed 7:23 p.m. Less than two hours ago, they'd been driving home from what they'd thought was a safe haven.

Doug's fingers trembled slightly as he advanced the footage. "Here...she's approaching the driver's side."

We watched the empty view as Potts moved toward the luxury SUV, invisible to the forward-facing camera. The Escalade's driver's window rolled down with mechanical precision. Through the rain-distorted footage, we could see movement inside—Jack's father leaning toward the window, probably reaching for his wallet like any law-abiding citizen during a routine traffic stop.

Then everything went to hell.

A muzzle flash erupted from beside the patrol car. The brief, brilliant flare was followed by the Escalade rocking slightly on its suspension. From this angle, we couldn't see inside, couldn't tell what damage had been done or who might have been hit.

"No," Doug breathed, his face pale.

Jack went absolutely still. Years of SWAT training had taught him to compartmentalize, to push personal feelings into a locked box so his tactical mind could function. I watched him make that shift in real time—from son to law enforcement officer.

"Can't determine the target from this angle," he said, his voice clinical. "Need to see movement, assess casualties."

The driver's door opened. Jack's father emerged with careful movements—hands visible, no sudden motions, the practiced compliance of a man who understood exactly what kind of danger he was in.

"Dad's mobile, responsive," Jack observed with professional detachment. "Following commands. Means the shooter's got him under control."

Richard Lawson moved toward the rear of the

Escalade, maintaining visibility of his hands. The rain continued to pour, turning the highway into a river. Potts had chosen her location well—isolated, dark, with perfect sight lines and no witnesses.

The rear door opened, and Richard began to climb inside. That's when Potts struck—a swift blow from behind. We couldn't see the weapon from the dash cam angle, only Richard's body jerking forward before he collapsed into the back seat.

My stomach clenched. Even after all my years in medicine and forensics, watching someone I cared about being brutalized made bile rise in my throat.

"Textbook takedown," Jack said, maintaining his clinical tone. "Nonlethal force, immediate compliance. She's maintaining two hostages."

The Escalade rocked as Potts secured her prisoner. Then she walked directly toward the dash cam, moving with purpose through the rain. Her dark hair was plastered to her skull, water streaming down her face. But it was her expression that made my blood run cold. Even through the rain and grainy footage, her smile was clearly visible—wide and bright and absolutely insane. The smile of someone who'd been planning this moment for a very long time.

She looked directly into the camera with focused intensity. Her lips moved, forming words we couldn't hear over the storm, but the malicious joy in her expression was unmistakable. She was talking to

Jack, knowing he would see this, knowing it would tear him apart.

"She knows," Doug said, voice tight with realization. "She knows we're watching. She wants us to see."

Potts raised her service weapon with deliberate slowness, pointing it directly at the camera lens. For a heartbeat, she held that pose—gun aimed, that terrifying smile never wavering, rain streaming down her face like tears of joy.

Then she pulled the trigger.

The screen exploded into static, white noise filling Jack's office like electronic screaming. Doug frantically worked the controls, but the dash cam was dead, the connection severed by a well-placed bullet.

"That's it," Doug said quietly. "The feed ends there."

Jack stood frozen, staring at the wall of static. The silence stretched between us like a taut wire, broken only by the storm outside and the hum of equipment.

When he finally spoke, his voice was barely audible. "She shot into the car first. Before she took Dad. Can't tell what the target was from this angle."

My chest tightened, but I kept my voice steady. "Your father got out under his own power. That's something."

Jack was already reaching for his phone. "Doug, send Cole and Martinez the GPS coordinates for Unit 47. They need to locate that patrol car."

Doug's fingers flew across the keyboard. "Sending now. Last ping shows it stationary at mile marker 47 on Route 218."

Jack put the call on speaker. "Cole, coordinates coming to you now. I need you and Martinez to locate Unit 47 immediately."

"Copy that, Sheriff. En route now." Cole's voice was crisp, professional. "What are we looking for?"

"Abandoned patrol car. Potts used it to take my parents, then ditched it for their vehicle. Process it as a crime scene but don't touch anything until Daniels gets there."

"Understood. We'll call as soon as we locate it."

Jack ended the call and looked at Doug. "I need continuous monitoring on all emergency frequencies. If she tries to communicate, I want to know immediately. And Doug—keep this off the main channels. Potts is one of ours. She could be monitoring our systems."

The wait was excruciating. I watched Jack pace his office with controlled energy, every muscle coiled tight. Twenty minutes felt like hours before his phone finally rang.

"Cole, report."

"Found the patrol car at mile marker 47, exactly

where Doug's GPS showed. Vehicle's abandoned, keys still in the ignition. No sign of Potts or your parents."

"Evidence?"

"Clean scene on the patrol car itself. But we found a cell phone on the front seat, deliberately placed. Looks like she wanted us to find it."

Jack's expression remained unchanged. "Don't touch it. Daniels will process it. Any sign of the Escalade?"

"Negative. No trace."

"Copy that. Return here immediately. We're establishing a command post."

Jack ended the call and immediately dialed another number. "Daniels? I need you at my location. Just you and one person you trust completely—pick someone who can keep their mouth shut. We've got two active crime scenes and a kidnapping in progress, but the suspect is one of ours. Potts. We need to keep this tight."

The house felt different with a command post taking shape in Jack's office. What had been our sanctuary was now ground zero for a manhunt, with laptops, phones, and evidence boxes transforming the space into something that belonged more in a precinct than a home.

Cole and Martinez arrived within minutes of each other, both soaked from the storm that continued to rage outside. Derby came next, his equipment bags slung over both shoulders, glasses immediately fogging from the temperature change. Daniels arrived next, having stopped to collect evidence from the abandoned patrol car. She'd brought one of her CSI techs with her —the guy introduced himself as Pete Rogers—and Daniels said he was someone she trusted completely.

Plank, Chen, Riley, and Cheek rounded out the group. We'd all been in tough situations together before, and I knew more than anything that Jack could rely on them if things went bad.

"The phone Potts left was wiped clean," Daniels said, setting an evidence bag on Jack's desk. "But she wanted us to find it. Staged it like a theater production. I have no idea why she left it. There were no other personal effects in the vehicle. It's been impounded. No sign of the Escalade."

Jack stood at the digital murder board, every victim's photo connected by a red line to locations, times, evidence. His parents' photos were now at the center, two question marks beneath them indicating their unknown status.

"Let's walk through this," Jack said, his voice

carrying that dangerous calm that meant he was thinking ten steps ahead. "Four days, three murders, one attempted murder, and now a kidnapping. The logistics alone are staggering."

He moved to the timeline they'd constructed, his finger starting at Monday evening. "Five thirty p.m.—Victoria Mills flees her medical practice. The woman at the insurance office next door, Dolores Hutchins, said Mills was loading her car like the devil himself was chasing her. Hands shaking so bad she dropped her keys twice."

"So someone got to her at work," Martinez said. "Threatened her. That kind of panic doesn't come from nowhere."

Jack nodded. "She races home, probably thinking she's got enough time to grab her things and run." Jack's expression darkened. "She meets her attacker in the garage on her way out. That's where we found the blood—still tacky on the concrete when CSI processed it."

"Attacker takes her and her Mercedes," Cole continued, building the narrative. "Meanwhile, less than two hours later across town, Thomas Whitman shows up at Judith Hughes's apartment for what he thinks is just dinner and a good time."

I felt the pieces clicking together as I studied the timeline. "Judith cooks—chicken and rice, opens a bottle of wine. They're talking, eating, and neither one realizes they're being poisoned. Belladonna—deadly nightshade. One of the herbs stolen from Evangeline's greenhouse." I traced my finger along the timeline. "At low doses, it causes hallucinations, confusion, nightmares—exactly what Judith described. She's been getting microdoses for weeks through those letters. The herb smell she mentioned? That's the delivery method. Just handling the parchment, inhaling the scent—it builds up in her system."

"Both get sick," Jack said. "Thomas leaves before nine, probably thinking it's food poisoning. Judith goes to bed. But the poison keeps working."

"Thomas is dying," I said quietly. "The belladonna weakens his heart. All he'd need is a sudden shock or surprise to trigger cardiac arrest. And then he's dead."

"Maybe she was hoping to kidnap him," Jack said. "But Thomas dies and the drugs wear off of Victoria too soon." Jack tapped his finger against his thigh. "Based on Whitman's estimated time of death around 3 a.m. we can assume he was alive in the trunk when the Mercedes pulled into the gas station at two forty-five. We have to assume she had another plan to kill him—she's got her service weapon—but luck gave her a hand and his heart gave out first."

"We can assume Potts used the gas station as a lookout to make sure the cemetery was clear," I said.

"Al Contreras didn't lock up like he was supposed to. Which she knew because she was at the gas station waiting for him to come by for his rounds."

"So she pulls into the cemetery and gets as close as she can to the grave. Dead bodies are heavy, but she gets him out of the trunk, strips him naked, and positioned the boards and stones. The lack of violence explains why his clothes were so clean."

"And somewhere else Victoria is still alive and waiting for her turn," I said. "Where would she keep her victims hidden?"

"She rents a house on James Madison," Doug said. "Looks like a two-bed, one bath."

"We'll get a couple of units to check it out," Martinez said, already on his phone.

"You won't find anything there," Jack said. "Someone like Potts thinks she's smarter than everyone else. She lives a quiet life, goes to work, does her job, all the while she's telling herself she's better than the rest of us, too smart to get caught, laughing every time she's working a crime scene. She'll have another location for her dirty work. She'd want to keep it compartmentalized from her life as a cop."

"We have a lot of unanswered questions," I said.

"The logistics of this are staggering," Jack said, studying the board. "One person couldn't possibly manage all this—threatening Victoria at her office, attacking her at home, keeping her captive, ensuring Thomas and Judith got poisoned at dinner, waiting for Thomas to die, then moving and staging his body with those heavy stones.

"Then Wednesday night," Cole continued. "Same pattern. Judith's attacked at her house—drugged with hallucinogens, terrorized. But she escapes into the woods."

Jack nodded and said, "All the while, Margaret Randolph is being lured to the mill. She's drugged, has her tongue cut out, drowns in her own blood. Her body is elaborately staged with all her books."

The room fell silent as everyone stared at the timeline.

"The Hughes plantation and Hawthorne Mill are on opposite sides of the county. Even if Judith's attack started early in the evening and Margaret was killed later, the timing is too tight."

"She had help," Jack said quietly. "Someone else who knows the history, has access to the drugs, can move freely without raising suspicion."

Doug's fingers were already flying across his keyboard. "Margot, run a cross-reference. Anyone connected to this case who has the means, motive, and opportunity to assist."

"Processing." Margot's voice filled the room. "I can help cross-reference databases," she offered.

"Though genealogical research of this depth will take time."

Doug's fingers flew across the keyboard. "I've been digging into this for the last hour. Let me pull up what I found." He opened multiple windows. "The Potter/Potts line is documented in Massachusetts records, but there's another branch I almost missed."

On the screen, a family tree began to populate. Bridget and Jedediah Ashworth, their daughter Mary who became Mary Potter, then Mary Potts. But there was another line—a son, born to Jedediah's second wife.

"Okay, this is weird," Doug said, hunched over his keyboard. "There's another kid. Samuel Ashworth Potter, born 1747—right before Jedediah got hanged for smuggling." His voice cracked slightly on "hanged," reminding me he was still just sixteen despite his genius-level intellect. "Jedediah remarried some woman named Catherine Bowman after he fled Virginia."

"What happened to him?" Jack's question came out sharp, focused.

Doug's fingers flew across the keyboard with the manic energy of a teenager who'd consumed too much caffeine. "Hold on, hold on...okay, it looks like Catherine Bowman remarried about a year after Jedediah was hanged. This is where things get a little hazy. Catherine Potter married a guy, name George Apthorp, who was a very well-to-do merchant in Boston at the time. In the 1755 census, George and Catherine Apthorp are listed, along with their three children—Samuel, George, and Charles Apthorp.

"It looks like Samuel joined the revolution and ditched the Apthorp name at some point, becoming Samuel Ashworth. George Apthorp was a loyalist, so it sounds like there were some daddy issues. I'm sure that made holidays exciting."

"Mary would have been an adult when Samuel was born," I said, working through the timeline. "Twenty-two when her father was executed. She might not have known she had a half brother."

"Track Samuel Ashworth's line," Jack ordered.

The genealogical software populated the screen with births, deaths, marriages—centuries of family history cascading like digital rain. Doug made little sounds of discovery, the kind of excited noises he usually reserved for breaking encryption codes.

"Whoa," Doug said, then immediately glanced at Jack. "Look at this. The Ashworth line stayed in Massachusetts forever, then split in the 1920s, meandering south for the next couple of generations." He pulled up another screen with the dramatic flair only a teenager could manage. "Until someone eventually came here. To King George County. In 1983."

"Who?" Jack's single word carried the weight of command.

Doug's fingers danced across the keyboard. "Someone named Evelyn Ashworth bought property on Marsh Creek Road." More typing, more screens. "But get this—two years later she marries this guy Joseph Toscano. He was navy, stationed at Dahlgren Naval Base.

"Marriage lasted less than a year," Doug continued. "But after the divorce, she starts going by Evangeline Toscano."

The silence that followed was absolute. I could hear my own heartbeat, the hum of Doug's computers, the storm still raging outside.

"Forty years," I said, the words barely a whisper. "She told us she'd lived here forty years. She's been here all along."

"Right under our noses," Cole said. "She knows how to use the plants—concoct her own hallucinogenic brew."

"Tag team," Martinez said. "One provides the methods, the other has the access."

Daniels's low growl made us all turn to her. "The greenhouse break-in. Three weeks ago. Potts processed that scene by herself. She's been at every scene. Her hands have been all over the evidence. We'll be lucky if we've got enough evidence to get a conviction on anyone by the time this is finished."

"Then we'll need to catch them red-handed," Jack said.

Jack hadn't moved, but I could feel the fury radiating off him in waves. When he finally spoke, his voice was soft, controlled, lethal. "Sheldon. She used him as a test subject."

"The séance that wasn't a séance," I said, remembering Sheldon's confused account. "The floating feeling, the memory gaps. She was dosing him, seeing how much it took to incapacitate someone without killing them."

"Are we sure he's still upstairs?" Jack asked Doug.

"Unless someone climbed the balcony and pulled him from the second story," Doug said, offhand.

I looked at Jack and then ran upstairs, Jack close behind me. When I got to the guest room Sheldon was staying in I knocked on the door, a little more frantic than I should have. And when Sheldon opened the door, eyes wide behind his lenses, and wearing a white undershirt and boxers, I almost hugged him in relief.

"Is it time for dinner?" he asked. "Doug said he was going to order groceries, but that was hours ago. What time is it? I've been playing *Elden Ring*. What day is it?"

"It's Thursday," I said. "We were just checking to make sure you're okay."

"I'm good," he said. "I broke up with Leena. She's taking it okay I think. She didn't text me back."

"That's wise," Jack said. "You'll meet the right girl one day. We're glad to have you stay with us for a while, Sheldon. Do me a favor and let one of us know if you need to go somewhere. Just in case."

"In case what?" he asked.

"In case Leena didn't take the breakup as well as you think," he said. "Women get crazy sometimes. You know how it is."

"True," he said, shaking his head. "When my Aunt Pam's husband left her she threw a hatchet at his head. Took off part of his ear."

"There you go," Jack said. "Enjoy your game."

We left Sheldon to his game and went back downstairs to the team who'd made themselves at home in the office.

"All good?" Cole asked.

"He's locked in," Jack said. "Pull up everything you can find on Evangeline Toscano's property."

"Margot has already started gathering the data," Doug said. "The Marsh Creek property's huge. About a thousand acres in all. A majority of it is wetlands. That's probably how she was able to buy it as a private sale. A developer couldn't do much with it." He pulled up the survey and a topographical map. "That's her home, and then there are a few outbuildings—greenhouse, shed, dock, and a boathouse. Those are the most identifiable."

"We had to park a good ways from the house," I said. "And then we had to walk across the bridge. Her house is built on stilts in the marshland. As far as I could see that bridge was the only way on her property. She saw us coming."

Doug showed a larger expanse of the map. "This is the east side of the property."

More satellite imagery filled the screens. The marshy property stretched for acres along the river, mostly wetlands and forest. But there were hints of other structures.

"What's that?" Daniels pointed to a clearing about a quarter mile from the main cabin.

Doug zoomed in. "Looks like an old structure. Maybe one that was torn down."

"Can Margot overlay a historical survey of that area?" Jack asked.

"I can do anything for you, sugar," Margot purred, making the team chuckle.

Margot hmmed absently, and not for the first time I shuddered at the thought of what the future looked like. Not nearly enough people had seen *The Terminator*.

She overlaid the historical survey on the map that was already on the screen. "This looks to be the original homestead on the property, but as you can see the waterline has changed dramatically over the centuries. There's also what seems to be a stone circle of some sort here."

"Stone circle?" Cole asked. "Like Stonehenge?"

"On a smaller scale, yes," Margot said. "During the witch trials, those who were knowledgeable about herbs and healing often sought stone circles at certain times of the year, believing that the natural gifts the earth had to offer—like the moon rising or the summer solstice—enhanced their healing gifts."

"Maybe Bridget really was a witch," I said.

Jack's phone rang, and I saw it was dispatch. He put it on speaker.

"Lawson," he said.

"The Escalade you requested the BOLO for has been found," dispatch said. "There's an archaeological site off Cedar Creek Road where it was abandoned. Walters and Durrant are responding officers."

"Patch me through," Jack said, and waited for dispatch to connect him.

"Sheriff," Walters said. "Durrant and I are here on scene."

"What do you have?" Jack asked.

"No one inside the vehicle. There's blood on the passenger seat, just a small amount. And there's a note. It says, *Where truth was buried, justice will rise.*"

Jack's hand flexed into a fist, and he punched the top of the desk. Jack wasn't a man to ever let his emotions get the best of him, and I knew he was hanging on by a thread.

"I want every available unit out there," Jack said. "Search every dig site. Look for recently disturbed areas. Coordinate with maintenance and get spotlights set up."

"Yes, sir," Walters said and disconnected.

He paced back and forth, like a tiger trapped in a cage, his mind lost in thought.

"Jack," I said, and I waited until he looked at me. "Remember what you said. She thinks she's smarter than everyone else. Do you really think she'd make it so easy?"

"No," he said. "But I can't take the chance. Just in case we're wrong. I want the team here to suit up. We're going to pay Evangeline a visit."

"You should go in by water," Margot said. "It will take you closest to the stone circle."

"Good thinking, Margot."

Jack's phone rang again, though it was a number he didn't recognize.

"Lawson," he said, and I could hear the weariness in his voice this time.

"Sheriff Lawson?" a deep voice asked. "This is Dr. Patel at King George Hospital. We have a situation with your witness, Judith Hughes."

Jack's expression darkened. "What kind of situation?"

"She's missing. The deputy posted outside her room was found unconscious about ten minutes ago. We believe he was drugged. Ms. Hughes is gone."

The room went silent.

"Security footage?" Jack asked, though his voice suggested he already knew the answer.

"Camera malfunction started thirty minutes before she disappeared. We're checking other angles, but whoever did this knew our blind spots."

"Lock down the hospital," Jack said. "Just in case our killer hasn't been able to get her out yet. Have hospital security stand guard at the exits. I'm sending a couple of units your way."

Jack ended the call and looked around the room at his assembled team. "They're splitting our resources."

CHAPTER TWENTY-FOUR

Doug hunched over his keyboards, pulling up databases and cross-referencing information with the methodical precision of someone who lived for complex puzzles. Derby stood by the communications equipment, coordinating backup units and emergency services. The controlled energy that came with an active manhunt thrummed through the room.

Jack paced behind his desk, cell phone pressed to his ear as he coordinated resources with surrounding counties.

The office door opened and Sheldon appeared in the doorway, wearing his white T-shirt and boxers with a bathrobe hastily thrown over them. He held an empty coffee mug and paused when he saw the room full of people, his expression mildly curious behind his thick glasses.

"Sorry," he said, adjusting his glasses with his free hand. "Didn't realize you had company. I was just going to grab some coffee." His gaze swept the room, taking in the laptops, maps, and general tension. "This looks official."

"It is," Jack said simply. "Help yourself to coffee. We might be here a while."

Sheldon nodded and headed toward the small coffee station. "Did you know that the average law enforcement officer consumes approximately three times more caffeine than the general population? It's a statistical anomaly that correlates with shift work and high-stress environments."

"Fascinating," Derby said without looking up from his communications equipment.

Sheldon poured his coffee, then turned back toward the group. "Margot, are you monitoring the situation?"

"I am providing analytical support as requested," Margot replied smoothly. "Hello, Sheldon."

"Hello back," he said, a small smile crossing his face. "I don't suppose you have any opinions on the boss fight mechanics in *Elden Ring*? I've been stuck on this one encounter for three hours."

"I have access to gaming databases and strategy guides," Margot said, and there was something almost pleased in her electronic tone. "Which boss encounter is proving problematic?"

"Margaery the Fell Omen," Sheldon said, settling into one of the extra chairs. "I keep getting caught in her AOE attack pattern."

"Area of effect attacks require precise timing and positioning," Margot replied. "I could analyze your combat approach and suggest tactical adjustments."

Martinez glanced up from his notes. "The AI's giving gaming advice now. She really does have better social skills than most people."

"I heard that," Chen called from where she was checking her radio.

"Did you know," Sheldon said, "that artificial intelligence was first theorized in 1950 by Alan Turing? He created the Turing Test to determine if a machine could exhibit intelligent behavior equivalent to a human."

"Fascinating," Derby said dryly. "Can we focus on the current crisis?"

"Sorry," Sheldon said, munching his crackers. "I get excited about learning new things. Margot, do you think you could pass the Turing Test?"

"I believe the more relevant question," Margot replied, "is whether humans could pass a test designed by artificial intelligence."

Cole looked up from his equipment. "That's either really profound or really disturbing."

"Both," Doug said without looking away from his screens.

That's when Jack's phone buzzed against the desk with sharp insistence. The unknown number on the screen made every person in the room go still.

Sheldon stopped mid-chew, cracker crumbs frozen on his lips.

Jack hit speaker, and the electronically distorted voice that emerged carried the satisfaction of someone who'd been planning this moment for years.

"Sheriff Lawson. Your parents are running out of time."

Jack's expression didn't change—fifteen years of tactical operations had trained that response out of him—but I caught the slight tightening around his eyes. The only tell he allowed himself.

"Potts."

"Finally figured it out. Took you long enough." The mechanical voice held layers of mockery. *"Every crime scene, every piece of evidence, every moment you trusted me with your investigation—I was three steps ahead of you."*

"Where are they?" Jack's tone was flat, professional. The voice of a negotiator, not a son.

"Where Bridget Ashworth grew her healing herbs. Where her blood first touched Virginia soil. The stones

have been waiting three centuries for justice, Sheriff. Tonight they'll finally witness it."

I felt the pieces shift into place—Evangeline's property. The stone circle on the survey maps.

"You have until eleven thirty," Potts continued. *"One hour and fifteen minutes should be plenty of time to suit up and find your way through the marsh. Unless you get lost. That would be unfortunate for everyone involved."*

The line went dead before Jack could respond.

Sheldon sat frozen with his mouth slightly open, cracker crumbs scattered across his pajama top. "Was that the bad guy?"

"That was the bad guy," I confirmed.

"She sounded really scary," he whispered.

The room stayed silent for exactly three seconds after that. Then Jack was moving with the controlled efficiency of someone who'd done this too many times.

"Everyone back to your vehicles. Full tactical gear—night vision, waterproofs, extra ammunition." He was already pulling his own equipment from a gun safe in the corner. "Martinez, Daniels—meet at the boat launch in thirty minutes. Cole, take your team to the front entrance. Coordinate through Derby."

The room emptied quickly. I could hear vehicles starting outside, radios crackling as they coordinated equipment pickup.

"Doug, I need satellite feeds on both approach

routes." Jack's voice remained steady as he checked his sidearm. "Derby, keep comms clean. Heavy tree cover will interfere with signals."

His gaze shifted to me as I laced up waterproof boots. "You're staying here with command."

"Your parents might need immediate medical attention. Smoke inhalation, drug overdose—an ambulance will have to take the long route." I met his eyes steadily. "I might be the difference between them walking out or being carried out."

Jack went still, and I could see him weighing tactical necessity against personal risk. His eyes flicked almost imperceptibly to my stomach—acknowledging the secret we shared without words.

"You stay with me. No heroics."

"Understood."

The boat launch sat wrapped in pre-dawn darkness, the Rappahannock a black mirror reflecting pinpricks of starlight. Fish and Wildlife had delivered two jon boats as requested—aluminum hulls that would move silently through shallow water.

Martinez and Daniels were already in position, their movements efficient despite bulky gear. Both wore tactical vests over waterproof clothing, night vision goggles flipped up on their foreheads, weapons secured in waterproof cases.

"Comms check," Doug's voice crackled through our earpieces.

"Copy," Jack responded, settling into the lead boat.

Plank took the oars in our boat, pulling us through black water without a sound. Behind us, Martinez matched the rhythm perfectly. The marsh closed around us—ancient cypress trees rising from dark water, their gnarled roots creating a maze of obstacles. Spanish moss hung in gray curtains that brushed our faces as we passed.

The night vision goggles turned everything into eerie green shapes, but at least we could navigate safely. Every shadow could hide danger, every sound might signal discovery. An owl's hunting cry made everyone tense. The splash of something large in the water had weapons swinging toward the sound.

"Visual on the dock," Plank whispered.

We secured the boats in absolute silence. Jack was out first, moving with the fluid precision of someone who'd learned that speed and stealth weren't mutually exclusive. The path wound through cypress stands, over rotting planks that groaned softly under our weight.

Then we saw it.

Seven weathered stones formed a rough circle about fifteen feet across—Bridget Ashworth's boundary markers, where she'd grown her herbs three centuries ago. Ancient oaks formed a natural amphitheater around the circle, their branches blocking out most of the sky.

In the center stood a pyre of old wood and fresh kindling, rising six feet high. Jeri and Richard Lawson were tied to a central pole, their heads lolling forward with unconsciousness.

Two figures in dark robes stood at opposite points around the circle. Potts at the north, weapon ready. Evangeline at the east, holding an unlit torch like some medieval executioner.

Something felt wrong about the setup, but I couldn't identify what.

That's when someone stepped from the shadows behind us.

"Hello, Sheriff."

I spun, weapon drawn, and felt reality shift sideways.

Judith Hughes stood twenty feet away, no longer the terrified victim who'd cowered in a barn. This woman held herself with calm purpose, a knife glinting in her hand, her eyes clear and focused.

"Surprised?" Her smile held sharp edges. "I'm a much better actress than anyone gave me credit for. Did you wonder how Thomas was poisoned? He was pathetically easy to manipulate. Promise a man sex and new information about his obsession, and he'll drink anything you put in front of him." Her smile turned predatory. "We never got to the sex part. Pity. He was quite skilled at it."

Jack's weapon tracked to her, but she was positioned where any shot risked hitting his parents. Professional calculation, not emotion.

"Welcome to the reckoning," Potts called out, finally turning to face us. "You're just in time to witness justice being served."

Evangeline touched her torch to the base of the pyre. The kindling caught immediately, flames racing upward through dry wood with hungry intensity.

"Let them go," Jack said. His voice carried absolute authority—the tone that made hardened criminals surrender without a fight.

"After the truth is heard." Potts gestured toward the tree line. "Richard Blackwood owes us a debt."

Blackwood stumbled into the clearing, his expensive suit torn and muddy, his face gray with terror. He clutched a leather portfolio like a shield.

"Read," Evangeline commanded. "Let everyone hear what your family did."

With shaking hands, Blackwood opened the portfolio. His voice cracked as he began reading from aged parchment—a confession detailing how his ancestor had fabricated evidence against Bridget Ashworth, murdered witnesses, stolen land while she was still warm in her grave.

The fire climbed higher. I could see Jeri starting to stir, coughing as the first tendrils of smoke reached her.

Jack made a subtle hand signal. Martinez and Daniels began shifting position. But as they moved forward, Potts swung her weapon toward the pyre.

"One step closer and I put a bullet in that kindling. It's soaked with accelerant—one spark and they go up like Roman candles."

Jack froze. Even if he took Potts out, her death grip could pull the trigger. The fire would spread faster than he could reach them.

"Smart choice." Potts's satisfaction was evident even through the electronic distortion. "You're learning not to be as reckless as your ancestor."

The flames were already climbing toward the center of the pyre. Every second meant less chance of rescue, but any aggressive move meant watching his parents burn alive.

I could see the calculation playing out in Jack's mind—angles, distances, probabilities. His training said move, but the tactical situation said wait. Either choice could be fatal.

The fire crept higher. Smoke began to curl around Jeri and Richard, and both were starting to cough more violently.

"Time's running out, Sheriff," Judith called mockingly.

That's when I noticed Jeri's hands moving. Not random struggling—deliberate, purposeful work. She was picking at the ropes with her fingertips, using techniques I recognized from her arthritis therapy sessions.

"Keep them talking," I whispered to Jack.

He caught the movement too, his stance shifting almost imperceptibly.

"So this was all revenge?" His voice carried across the clearing. "Three centuries of planning?"

"Justice," the three women said in unison. "The truth must be known."

"Victoria Mills figured it out," Jack continued, buying precious seconds. "That's why you killed her."

"She got too close," Judith admitted. "I handled it personally."

The DNA under Victoria's fingernails would match Judith, not Potts.

Jeri's hands were free now. She was still playing unconscious, waiting for the right moment while working on Richard's bonds.

The fire was getting dangerously close—another minute, maybe two, before it reached them.

Jack made his decision.

He pulled a flashbang from his tactical vest. "Everyone down!"

The explosion was pure sensory chaos—blinding

light, deafening noise, disorienting percussion that turned coordination to confusion. In that moment of chaos, Jeri proved why she'd raised a son like Jack.

She burst into motion, using her freed hands to finish untying Richard, then practically hauled him toward the edge of the circle with strength born of desperation.

"Now!" Jack shouted.

We rushed forward. Potts reached for her weapon, but Plank was already on her, driving her into the mud with professional efficiency. She fought with vicious strength, but training and fury won.

Evangeline tried to run, but Martinez caught her in three strides, bringing her down with a textbook tackle.

Judith fought hardest—she was the one who'd beaten Victoria Mills to death, and fanaticism gave her strength. But when she pulled the knife and went for Daniels, he broke her wrist with a sharp crack that echoed across the clearing.

Jack reached his parents just as burning wood began to scatter from the collapsing pyre. I helped drag them clear, checking vitals while he cut the remaining ropes.

Smoke inhalation, some drug effects from whatever they'd been given, but their airways were clear. They'd be fine.

"Mom?" For just a moment, Jack's professional mask slipped and he sounded like a worried son.

Jeri opened her eyes, focused on his face. "Took you long enough," she said hoarsely, then started coughing again.

The three conspirators were secured, hands zip-tied behind their backs. In the dying firelight, they looked older somehow, as if their failure had aged them years in minutes.

"It's not over," Judith said through split lips. "The documents are already uploaded. Everyone will know what your ancestors did."

"Good," Jack said simply. "The truth should be known. But you're going to prison for murder."

EMTs arrived as backup swarmed the scene. The smoke from the scattered pyre was dissipating quickly in the night breeze, no longer a threat now that the fire was contained to small, manageable piles of ash and ember.

"You okay?" Jack asked, his arm settling around me as we watched his parents argue with EMTs about not needing hospitalization.

"Fine." I leaned into his solid warmth. "It's over."

As we walked back toward the boats, I couldn't shake the feeling that something had finally been laid to rest. Not just the three-hundred-year-old injustice, but the weight of secrets that had been poisoning King George County for generations.

The truth was known now. The guilty had been exposed. Both past and present.

I pressed my hand to my stomach, thinking about new beginnings and futures free from ancient vendettas.

"Pancakes?" I asked as we climbed into the boat.

Jack actually laughed—really laughed—for the first time in days. "With extra syrup."

"And bacon," I added, suddenly starving despite everything.

"Definitely bacon." He settled beside me as Cole took up the oars. "Think your stomach can handle it?"

"My stomach and I have reached an understanding," I said. "We're going to get along just fine from now on."

Dawn was breaking as Cole rowed us back toward civilization, painting the marsh in shades of gold and green that made it look like something from a fairy tale rather than a crime scene. Behind us, the last wisps of smoke curled into the morning air, carrying away three centuries of buried secrets.

The storm had passed. The darkness had lifted.

And in King George County, maybe the past could finally stay where it belonged.

THREE DAYS LATER

I found Jack on the back porch at dawn, coffee steaming in his hands, staring out at the mist rising from the Potomac. The storm had finally broken, leaving the world washed clean and gleaming in the early light.

"Couldn't sleep?" I asked, settling beside him on the swing.

"FBI called me at four. They found more journals in Judith's apartment. She'd been planning this since she was sixteen." He took a sip of coffee. "Started when she learned she was descended from both sides—the Hughes who stole the land and Bridget Ashworth who was murdered for it. The conflict tore her apart."

We rocked in comfortable silence. The investigation would go on for months—testimony, evidence review, the slow grind of justice. But the killing was done. Potts, Evangeline, and Judith were in federal custody. The truth about the seventeen victims Thomas had identified was public. And Sheldon, somehow, had emerged from the whole ordeal intact, already asking Emmy Lu if she knew any nice, normal girls who didn't conduct séances.

"Mom called," Jack said. "She and Dad are coming for Sunday dinner. She says she wants to write a book about this."

"Of course she is."

"Patricia Whitman's leaving town. Donating Thomas's research to KGU."

"Can't say I blame her."

A cardinal landed on the porch railing, its red breast bright as fresh blood. It studied us with one black eye, then flew off toward town.

The sun climbed higher, burning off the mist. Somewhere across King George County, people were waking up to ordinary lives, making coffee, reading the news about our extraordinary week. But here on our porch, in the quiet between night and day, I thought about Bridget Ashworth.

Not the legend or the ghost story, but the woman. A healer who grew herbs by the river, who helped her neighbors until they turned on her for her land. She'd died refusing to confess to crimes she hadn't committed, the weight of stones crushing the life from her while men who called themselves righteous divided up her property.

Three hundred years later, her descendants had tried to balance those scales with blood. They'd failed, becoming the very thing they'd sought to punish—killers who destroyed innocent lives for their own purposes.

But maybe that was the real lesson. That vengeance was just another kind of weight, crushing the life from anyone who carried it. That justice delayed too long became poison. That the truth, when it finally surfaced, was usually uglier than the lie.

"Ready to go in?" Jack asked.

"In a minute."

I watched the mist disappear completely, leaving King George County exposed in the morning light— all its beauty and all its blood, its history and its hauntings, its old wounds that never quite healed.

Somewhere in the cemetery across town, fresh flowers lay on Bridget Ashworth's grave. Anonymous tributes from people who finally knew her story. The real story.

After three hundred years, she could rest in peace.

Fighting Dirty

March 24, 2026

A BONE TO PIC - A MABEL MCCOY MYSTERY

Chapter One

I had no plans to become a widow at the tender age of twenty-four.

I also had no plans to own a tea shop on a sleepy South Carolina island, but I've discovered life doesn't give two figs about my plans. Life on Grimm Island taught me that lesson. Here, the oak trees drip with Spanish moss and secrets hang just as heavy in the humid air.

The Perfect Steep—my tea shop and little kingdom of mismatched chairs and organized chaos —sat on the corner of Harbor and Lighthouse. From the outside, it was Grimm Island gentility personified —soft blue paint with crisp white trim, black shutters, and a sweeping wraparound porch where two rocking chairs waited patiently as if ready for Southern hospitality itself.

Inside was a different story entirely. Inside was pure me.

My name is Mabel McCoy, and I'd done a good job of pretending to be gentility personified since my husband died ten years ago. But I'd noticed lately there were times when I was starting to feel a bit frayed around the edges, and I wondered how long it would be before people started to notice.

My tea shop was what I affectionately called organized chaos with a tea obsession, a phrase that would have made Patrick smile if he'd lived to see it. Shiplap walls that should have been pristine white were instead painted a pale yellow on one wall, mint green on another, and a soft lavender on the third— the result of my inability to choose just one color and my stubborn refusal to start over once I'd begun. The heart pine floors creaked like they were telling secrets, especially in the three spots by the register that I'd learned to hop over during busy hours.

Ceiling fans with blades shaped like giant leaves spun lazily overhead, stirring the air that always smelled of whatever tea blend I was experimenting with that day. Today it was something with bergamot and cinnamon that made the whole place smell like Christmas morning, even in the middle of May.

I glanced at the hideous cherub clock on the wall

—a wedding gift from Patrick's grandmother that I couldn't bring myself to take down despite its beady-eyed stare. Five-thirty. The afternoon crowd had thinned out, and I had about thirty minutes before the Silver Sleuths would arrive for their monthly book club meeting.

I caught a glimpse of myself in the mirror and smoothed back a stray blonde curl. At least the island's humidity was good for something—my vintage waves actually seemed to like it. I reapplied my red lipstick, the one bit of glamour I never skipped, and hummed along with Frank Sinatra as he sang *I Get a Kick Out of You* through the speakers.

I'd just finished boxing up a special tea blend to deliver to Mrs. Pembroke when the bell above the door jingled. Deputy Mark Reynolds strolled in, his uniform crisp despite the late hour, that easy smile crinkling the corners of his eyes.

"Just in time," I said. "It's almost closing time."

"My timing's always been impeccable," he replied, removing his hat. His rust-colored hair had gone silver at the temples since I'd known him, but his pale blue eyes still held that same kindness they had since I'd been a kid. "Got any of that cinnamon tea left? Been a day."

"For you? Always." I turned to prepare his usual as he settled onto his regular stool at the counter. "Rough shift?"

Reynolds sighed, running a hand through his hair. "Milton left us a mess to clean up. This new sheriff's asking a lot of questions and digging through files none of us even knew existed.

"And that's a problem?" I asked, sliding his to-go tea across the counter.

"Can't say I blame him," he said. "But it's just stirring up the past. Sheriff Milton did a lot of damage and people are hurting. He even went through the case files from when those three girls went missing. That might have been before you were born. But those girls' families still live on the island. No need to dredge it all up and put them through that again. Some things are better left buried, if you ask me."

He took a sip of tea and closed his eyes in appreciation. "Perfect as always, Mabel. Don't know what I'd do without my evening fix."

I smiled. Reactions like his to my teas were my favorite part of the job. It might seem boring by most people's standards, but I didn't need much. I considered myself a simple, easy-going woman.

"So how's the new sheriff working out?" I asked, wiping down the counter.

"Beckett?" Reynolds shrugged. "By the book. Bit of an outsider, but seems decent enough. Time will tell if he sticks around." He glanced at his watch. "Guess my break is over. You closing up for your book club tonight?"

"How did you know about that?" I asked, though I wasn't really surprised. Nothing stayed secret on Grimm Island for long.

He tapped the side of his nose and said, "Hey, I'm a cop. I know things." He finished his tea and slid a five-dollar bill across the counter.

"On the house," I told him.

He put the five in the tip jar anyway and gave me a wink. "See you tomorrow."

As the door chimed behind him, I went to clear china cups from a corner table, wiping it down and giving my last customer a side-eye because he'd been sitting there for three hours and kept filling up his tea cup with whatever was in the thermos he'd brought from home. I was getting ready to shoo him along when he hurriedly shoved his things in his bag and hurried out the door.

"Rude," I said, cleaning up his mess. "Almost time, Chowder," I said to my French bulldog, who was sprawled across the window seat, his wrinkled face looking particularly judgmental today. "The Silver Sleuths will be here soon."

Chowder snorted and rolled onto his back, his stubby legs in the air.

"I'll take that as excitement. Just try not to con Walt out of all his treats this time. You

know what the vet said about your cholesterol."

I wiped down the large round table by the front

window—the Silver Sleuths' preferred spot for their meetings. They liked to see and be seen, a requirement for five seniors who considered people-watching a competitive sport. I'd arranged six chairs around it, knowing that somehow they'd rope me into joining, despite my protests.

I gave my sea-green dress a final smoothing. It was vintage, with those puffed sleeves I loved, and paired perfectly with the pearl pendant Patrick had given me on our first anniversary.

Frank's crooning faded, and Ella and Louis came on, deciding whether or not they could be friends as they debated the correct pronunciation of the word tomato. Chowder gave a soft woof and rolled to his side so he could look at passersby out the window.

"I agree," I told him. "I could never fall in love with someone who says tamahto. A bit too pretentious for my taste."

Chowder woofed again in agreement. There were some moments when Chowder and I were in perfect accord.

I'd just finished arranging a fresh bouquet of flowers in the center of the table when the bell above the door chimed again.

"Do I smell lemon scones?" Deidre Whitmore called as she bustled in, fifteen minutes early as usual. Her silver hair was secured in a haphazard bun with what appeared to be a pencil, wayward curls flying in all directions. She carried an enormous tote bag, and I knew it was filled with books and enough butterscotch candies to survive an apocalypse.

"Fresh out of the oven," I confirmed, smiling despite myself. Ms. Whitmore had been Grimm Island's librarian for most of my life—a woman who had seemed positively ancient when I'd been a kid—only to finally retire a few years ago. Somehow, she looked exactly the same as she had twenty years earlier. I still couldn't quite shake the feeling that I should whisper in her presence. I also had trouble remembering to call her Deidre instead of Ms. Whitmore.

"Wonderful! I brought some of my lavender shortbread to share," she said, extracting a tin from her bag. "The recipe's from 1897. Found it in the historical society archives."

I smiled and took the tin from her. "You know you don't have to bring food, Ms. Whitmore. This is a tea shop. I'm happy to provide all the refreshments."

"Call me Deidre, dear," she reminded me for what had to be the hundredth time. Her bright red culottes were a blur as she made her way to the prepared table. She untied her red and white striped sweater from around her shoulders and put it on the back of her preferred chair to save her spot. "And nonsense. It's a book club, and book clubs have potlucks."

The bell jingled again, and Walt Garrison marched in with military precision, followed closely by Dottie Simmons and Hank Hardeman.

"Five forty-two," Walt announced, consulting his ancient waterproof watch. He wore pressed navy slacks with sharp creases, a matching windbreaker, and the thick soled shoes his orthopedist insisted he wear for fallen arches. "Right on schedule."

"We're early, Walt," Dottie corrected, adjusting her green cat-eye glasses. "The meeting doesn't start until six."

"Early is on time, on time is late," Walt replied with the air of someone who had been saying the same thing for at least seventy years.

"And late is unacceptable," Hank finished with a sigh. "We know, Walt. We've known since 1972."

Hank had spent a good part of his career as a federal judge and had finally retired a few years ago at his wife's urging. He was a no-nonsense sort of man, but he'd taken to wearing shorts since his retirement, showing off knobby knees and the black dress socks he wore pulled up to the middle of his shins.

"Where's Bea?" I asked, noting the missing member of their quintet.

"Picking up Mr. Whiskers from the groomer,"

Dottie explained. "That cat gets more salon appointments than I do." She patted her freshly cut bob that had been dyed the jet black of her youth.

"Tea will be ready in a minute," I said. "I've got Earl Grey for Walt, oolong for Deidre—"

"And chamomile for me," Dottie finished. "You're a dear to remember."

"It's not exactly difficult," I said. "You've ordered the same thing for the past three years."

"Consistency is the foundation of character," Hank declared.

I retreated to the counter to prepare their tea. This monthly ritual had become so familiar I could probably do it in my sleep. First Thursday of every month, the Silver Sleuths Murder Society would descend upon my shop for their book club meeting, which inevitably dissolved into island gossip and wild speculation about whatever mystery novel they'd selected.

The bell jingled again, and Bea Livingston swept in like a tropical storm. Today she wore a flowing caftan in a peacock print so bright it had its own weather system, paired with earrings the size of small chandeliers. Her red hair sizzled with electricity.

"Sorry I'm late," she announced, though she was actually ten minutes early. "Mr. Whiskers was uncooperative." She held up her hands to display several small scratches. "Battle wounds."

"I have some antiseptic cream," I offered.

"Don't bother. I've survived three husbands and more hurricanes than I can count," she said with a dismissive wave that sent her bangles jangling. "A few cat scratches are nothing."

She settled into her usual chair and immediately leaned forward. "Now, before we start, has anyone seen our mysterious sheriff today?"

I rolled my eyes. The whole island was fascinated by the new sheriff. Maybe because he'd been brought in because of a scandal. Maybe because he wasn't a local. Or maybe because none of the gossips could get any personal information out of him. But the Silver Sleuths' sheriff watch made the CIA look like a bunch of amateurs.

"Not since yesterday," Walt reported. "He was at the pharmacy picking up a prescription."

"Did you see what for?" Deidre asked, leaning in so eagerly she nearly knocked over her teacup.

"Couldn't tell," Walt said, clearly disappointed by this gap in his intelligence gathering. "Brown paper bag, folded at the top. Very discreet."

"Blood pressure medication, most likely," Hank declared with authority. "Law enforcement has the highest rate of hypertension of any profession."

"Could be pain medication," Dottie countered,

tapping her fingers thoughtfully on the table. "Did you notice how he rolls his neck? I bet it's arthritis. Unless he's addicted to pain pills. That's a whole other problem."

"Maybe it's something more...personal," Bea whispered, raising her eyebrows.

All I could do was shake my head. The poor sheriff would have an interminable disease by the time they got through with him. "Or it could just be allergy medicine," I offered. "I've seen him sneeze every time he walks past the magnolias on Harbor Street."

"Interesting that you've noticed his sneezing habits, Mabel," Bea said, her smile spreading like warm butter.

I felt my cheeks flush. "We live on a four thousand acre island. Everyone knows everything."

"Clearly not everything," Walt said, rubbing his chin thoughtfully. "Otherwise we'd know what was in that prescription."

"You all do realize that stalking the sheriff is probably illegal, right?"

"It's not stalking," Deidre protested. "It's community awareness. You should just ask Jerry, Hank. Don't you two play golf together?"

Hank grunted. "Jerry holds confidences better than a Catholic priest. He's a pharmacist with scruples."

"Imagine that," I murmured.

"He'll be here any minute." Dottie said with a meaningful glance at the clock. "It's almost closing time."

She wasn't wrong. For the past three weeks, ever since Sheriff Dashiell Beckett had been appointed to replace our disgraced former sheriff, he'd developed a habit of stopping by The Perfect Steep just before closing time for his evening tea. Black, strong, no sugar, splash of milk. It was the most predictable thing about him.

"He's very consistent," I said, trying to sound casual. "Professional habit, I guess."

"Or he likes the view," Bea suggested with an exaggerated wink in my direction.

I pursed my lips. "He likes the tea, Bea. That's all."

"Mmhmm," all five seniors hummed in unison, with identical expressions of disbelief.

"So what's the book this month?" I asked, desperate to change the subject.

"The Graves of Walter County," Deidre said, producing a worn paperback from her bag. "About a series of cold cases in a small Texas town in the 1960s."

"How many victims?" I asked, despite myself. These murder mysteries were admittedly a guilty pleasure.

"Seven," Dottie replied eagerly. "All buried in the woods behind the killer's house. But he didn't bury them deep enough and when heavy rains came one spring one of the bodies was washed into the creek and floated all the way downtown. Victim was a girl that had gone missing from the college in the next town."

"The killer strangled all his victims with his belt," Walt said. "Had a real unusual belt buckle that left an impression in the tissue."

"The author's research was impressive," Hank added, reaching for a scone. "Though I found myself quite irritated by his abbreviations of words. He kept using the word anal for analysis, as if that's some kind of shorthand those of us who deal in crime use on a daily basis. I can tell you I've never uttered the word anal in my courtroom."

I stifled a laugh, entertained by the absurdity of the conversation.

"Pass the clotted cream," Walt said, unfazed. "I enjoyed the book. It reminded me of a case in Annapolis back in '82."

The bell above the door jingled, and I didn't have to look up to know who it was. A hush fell over the Silver Sleuths as Sheriff Beckett entered, right on schedule.

He was still in uniform, dark pants and a short sleeved button-down that fit well across his broad shoulders and hugged his biceps. His dark hair was slightly tousled by the wind. A thin scar ran along his right jawline, barely noticeable unless you were looking for it because of the stubble he'd let grow.

"Evening, ladies. Gentlemen," he nodded.

"Sheriff," Walt replied.

"Good evening, Mrs. McCoy," Sheriff Beckett said, turning to me with a polite nod. "Hope I'm not interrupting."

I smiled at the formal address. After ten years as a widow, "Mrs. McCoy" felt like a well-worn sweater—comfortable, familiar, and something I had no desire to take off.

"Not at all, Sheriff," I replied. "Just in time for your usual?"

"Please," he said with a small smile that didn't quite reach his eyes.

Sheriff Beckett smiled with his mouth, but his eyes always remained watchful, alert. It was slightly unnerving and, if I was being honest with myself, slightly fascinating.

"Book club night?" he asked, glancing at the table where the Silver Sleuths had spread out their books and notes like battle plans.

"First Thursday of every month," Deidre confirmed, straightening her glasses with a librarian's precision. "We're discussing The Graves of Walter County." She held up the book.

"True crime?" he asked, raising an eyebrow. "I saw a TV special on that case. It was fascinating."

"We only read true crime," Dottie explained with a dismissive wave. "Fiction is too..." She paused, nose wrinkling like she'd smelled something unpleasant. "Unrealistic."

The corner of Sheriff Beckett's mouth quirked up. "How so?"

"Too many coincidences," Hank declared. "And the detectives—" he jabbed a finger toward Beckett, "—are too incompetent, so the amateur sleuth ends up solving the case. It's ridiculous."

"Unlike real detectives, who welcome civilian input," Beckett said dryly, his eyes crinkling at the corners despite his deadpan delivery.

Walt leaned forward, elbows on the table, entering what I'd come to think of as his intelligence briefing posture. "Depends on the detective," he countered. "And the civilian. Some of us have relevant expertise."

"Is that so?" Beckett asked, accepting the to-go cup I handed him, his fingers briefly brushing mine.

Deidre sat up straighter, fairly bursting with pride. "Walt was career military. He spent thirty years in Navy intelligence," she said, patting Walt's arm. "Worked for the Department of Defense before he retired. Appointed by the President."

"Really?" Beckett asked.

Walt nodded. "If I told you about it I'd have to kill you. Top secret security clearance."

"And of course Dottie was a pathologist with the Charleston medical examiner's office," Deidre continued.

"It's true," Dottie said, cleaning her glasses. "I've had my hands in a lot of bodies."

Deidre's eyes widened comically, but she continued as if that were a perfectly normal thing to say. "Hank was a federal judge."

"They called me The Hammer because I liked to put the final nail in a criminal's coffin as I sentenced them," Hank added.

Dottie rolled her eyes. "I've known you for forty-five years, and I've never heard anyone call you The Hammer." She patted his hand to soften the blow. "But you were tough on those criminals."

"I spent almost fifty years as a librarian," Deidre said. "But my true love is research. I can get lost for days in research. And then there's Bea..." Deidre paused, looking like she was unsure what to say. "Bea—"

"Had access to more secrets than the CIA," Bea said with a theatrical flourish of her bangle-laden wrist. "Society columnist. You'd be amazed what people will tell you at charity galas after two gin and tonics. I've got the dirt on every player in town if they've been here long enough. Of course, I've got the dirt on anyone who thinks they're anyone in the whole state. The south loves old money and family secrets."

Beckett looked thoughtful as he sipped his tea, his eyes moving from one Silver Sleuth to another as if reassessing them. "That's an interesting combination of skills."

"You never want to watch mystery movies with us," Dottie said. "We always figure out who did it."

"We call ourselves the Silver Sleuths," Walt said, puffing out his chest slightly.

"Catchy," Beckett commented, but he was looking at me as if he were waiting to hear what my special skills were. I hated to disappoint him, but I didn't think he'd be too interested in my ability to do crossword puzzles or how I can memorize song lyrics the first time I hear them. Neither of those things is helpful when watching mysteries on T.V.

"Storm's coming in," I said for lack of anything better, nodding toward the windows where dark clouds were gathering on the horizon. "Looks like it could be a bad one."

Beckett followed my gaze. "You're right about that," he said. "Weather service issued a severe thunderstorm warning not long ago. You might want to wrap up your meeting early tonight."

"Nonsense," Deidre said dismissively. "We've weathered worse. Remember Hurricane Matthew?"

"I remember you showing up on my doorstep because you ate all your hurricane snacks before the storm hit," Dottie said.

Beckett turned to me. "What time will you close up here?"

"We usually finish at seven," I said.

He nodded. "You'll be cutting it close. You'll want to get home before it gets too bad."

"I'm just three blocks away," I told him. "The white corner house with the piazza at the end of Harbor Street. I'll have time before things get too bad. Those clouds are still a good ways off."

"You can predict the weather?" the sheriff asked, arching a brow.

"I'm my father's daughter," I said, and left it at that.

"Right." His eyes met mine with that dark, direct gaze that never seemed to waver.

He paid for his tea, leaving his usual generous tip in the jar by the register, and then he nodded to the group. "Enjoy your book club. Try not to solve too many crimes in one evening."

"No promises," Bea called after him as he headed for the door.

"Have a good night, Sheriff," I said.

He paused at the door, glancing back. "Dash," he corrected quietly. "After hours, it's just Dash."

Before I could say anything else, he was gone, the bell chiming in his wake.

Five pairs of eyes immediately swiveled to me.

"After hours, it's just Dash," Bea mimicked in a deep voice. "Well, well, well."

"Don't start," I said with a small smile. "It's just tea and manners. That's all."

"I certainly didn't notice any arthritis in his neck," Hank said observantly. "He was able to turn his head to look at Mabel just fine."

"Did you notice the scar on his jaw?" Deidre asked, leaning forward conspiratorially.

"Bar fight in Charleston," Walt declared.

"Knife fight with a drug dealer," Bea countered.

"Military," Dottie guessed. "He has the posture."

"You're all ridiculous," I said, returning to the table with a fresh pot of tea. "He probably cut himself shaving."

"No way," Walt shook his head. "That's a knife scar. Clean, deliberate. Man's seen action."

"I heard he's from Virginia originally," Deidre offered. "Old family, fell on hard times."

"I heard he was FBI before this," Bea said, not to be outdone. "Undercover work. Very hush-hush."

"I heard he's just a normal person trying to do his job without being the subject of wild speculation," I suggested.

"Boring," Bea dismissed. "My version is better."

"We should invite him to join the book club," Dottie suggested suddenly. "He seems interested in true crime."

"Occupational hazard, I imagine," I said dryly.

"No, it's perfect," Deidre agreed, warming to the idea. "We need fresh perspectives."

"And it'd give him a chance to stare at Mabel more," Bea added with a wink.

"He's probably very busy with sheriff duties," I said, adjusting my pearl pendant.

"Not too busy for tea, apparently," Deidre pointed out, patting my hand.

"Mabel should consider courtship," Hank announced to the table, as if I weren't sitting right there. "A respectable widow of her standing would be quite eligible."

Bea nodded sagely. "In my day, ten years was more than sufficient mourning period. I married my second husband six months after my first had been buried. Of course, Leonard and I had something of a past if you know what I mean."

"If you mean you were having an affair with him while Earl was alive then we know what you mean," Deidre said, shaking her head. "The whole island knew."

Bea pursed her lips tightly, but she didn't dispute it.

"Patrick would have wanted you to move on,"

Dottie said softly, using the exact phrase she'd repeated at years two, five, and seven.

Walt cleared his throat. "Sheriff seems like a decent sort. Responsible. Reliable pension. Good posture."

I glanced between them, fighting both amusement and exasperation. They'd decided my future with the same certainty they used to plan the church bake sale or determine who was stealing Mrs. Peterson's newspaper.

So I did what I always did when I didn't know what to say. I started singing.

"Don't know why there's no sun up in the sky, stormy weather..."

"Ethel Waters or Lena Horne?" Walt asked immediately.

"Lena," I said. "Though Ethel did it first."

"Good taste," he approved. "My Margaret loved Lena Horne. Saw her perform in New York once, before we were married."

And just like that, we were back on safe ground, with Walt launching into one of his stories about his late wife that somehow always involved either naval intelligence or jazz music, often both. The tension dissolved, and I found myself relaxing back into the familiar rhythm of their conversation.

Outside, thunder rumbled in the distance. I sipped my tea and half-listened as Deidre started discussing the book, with frequent interruptions from the others. The storm was building, but in here, in this moment, everything felt comfortingly normal.

I'd spent ten years building this life—the tea shop, the routines, the careful distance I maintained from anything too emotional or complicated. Ten years as Mabel McCoy, young widow, tea shop owner, honorary senior citizen.

But as another rumble of thunder shook the building, I couldn't help wondering if maybe, just maybe, I was ready for a little storm in my life.

Not that I was thinking about Dash Beckett when that thought crossed my mind.

Not at all.

A Bone to Pick: A Mabel McCoy Mystery Book 2
December 9, 2025

ACKNOWLEDGMENTS

Getting a book to publication takes an amazing team of people. I'm fortunate to have had these people in my corner for years.

To my editor—Imogen Howson for always making me better.

To my cover designer—Dar Albert for always blowing me away with your talent.

To my children—You're all so special. You have gifts and abilities beyond measure, and I'm excited to see what God has in store for each of you.

To Scott—thank you for answering a ridiculous amount of law enforcement questions and acting out weird scenarios with me. Any mistakes are mine alone.

ABOUT THE AUTHOR

Liliana Hart is a *New York Times*, *USA Today*, and Publisher's Weekly bestselling author of more than eighty titles. After starting her first novel her freshman year of college, she immediately became addicted to writing and knew she'd found what she was meant to do with her life. She has no idea why she majored in music.

Since publishing in June 2011, Liliana has sold more than ten-million books. All three of her series have made multiple appearances on the *New York Times* list.

Liliana can almost always be found at her computer writing, hauling five kids to various activities, or spending time with her husband. She calls Texas home.

If you enjoyed reading this, I would appreciate it if you would help others enjoy this book, too.

Recommend it. Please help other readers find this book by recommending it to friends, readers' groups and discussion boards.

Review it. Please tell other readers why you liked this book by reviewing.

Connect with me online:
www.lilianahart.com

facebook.com/LilianaHart
instagram.com/LilianaHart
bookbub.com/authors/liliana-hart

ALSO BY LILIANA HART

JJ Graves Mystery Series

Dirty Little Secrets

A Dirty Shame

Dirty Rotten Scoundrel

Down and Dirty

Dirty Deeds

Dirty Laundry

Dirty Money

A Dirty Job

Dirty Devil

Playing Dirty

Dirty Martini

Dirty Dozen

Dirty Minds

Dirty Weekend

Dirty Looks

Dirty Liars

Dirty Valentine

Addison Holmes Mystery Series

Whiskey Rebellion

Whiskey Sour

Whiskey For Breakfast

Whiskey, You're The Devil

Whiskey on the Rocks

Whiskey Tango Foxtrot

Whiskey and Gunpowder

Whiskey Lullaby

The Scarlet Chronicles

Bouncing Betty

Hand Grenade Helen

Front Line Francis

The Harley and Davidson Mystery Series

The Farmer's Slaughter

A Tisket a Casket

I Saw Mommy Killing Santa Claus

Get Your Murder Running

Deceased and Desist

Malice in Wonderland

Tequila Mockingbird

Gone With the Sin

Grime and Punishment

Blazing Rattles

A Salt and Battery

Curl Up and Dye

First Comes Death Then Comes Marriage

Box Set 1

Box Set 2

Box Set 3

The Gravediggers

The Darkest Corner

Gone to Dust

Say No More

Laurel Valley

Tribulation Pass

Redemption Road

Midnight Clear

Forgiveness River

Atonement Trail

www.ingramcontent.com/pod-product-compliance
Lightning Source LLC
Chambersburg PA
CBHW061045310726

48969CB00004B/1094